São Paulo Noir

São Paulo Noir

Edited by Tony Bellotto

Translated by Clifford E. Landers

AKASHIC
BOOKS

BROOKLYN, NEW YORK, USA
BALLYDEHOB, CO. CORK, IRELAND

This collection comprises works of fiction. All names, characters, places, and incidents are the product of the authors' imaginations. Any resemblance to real events or persons, living or dead, is entirely coincidental.

Published by Akashic Books
©2018 Akashic Books

Series concept by Tim McLoughlin and Johnny Temple
São Paulo map by Sohrab Habibion

ISBN: 978-1-61775-531-6
Library of Congress Control Number: 2017956553

Akashic Books
Brooklyn, New York, USA
Ballydehob, Co. Cork, Ireland
Twitter: @AkashicBooks
Facebook: AkashicBooks
E-mail: info@akashicbooks.com
Website: www.akashicbooks.com

ALSO IN THE AKASHIC NOIR SERIES

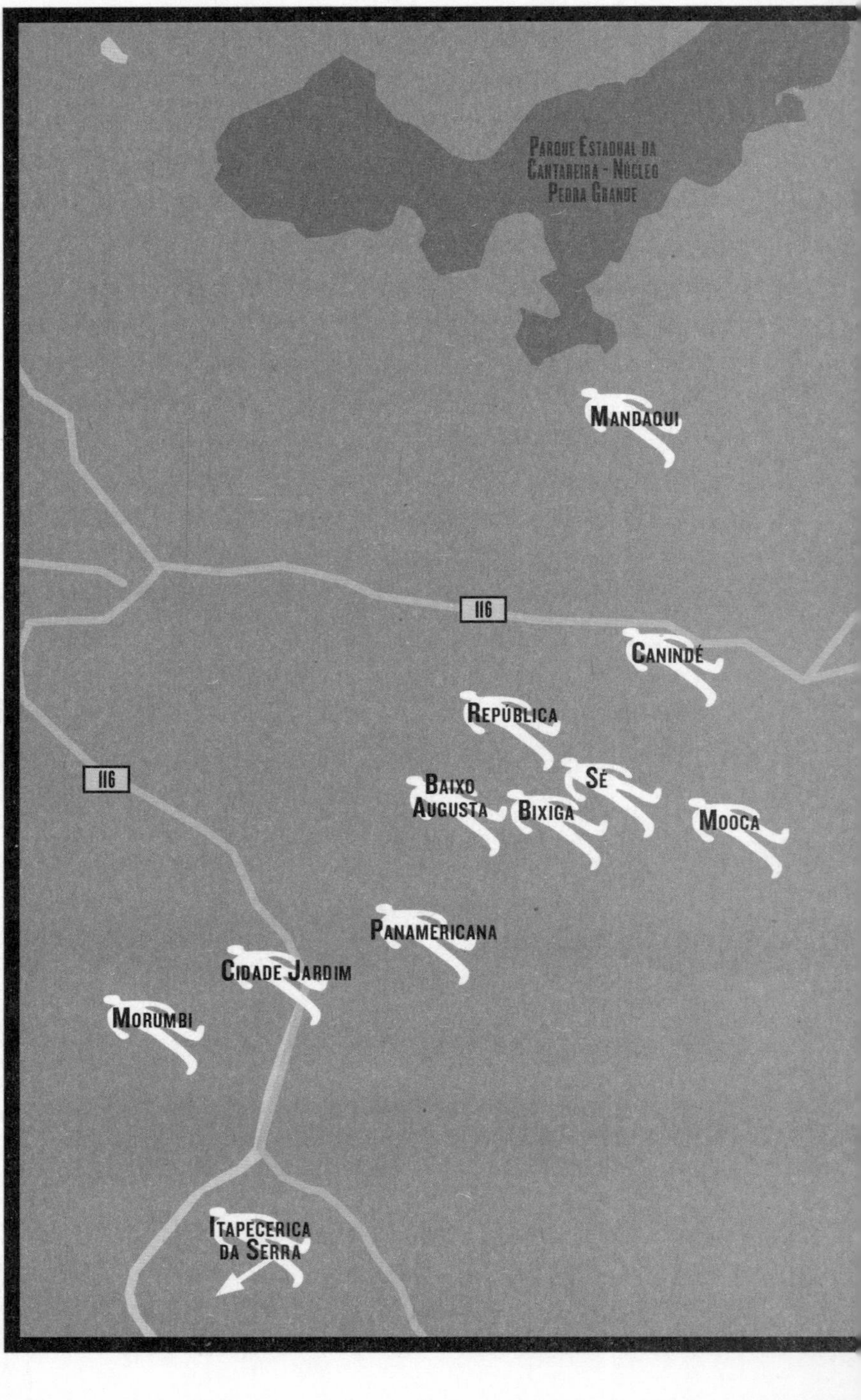
Parque Estadual da
Cantareira - Núcleo
Pedra Grande
Mandaqui
116
Canindé
República
116
Sé
Baixo
Augusta
Bixiga
Mooca
Panamericana
Cidade Jardim
Morumbi
Itapecerica
da Serra

SÃO PAULO

116

SP-070

VILA CARRÃO

GUAIANASES

TABLE OF CONTENTS

PART III: DISCREET INELEGANCE

INTRODUCTION
LAND OF MIST

E ncyclopedias will say that São Paulo is the main financial, corporate, and commercial center of South Amer-
ica. The census will show that São Paulo is the most
populous city in Brazil, the Americas, the Portuguese-speaking
world, and the entire Southern Hemisphere.

Calculations will indicate that São Paulo is the seventh-
largest city on the planet and that its population of twenty
million is the eighth-largest urban agglomeration. Research
will state that São Paulo is the most influential Brazilian city
on the world scene, considered the fourteenth most globalized
city in the world. The Globalization and World Cities Study
Group and Network classify it as an alpha global city.

On its coat of arms appears the Latin phrase, *Non ducor,
duco*, which means, *I am not led, I lead.* Publicists will affirm
that São Paulo is the city that can never stop. Specialists will
conclude that in its streets moves (or fails to move) the worst
traffic in the world.

Scholars will inform us that São Paulo is the most multi-
cultural city in Brazil, having received, since 1870, millions of
immigrants from every part of the planet, and that it is the city
with the largest populations of people of Italian, Portuguese,
Japanese, Spanish, and Arab origin outside their respective
countries. Anthropologists will emphasize that the city is the
destination of thousands of immigrants, who each year leave
the poorest regions of Brazil in the north and northeast in

search of better living conditions, and that around 30 percent of the population is of African descent.

Experts will assure us that São Paulo has a high crime rate. Sociologists will confirm that the city has an area known as Cracolândia (Crackland) and that among the violent and neglected communities spread along its periphery, one bears the ironic name Paraisópolis (Paradise City). Politicians will roar that São Paulo is the engine that drives Brazil.

Poets will dub it "Hallucination City," songwriters will nickname it "Sampa," and the nostalgic will remember it was once called the "Land of Mist."

All this information, however, will not aid the reader in understanding the city. I myself, born in Jardim Paulista, know little of the great metropolis that comprises it.

It is with the help of Olivia Maia, Jô Soares, Vanessa Barbara, Drauzio Varella, Beatriz Bracher, Marçal Aquino, Maria S. Carvalhosa, Mario Prata, Ilana Casoy, Marcelo Rubens Paiva, Ferréz, Marcelino Freire, and Fernando Bonassi that I have tried to better understand the city where I was born.

More than historians and sociologists, writers have always been able to transform cities into great characters. This is the way we decipher devouring sphinxes.

Tony Bellotto
March 2018

PART I

HALLUCINATION CITY

CROSS CONTAMINATION

BY VANESSA BARBARA

Mandaqui

"See: I used to fold the corner of the toilet paper, leave the chocolate mint on the pillow, make a swan with the towel. A towel swan! Know what that is? The towels folded on top of the bed in the form of a heart? Now they give me twenty minutes to clean a room where obviously a funk party went down, with like eight guests, a dozen crack pipes, and half a dozen voodoo chickens—and what do they want me to do, spray some lemongrass essence in the air? Or arrange the little bars of soap according to feng shui?"

That wasn't right, no sir, exploiting a well-bred chambermaid like that, with experience in the finest hotels in São Paulo, like that five-star in Jardins that hosted international pop stars and where lobby security has to contain crowds of obsessed teenagers who pay up to five hundred reais for the pillowcase Justin Bieber slept on. Not that Cléo was fired just for that; the black market for pillowcases supposedly used by celebrities was just one of the reasons the management of the chic hotel let the maid go. Before that, there were suspicions that she didn't vacuum the corners and, worse, that she ate the room service leftovers. But none of that was ever proven. And what do half a dozen pillowcases matter to an establishment that charges a thousand reais a night? When her entire month's salary was barely more than that?

In any case, Cléo was fired from the luxury hotel in Jardins and, without prospects of working in establishments with sheets of Egyptian cotton and a selection of pillows, she ended up at the Hotel Five Stars in the Mandaqui district. Not that the hotel was rated as such—it was merely the name. The recently inaugurated establishment had forty-four rooms on three floors, fifth-class towels, abrasive toilet paper, a few suites with round beds, and some electrical outlets in strange places that no one could explain. At first it attracted curiosity-seekers from the neighborhood, especially elderly folks who stayed there for a change of air and to have something to talk about at the local bakery. They usually stole the miniature shampoo and soap, drifted off early in front of the television at high volume, and loved ordering room service. They would spend all day in their rooms and liked to supervise the cleaning, even when Cléo asked them to wait in the hall.

Little by little, the clientele became more diverse. The grannies and grampas from Mandaqui were joined by couples from the Lauzane Paulista, bocce lovers from Imirim, numerous families from Jardim Peri, bachelors for extended stays, prostitutes, taxi drivers, card readers, writers, and all types of bad elements looking for privacy to carry out their nefarious businesses. And Cléo, having daily access to the filthy rooms, knew everything.

"Can lemongrass spray disguise the smell of a cadaver?"

One fine day, a man turned up dead in room 33. He was a commercial representative for a firm in Campinas, a loyal guest of the Five Stars who came almost monthly for meetings and trade shows in Anhembi. Dr. Otávio was known to all the staff. Normally he would spend only one or two nights in the hotel, sometimes with a woman he knew in the city who he would call to keep him company. He would leave early for work, was discreet in his extramarital adventures, and didn't quite mess up the place—except when he became irritated with his lover and slapped her around, causing some damage to the room.

But he always paid for the damages and left a good tip for Cléo, who didn't mind cleaning up the bloodstains from the previous night, the broken glasses, and the tufts of blond hair that the man sometimes yanked from his lover's head. He also said good morning and left a tip of twenty reais when the mess was excessive.

Therefore it was annoying when he was late checking out and the maid had to enter the room around two in the afternoon and found the following scene: Dr. Otávio lying on the floor beside the bed in a dark pool of wine and blood, with a corkscrew in his jugular. The bedside lamp on the floor, the sheets disheveled and dirty. The body was already cold, pallid, and rigid. In the air, a slight smell of garlic. There was no one else in the room.

Cléo didn't let herself be shaken by the scene, merely closing the door and calmly notifying the management, who brought in the police. She continued cleaning the other rooms while detectives photographed the crime scene. At dusk, with the body already removed, Cléo was asked to work overtime and handle the cleanup along with the other maid. But she was left in the lurch, as the other woman had a panic attack and quit, unable to deal with the situation. She said disinfecting a room where someone died wasn't in her job description. A kitchen aide was summoned to help Cléo, while the cleaning staff brought mops and attempted to calm the remaining guests. They worked three hours without a break, scrubbing the walls and the floor, removing the torn curtains, and sending for more material.

While she wrung the cloth, Cléo complained of the way management exploited her, her of all people, an experienced professional who knew how to make a bed with ninety-degree corners—but not with those cheap sheets. And not under those terrible work conditions, having to put in overtime in a pool of blood. And she told the kitchen employee, a young woman named Lena: "You have no idea what I have to put up with around here. Like, I once went into the room of a couple I thought were normal, people who seemed refined, who lived near Santa Terezinha. I was sure I'd finish the cleanup in fifteen minutes, but no way. The walls were covered in jelly, there was a video camera pointed toward the bed, and I think others had been through there too. I saw a lot of suspicious puddles on the carpet. I also picked up several hypodermic needles from the floor and two DVDs: *Free Willy 1* and *2*. Seriously. They filmed an orgy, got high, and watched *Free Willy 1* and *2*."

Since the kitchen helper did the cleaning with care, with focus, and without getting sick, the manager promoted her to the second chambermaid position. Which wasn't exactly good news for Cléo, who now, in addition to having to clean more than twenty rooms a day in that hole, had to train the novice. Lena was so inexperienced that she didn't even know it was necessary to remove the dust starting from the top in order not to leave dirty streaks on the area already cleaned. She also didn't know it was forbidden to hold the pillow under your chin, as that was considered unhygienic. Not that this mattered at the Five Star, where a guest swore on TripAdvisor to have seen fungus growing in the closet of her room.

They began the rounds very early, with Cléo giving instructions: "Careful removing the dirty sheet from the bed, there may be hypodermic needles hidden there and you'll hurt yourself. And condoms too. The first thing we do when we enter a room is take away all the sheets, pillowcases, and dirty towels. But only the ones that are visibly dirty. Throw them in the basket on the cart."

Lena stared at Cléo with the cold expression of someone who wasn't there to make friends. She followed the maid into the bathroom, where she picked up two soiled towels.

"Know what these stains are?" Cléo asked, without expecting a reply. "Blondor. Blondor is hydrogen peroxide. The woman thought it was time to lighten her pubic hair, so she sat on the towel and ruined everything. See? She used the glass to mix it in. Hard to believe. What animals. From time to time you get women who dye their hair and ruin the towels."

She explained that theoretically the maids should wear caps and masks. But at the Five Stars everything was just theoretical. Besides, in the chic hotels it was forbidden to use the same pair of gloves for cleaning the bathroom and the bedroom, as that could lead to cross contamination. The same logic applied to the mops. In the Mandaqui hotel, however, the glove touching the toilet was the same one that touched the sheets.

"Glasses you just give a quick rinsing in the sink or use a cloth with glass cleaner so they don't show any stains. And try not to use the guest's toothbrush to scrub the drains, because that's really low."

Inspired by the work of the police, who were still investigating the corkscrew killing and trying to discover the whereabouts of the victim's lover, Cléo pointed out stains and guessed their provenance, showing off for the benefit of the newcomer.

"Let me show you something else here in 24. Come take a look at this dark circle near the bed. Know what it is? No?

Dried vomit. This here was covered in vomit when I came in, about two months ago, and there was no way to get rid of it. The manager said he wasn't going to change the carpet. So there it is. To this day."

Cléo explained that the vomiting guest was a tall bald man and a Rotarian by the name of Osvaldo Oliveira. The Blondor woman was young, a little over twenty, dark, and a business administration student at a college in Vila Maria. She knew this because she never stopped rummaging through the woman's belongings, opening her luggage and everything. She said she knew the slightest details of the lives of every guest: if they were married or single, adulterers, had fetishes, used dental floss, had a fight the night before, and whether their intestines were in working order.

"This woman wears a size 5 shoe, she's fashion-conscious and only buys designer clothes. She has very long hair (or else she accidentally dumped out half a bottle of shampoo) and her perfume is Air de la Vie. Counterfeit. She takes a lot of prescription medicines, like this one here, which I later discovered is for a bipolar disorder."

Lena didn't reply. Cléo suspected the new girl wasn't exactly enthusiastic about her new job, but that hardly mattered. She continued with her monologue.

"She brought a guy here but sent him away in the middle of the night so she wouldn't have to pay the extra occupant charge. They drank five cans of beer, ordered a pizza from Bola's, broke the remote control, and smoked marijuana in the bathroom, because the bedroom doesn't have a window. People think we're stupid. She probably had to stand up on the toilet and smoke with her arm outside the window, but the smell sticks to the walls and if we look in the trash we'll find the roach . . . There! Didn't I tell you?"

Lena limited herself to scouring the toilet, quiet like one who had seen worse.

"Here there's none of that business of always changing the bedsheets. If it doesn't look very dirty, all you have to do it turn the sheet over and everything's fine. If the mattress is stained, you can flip it too. Just be careful, 'cause sometimes a flea jumps out."

The basic rule of management, according to Cléo, was to look clean and never worry about anything. For example, some time ago a woman tried to abort in the bathroom, failed, and left the tiles covered in blood and feces. "None of my business," said Cléo. Sometimes she found rooms totally turned upside down with dark stains and tufts of hair on the table corners, or heard screams from women being attacked, like Dr. Otávio's lover—none of it was the maid's concern.

Lena flashed an angry look in Cléo's direction but said nothing.

"It does no good to look at me like that: your role here is to mop. That's all. If the guest is given to satanic rituals and likes to sacrifice chickens, for example, or make a pentagram on the floor with lit candles, that's his problem. You advise the manager to charge the damage against his preauthorized credit card, and that's that." In a softer tone, she added: "That's how we survive in this damn job."

The newcomer didn't ask, but during the rounds Cléo said that nothing could get to her. Almost nothing. She once read in the paper a story that made an impression on her for several days.

Years earlier, a body was found in the bed frame of room 222 in the Budget Lodge Hotel in Memphis, Tennessee. A twenty-eight-year-old woman had been strangled by her boyfriend, the father of her five children, with the cable that connected the television to the DVD player. The body remained hidden for six weeks in the bedframe, under the side rails and mattress.

"It was a bed just like ours, you know? Notice that there's no space underneath because the bedframe is completely enclosed down to the floor. Which I think is great: one less thing for us to clean. The killer lifted the mattress and stuck the body inside. Then he put everything back the way it was and left without checking out." At least five people slept in the room before someone complained about the smell. "Just think: a body in here for all that time! And couples sleeping on top of it!"

Cléo shuddered and Lena remained silent as she replaced the toilet paper. Still without making a sound, she folded the top ply, as if it meant something.

In room 25, the cleanup was lighter. The guest was a known trafficker in the region who sometimes used the hotel for rendezvous with lovers. Despite his bad reputation, he was clean and tidy—Cléo thought he had a touch of OCD. He must have had a cold, as the two women found a pile of used tissue and an empty cold-medicine box in the trash. The trafficker usually separated the plastic bottle for recycling and suffered from hair loss.

Room 26 was unoccupied, and in 27 they found only a few drops of some type of bodily fluid on the sheets, in addition to toenail clippings scattered on the floor. Cléo rummaged through the receipts on top of the table, opened the drawer, found a watch and a chaplet, and deemed the guest very uninteresting. Probably an orderly at the Mandaqui Hospital. She asked Lena to remove the hair from the sink while she swept the floor.

"I know everything, everything about these people. Like, Dr. Otávio's lover—nobody knows anything about her, no one has ever seen her come in or go out, probably because the night shift at this hotel is a madhouse. No one awake at reception. But I know: she's a bleached blonde, on a diet, wears pink lipstick. I think she's left-handed. And she likes red wine."

It was strange that, in all those months, no one had more information about the woman, who barely cried after a beating and hid in the bathroom when room service showed up with ice. Cléo, however, bet she was tall and straightened her hair, and she couldn't wait to find out if she was right.

As a kind of demonstration of her investigative abilities, in the next room she made a great discovery: the female guest in 28 was having an affair with the man in 34. She got excited and proceeded to show the proof.

"He slept here! Beyond a doubt. I recognize that toothbrush, it's classy, Swiss, and costs nineteen reais at the pharmacy. And it's yellow with green bristles. This slipper is his too: surfer style, with thick straps. They're both married. She's a publicist, he's a salesman. Maybe they met in the lobby and decided to have a fling at night in her room. Notice there's an extra blanket? He brought it from his room. You'll have to take it back later."

The maid tossed the blanket on top of the dirty sheets, in the cart. Still in 28, she saw that Lena had some sort of problem with her left shoulder, judging by how she handled the mop. She must have hurt herself in the kitchen, where accidents were always happening with the large kettles. Cléo could even see a few purple bruises near her collar.

For some reason, she didn't mention what she had observed. Somewhat awkwardly, she continued talking: she said that some of the rooms were used for gun-running; others, for meetings of evangelical groups. Maybe the latter prayed for the salvation of the former, and in the end everything might balance out. In any case, so far she'd never seen a meth lab set up in a suite, or traces of exorcisms. She was, however, constantly covering up signs of some abuse or other and of countless acts of aggression, which for her was more than unpleasant enough.

They went to room 29, and there Cléo couldn't stand it any longer.

"What's your problem, huh? You don't say anything and you look at me with that expression. I don't even know if you understood my instructions, whether I can trust you with the rest of the rooms . . . You think you can handle it? Do you remember which room you're going to take this blanket to?"

As always, Lena did not reply. That afternoon, by the end of the shift, the newcomer would have to take care of rooms 30 and above, on her own, since Cléo had been called to the police station to testify about the homicide. She was feeling important because she had been the one to discover the body and also because she had retained so much information about the victim and the likely killer; she would impress the cops with her gifts of perception. Who needed DNA when they had a witness like her? They might even begin to call on her as a consultant at other crime scenes, with the advantage that she could also lend her services in cleaning up the location after the evidence had been gathered. Consultants must make a good salary, even more if they actually solved the crimes. This was finally the way out she had been seeking for such a long time. She would start a new life in a less humiliating profession, and perhaps she could even stop closing her eyes in the face of injustice.

She would do like those FBI psychologists and compile a complete profile of the killer, starting with the small clues he left on the carpet that could go unnoticed by someone who wasn't trained by the management of the most renowned luxury hotels in the Jardins.

"If there's anyone able to recognize the killer, it's me," she stated proudly. But as soon as she said this, she realized she'd made a huge mistake.

This time, Lena moved the cart away from the entrance and closed the door. Cléo felt her gloves grow sticky with sweat.

Then she understood: no one had ever seen Dr. Otávio's lover entering or leaving because she lived there. She would go up through the service elevator, coming directly from the kitchen with a bottle of wine. Thus the smell of garlic at the scene of the crime. Thus the dyed-blond hairs and pink lipstick of Lena, who had probably grown tired of being beaten and decided to resist with the corkscrew. It would have been a well-executed crime were Cléo not a first-class chambermaid, a good observer, a perfect witness to the clues the kitchen helper had left behind.

In any case, Lena had been trained by Cléo and would do an impeccable cleanup of room 29, with hydrochloric acid and lemongrass essence to disguise a smell that over time would become permanent. Perhaps her recent lessons in hotel order and asepsis would give her a six-week head start on the police, which would be more than enough for her to flee before being discovered. She would finish the job by folding the end of the toilet paper and attempting a pair of towel swans.

Ripping away the television cable with her left hand, Lena remained quiet, but now she had a resolute air and her head was erect. She had seen worse things. Before approaching Cléo, she put on a new pair of gloves, to avoid cross contamination.

BONICLAIDE AND MRS. ALS

BY ILANA CASOY

Cidade Jardim

I t was a day like any other in the home of Amélia Lins e Silva, or Amelinha, as everyone knew her. She had lived in the same neighborhood since childhood, even when her father was still alive and Cidade Jardim was the symbol of a place of success. Nowadays it was a bit in decline, many houses for sale were so old that only the land had any value. In bed, as she had been for a long time, she looked at the clock a thousand times, lamented the delay of Boniclaide, her maid for over fifteen years. Mornings were always difficult when she didn't arrive on time. She noticed the vexed mood of the night nurse, dying to vacate the scene but unable to abandon his shift. And she could never be alone, so for the long nights her son had contracted one of those firms of companions, now known as Home Care, efficient but impersonal. Better that way—she didn't need to engage in idle chatter and hear about a slew of other people's problems. At least they came and went at the appointed times, without drama. And if one professional couldn't come, another was quickly sent in his place. She didn't care whether the caregiver was a man or a woman, she didn't get attached. You get what you pay for. Excellent. With no debt of gratitude. But with Boni it was different.

Amelinha suffered from a rare disease that developed gradually but inexorably. It was a slow and painful neuromus-

cular degeneration. At the beginning she accepted the diag-
nosis with courage and bravery and even soothed her family,
but as the disease progressed, it was impossible not to rebel.
What she had done to deserve this punishment was the question that never went away. It was painful to remember the
feeling of sand under her feet, cooking a favorite dish, shopping at a crowded supermarket, going to the bank—she even
missed waiting in line. Many days, when she opened her eyes,
her brain forgot for an instant that she was immobile forever.
It had the impulse to be normal, to get up without thinking
how, and almost pictured turning on the night-table lamp
and leaping out of bed, but nothing happened. She remained
there, shrunken, paralyzed, with a tube in her trachea helping
her to breathe. Breathing! Not even that could she do on her
own. How much longer would she have to face this torture?
Lately saliva and phlegm, the product of the immobility itself,
had gathered in her throat, making just staying alive more
difficult. It was as if she was dying! She needed the caregiver
on duty to siphon away the excess, using a small machine; for-
tunately, she could pay for all of it. There were pleasures she
wasn't ready to abandon. She had a state-of-the-art computer,
with a special program that let her write with her eyes, the
only part that moved in the prison of her body. It was in this
manner that she read articles from friends in her profession,
saw the updates on social media, kept up with the life of her
grandchildren, watched films and television programs. And
wrote. Amelinha loved to write. In recent months, even that
had become complicated as she took too long to hit the right
letters. All things considered, she lived in a cell worse than
where criminals go.

Boniclaide was the person who most easily communi-
cated with her. She used a chart with the alphabet and cer-

tain words like *cold, hot, thirst, tomorrow*. Boni would point to them one by one, and when Amelinha blinked, the sentences would take shape. The method they developed was nothing new, but it was quick because they were quite accustomed to each other. Accustomed to many other things as well, from so much time together. Each understood the other through looks. Boniclaide began working there while still a young woman, and Amelinha was her adviser and guardian angel. She had seen Boni's daughters grow up, she never let anyone go wanting for medicine. It couldn't be said that Boni was like a daughter to her, because each of them knew her place, and it wasn't healthy to mix the personal with the professional. Nonetheless, they were friends, though there was a day when she had to explain to Boni the matter of separate chinaware, as she had learned from her mother. Respectful of Amelinha's possessions, she never used anything without first getting permission. Also, Amelinha couldn't complain about the affection with which the maid took care of her now, in this phase of her life. There was no comparison with the orderlies; she even got their names mixed up. But today she wasn't inclined to sing the praises of her employee. Precisely today, when she was hosting some friends for dinner. Boni was late. She just wasn't the same as before. Since that man, Zen, had started living with her, Boni was over the moon, had lost her focus. Amelinha didn't know much about the life of her maid— in her family they had been taught to avoid intimacy with the servants—but she did know her employee had changed, and for the worse. She couldn't lose Boniclaide, and she had done everything to help that Zen fellow find a decent job. He even had a nice appearance. Yet when Amelinha suggested that Zen fill out an application using her as a reference, Boni changed the subject, saying that he was going to do so, but then he didn't. She couldn't understand it. Amelinha would have liked to see him employed at the Isle of Flowers, which in the 1960s was the leading market in the region, since then sold to become a successful restaurant. She could easily have a word with the owner, a friend of hers. Boniclaide evaded. Then Amelinha thought of an opening at Veranda, a high-end supermarket on the Cidade Jardim Bridge. She still recalled Argeu and Elias, with their fruit stand beside the favela that had sprung up at the edge of the Jockey Club. Jânio Quadros, mayor of São Paulo at the time, demolished it all in 1985, but not the stand, which prospered and was today almost a tourist attraction for the city's coconut water. She asked several times for Boni to find Argeu's e-mail, but she always forgot. In the end, she accepted giving the young man a reference as a dog walker for the pets in the neighborhood, since she knew several families. It seemed that the pet-walking business was a success. Zen had more and more clients and was already subcontracting, but her maid wasn't the same. She thought of nothing but him, was rather spaced out, didn't remember the simplest things. Amelinha needed to have an urgent talk with Boniclaide!

The clock was already showing 7:20 and the woman hadn't arrived. Given the level of dependency to which she was subjected, anguish and anger grew in Amelinha's breast, knowing the chaos there would be if Boni didn't come. What hatred she felt being dependent on someone!

In the middle of a bunch of people packed onto the bus, Boni saw the Paineira stop approach, where she descended daily. The corner of Avenida Vital Brasil and Francisco Morato. According to legend, a silk-cotton tree once stood there. It was a stop for workers coming from all over, the North, South, and

East Zones, and from there each spread out to his or her destination—heavens, they had to take two buses to arrive, two more to return, besides having to walk a good part of the way. No one deserved to spend so much time commuting in order to earn a living, but everyone there faced the same situation every day, impossible to pay the rent near the districts where the upper class lived, and they didn't want to live in the favela, since they'd had enough of that in childhood. They might be poor, but they never gave up having a street address and a number so mail could arrive.

She pushed herself past butts and thighs to get off the bus, after hours of rattling around. Enormous and unstable! She was late and still had a twenty-minute walk to her mistress's house. She liked working for Dona Amelinha, but lately she was always tired, and with Zen's dog-walking business going so well, she wondered whether it was time to slow down and enjoy life more. Zen, the love of her life, the carefully hidden secret.

As she walked along the avenue by the Jockey Club toward her job, she reminded herself that Dona Amelinha must never know the truth about Zen. She would never understand; it was better for her to think he was a new love after years of loneliness. Or not? She had always been good, had helped with the girls' things . . . Well, omission isn't lying, is it? No, she hadn't done anything wrong.

She continued walking and greeted several cross-dressers, many of them her friends.

"Good morning, Morena," said Shirley, standing on the corner. Shirley Caveira. She was beautiful to die for, but her ID read *Ernesto Correia*. Boni had a special affection for the transvestite. Boni had a "great ass," and several times on her way there she was approached by men in very expensive cars.

At first, some of the drag queens thought she was a competitor, and she was afraid to come and go by that route until Shirley talked to them and adopted her. She never had any more problems. Today she even laughed when a "sugar daddy" stopped his car beside her and rolled down the passenger window. She felt pretty.

"Good morning, friend. How's Marcos, has he 'watered the flowers' today? May I get by on the sidewalk?"

They both burst out laughing. The only danger they faced daily was from a half-crazy resident, the owner of one of those enormous mansions across from the Jockey, who used a garden hose to roust the transvestites from his corner, soaking anyone standing there. It was enough to provoke laughter witnessing the scene, but it wasn't at all funny when you were the one getting drenched.

Boni continued on her way, daydreaming to pass the time more quickly. She always went along the sidewalk where the cross-dressers were. She had never had an agreement with the whores and they were overly aggressive. São Paulo Jockey Club, the horse races, and such. And an endless wall, all beige with a few green details. She'd never been inside and was dying of curiosity, but she had seen the bustle on Grand Prize day, women in hats, extremely chic, accompanied by those guys you only see on television. Dona Amelinha proudly told of her high school inside there, the Jockey Club School of São Paulo, where the pupils were a mix of employees' children and those from the noblest families. Just think, the stableman's daughter dating the rich man's son from Cidade Jardim! Dona Amelinha said she couldn't imagine herself paying attention to a poor man. Lineage! She had heard a lot about that. Rich people think they're better than others, Boni was accustomed to it. She had been trained by her godmother, who said: "Stay in the shadows and make yourself indispensable." The anger she felt toward such people! They did charity for the church, but at home no one was as good as them. Sometimes even the puppy was more important than everyone. She wasn't talking about Dona Amelinha, just the opposite, the old lady was actually very kind to her, but from there to understanding Zen's problem was too much to ask. At times she regretted not having said anything, though she tried not to think about that. Not a lot.

She crossed the intersection at the end of the avenue—which was always hard because the traffic lights had multiple phases—avoided the confusion at the entrance to the American school on the corner, made the sign of the cross as she saw the Parish of Saints Peter and Paul, and entered the pedestrian-only street that began at the avenue. Now she was inside the neighborhood.

"Good morning, Boni!" It was Dutra, the head of security at Colinas das Flores, the firm that patrolled the district in vehicles. All the streets had names of plants: Maidenhair, Manacá, Acacia, Blackberry, Peach, Begonia.

"Hi, Dutra! Let's hope for a good day," Boni said, smiling.

"Is Zen working today?"

"He'll be here soon. I think his clients don't get started till eight."

"Cool."

Dutra waved, getting into the car to answer a call on the radio. They kept watch over the residents entering and leaving their garages, the moment when most attacks took place. What would Dona Amelinha think if she knew in fact who Zen was? Convicted of robbery and murder. He didn't pull the trigger, but in the eyes of the law that didn't matter. The thing went south, an idiot in the gang lost control, and that's all it took! Killed the security guard. And everyone paid the price. Oh, Zen, the love of her life . . . He couldn't kill a fly. His wide smile whenever he saw her was filled with emotion; her brow furrowed with the constant humiliation of each body search she suffered in visits to the prison. Boni always took special snacks and treats just to see the childlike delight on his face when he opened the bag that she brought for everyone in the cell. Almost fifteen years of that life, away from home, not even seeing the girls born, but she couldn't deny they had never gotten on as well as during this time. They never fought. The prison visits were always full of love and sex, promises and dreams for when he got out. When his parole came through and Zen walked out into the open, they couldn't believe it! Finally it would be every day, whenever they wanted.

Dona Amelinha had even tried to help Zen find a job when he got out, but Boni couldn't run the risk. It wouldn't do, especially since it was a matter of robbery. The old lady would immediately think there would be a robbery in the district, that Boni was involved with criminals, and so on. She suggested looking for a job as a waiter, a bagger in a supermarket, but Boni dodged the subject because Zen's past mustn't be discovered. What if she were fired because of it? Both of them unemployed?

Boni went in quickly. She donned her uniform and immediately headed to Dona Amelinha's bedroom. The list of the day's tasks must already be on the computer screen. She opened the curtains to let light in.

"Good morning, Dona Amelinha!"

Amelinha let out a sigh of relief when Boni came into the room. She indicated to the maid all the tasks, chose the dinner menu, the chinaware to be used, and the wine for Boni-claide to bring from the cellar. Then she concentrated on the reading she was doing, pausing now and then to listen to the news. She lunched frugally and took her nap. It was then, as in a nightmare, that she was awakened by a hail of gunshots, explosions, the sounds of cars braking, police sirens. She could neither move nor scream, but she was in a panic! What if she were assaulted? How could she convince anyone that she really couldn't move, that she couldn't open the safe, that no sound came out of her mouth? Terrified, she activated the button that summoned the maid. Nothing—she didn't come! She heard the doorbell ring. And waited. And nothing happened, no sign of Boniclaide; phlegm began to rise from her throat to her nostrils, saliva gathering in her mouth. That happened sometimes when she was nervous. Amelinha couldn't remain very long without the aid of the suction device. Where was Boni? She didn't know how long she could hold out. She focused on the news, changing channels with her eyes in an attempt to understand what was going on. The crime programs were sensationalist, trashy, but at that moment they were all she had. Many reporters were now live, with cameras out there near her corner. Robbery, a stray bullet, a death. Amelinha mentally reconstructed the action that had unfolded a few meters from her. It was then that she heard—it couldn't be the same person, it couldn't! Had Boni been lying to her for so long? Could a killer have come and gone freely in her house all that time? What a betrayal Boniclaide had done to her! The shameless woman dissembled her entire life. That's why this country didn't progress: an individual commits a crime and before long he's back on the street, ready to perpetrate another. The police were useless! How was it someone doesn't serve out the full term to which he was sentenced? Didn't he get twenty years? Let him rot in jail until he paid for what he did! American law had it right, it doesn't want to know and doesn't care—the death penalty, and three strikes is life imprisonment. She couldn't resign herself to the lie, she could put up with anything except lying. Lying was betrayal. Omission was lying. And she thought Boniclaide was her friend, what a dream. She should have listened to her mother, who always told her not to take a liking to servants, they'd change jobs for an extra two cents. It wasn't going to end like this, not at all. Her eyes, now furious, began to "hammer" the letters on the computer keyboard. She wanted an explanation for such a betrayal of trust.

Boni was preparing lunch when the gunfire began. It was as if she were in the favela. She looked out the kitchen window and saw a line of Colinas vans pass by, heard the police sirens, total pandemonium. Something was obviously wrong on Avenida Cidade Jardim. The area was packed with banks and stores, one after the other. She heard a series of gunshots of different calibers, accustomed as she was, shouting, cars braking, people running. And when she heard the doorbell, she went directly to open it for Zen, who must already be tending to the dogs and could only be arriving to have his daily "snack" before leaving for home. Dona Amelinha didn't even know he had lunch with Boni every day, nor did she need to know, it wasn't going to be missed, in that house food was always plentiful. She opened the door, anxious to find out what had happened, holdups in the district were nothing unusual, but her soul froze when she saw Dutra standing there, a frightened look on his face, the door to the security van still open.

"Talk to me, Dutra, talk! What happened? Where's Zen?"

"Calm down, Boni, calm down. You need to be strong."

"Why strong, Dutra? You're scaring me!"

"Boni, there's been a robbery—"

"But is Zen involved? Is he a suspect? Don't tell me something like that, Dutra, he's gone straight, he works every day . . ." She spoke breathlessly; my God, a robbery and they would immediately suspect him, she was going to lose her job too. She wiped her hands on her apron, desperate, with Dutra more and more tongue-tied.

"Talk, Dutra, talk! You're killing me!"

"Boni, what are you saying, woman? Zen was shot! Zen is the victim!"

Boni stopped talking. A drop of sweat ran down her back to her butt. She pushed Dutra aside.

"Out of my way." She ran, ran, clearing bystanders from her path. There was a body stretched out on the ground. It was him. She grabbed his face, imploring him not to die. She called his name, cried, embraced him, stained herself with blood.

"It was a gun, a gun!"

She heard everything that was said, but the sound was far away, disjointed words, murmurs . . . there were four black blazers . . . a bomb . . . glass at the door of the bank . . . a stray bullet . . . A stray bullet? They were joking, weren't they? To have the life Zen had, to survive in a gang, with him carrying a gun, facing prison and the worst people in the world, paying his debt, reforming, finding work—only to die from a stray bullet while walking other people's dogs in Cidade Jardim? God must have a diabolical sense of humor, this couldn't be happening! Not now, not with everything going right, they didn't deserve this! Dazed, she let herself be taken home— that is, to Dona Amelinha's—called her mistress's son to notify the assisted-living agency to send someone urgently, went to Dona Amelinha's room desperate to leave, though not without first letting her know. Amid weeping and memories, not fully understanding what was happening, she removed her uniform and put on her street clothes. She would not go away in the middle of the swarm of people like every day. She would go alone, the protagonist of the day's tragedy.

Almost at the entrance to Dona Amelinha's room, she heard the last of the coverage on the TV: ". . . *bank robber killed by stray bullet in attack in Cidade Jardim.*" With her hand on the doorknob, she stood paralyzed. She needed to go in, she knew. Dona Amelinha's eyes were fixed on her, then on the computer. On the screen was written:

You lied! Betrayal! You brought a psychopath into my house? My God, the risk! A robber and a killer! Good thing the bullet didn't kill an innocent person, divine justice speaks louder! The two of you deserved each other, you hypocrite! You have a lot to explain to me, this isn't the end of it. And you know something? It was God Himself who freed you of him! Each one gets what he deserves. Serves him right!

Boni opened and closed her mouth without emitting a single word. Amelinha went on writing, as red as a beet, but Boni didn't see anything more. She was stunned. What a vulgar, vile, spiteful old woman. Granddaughter of the Baron of Quental, blah-blah-blah, so what? Heartless. After everything she had done for her, she had put up with so much! She had given Dona Amelinha her best years, my God, how she had deceived herself. To "say" all of that at such a time, with Zen lying on the ground bleeding, dead, still warm, waiting for forensics. The sons of bitches! Damn her, damn the newscast;

she ran out, stifling her sobs. She couldn't think about that now, not now. Zen needed her.

Dona Amelinha. Dona Amelinha . . . Boniclaide had never suffered such humiliation in her entire life. Hypocrite? After twenty years! Her blood boiled, she could even hear her heart beating. *Take it easy, Boniclaide, take it easy,* she had been repeating to herself since that fatal day. The dust hadn't settled, she hadn't calmed down. She had been working that job for so long, never missing a day, to end up "hearing what she heard." She wasn't resigned to it!

She took the closed-off street beside the Bradesco Bank, greeting the Colinas security man stationed there. Of course, a rich people's area is going to have a security guard. What irony! She entered her neighborhood—that is to say, Dona Amelinha's, but it was as if it were hers as well. She spent more time there than in her own home. Cidade Jardim. All the workers arriving and leaving together. If you sat on the bench at the corner in the morning, you could see the movement, the housekeepers, maids, day workers, security men, gardeners, pool cleaners, coming and going through the blocked-off streets, each heading to his or her livelihood, where the bus doesn't enter. At afternoon's end everyone scattered.

She stopped at the corner of her mistress's house. She looked, trying to remember how it was before, but couldn't. She only saw Zen dead on the ground and heard Dona Amelinha's *Serves him right!* She only saw a body, the body of her love. *My love, my love, how did it happen?* Boni, the well-raised, well-behaved daughter who had her future planned and her trousseau already bought. Boni, who entered the penitentiary mute and left silent, who disdained those criminals—her, of all people, whom her mother forced to visit her brother in jail, fell in love with his cellmate. She had fought against the feeling as much as she could—how could it possibly work out?—but Sunday by Sunday, smile by smile, glance by glance, she slowly yielded. Until she gave herself. Never again would she feel as loved, never again would she give so much of herself. No one has two soul mates. Her eyes filled with tears that flowed freely at the mere recollection. The security guard at the house across the way looked at her, downcast. She stared at the ground. She was cursed, damned, the wife of a criminal. She clutched the bag under her arm and thought again. Seethed again. Better to not even go inside. How was she going to take care of her after all this? Of course, she could quit. Zen—Zen had won his freedom from prison but was never going to overcome prejudice. Now everyone knew her greatest secret. The weekend had been a nightmare. People looked upon her with different eyes. She wanted to feel her pain in peace. With a mixture of sadness and shame, she imagined herself gathering all her things, packing her bags, and leaving forever that house that was also a little bit hers. She softened as she glanced around, how hard it was to say goodbye to what had been hers for such a long time. No, she couldn't weaken now. Damn Dona Amelinha, she didn't deserve Boniclaide's dedication. Never again would she submit to being humiliated for money. She would have courage, the girls were older now, everything would work out. But how was she going to say this to Dona Amelinha? How to start? Despite her anxiety, it shouldn't be too difficult, the old woman deserved it.

She decided to go down Blackberry and cross into the woods. She wasn't ready yet. She passed by the home of the famous TV personality, Hebe Camargo. On the other side, the Morumbi woods. What did the sign say? *Alfredo Volpi Park*. She had no idea who he was, but the rich liked to complicate things. She entered through a path filled with shadow and light. Going through these trees always calmed her, even when she was in her uniform, a bit embarrassed, pushing Dona Amelinha's wheelchair. Heavens, she kept thinking about Dona Amelinha, didn't she? *Good Lord, I need to stop this habit of putting her into everything I remember.* She picked some flowers along the path and took them to the wooden cross up above. She prayed, deposited the bouquet at the foot of the cross, and asked for understanding. She asked for calm. Rage was taking control of her. All right, she had hidden Zen's past from her mistress, but what alternative did she have? It was something out of a soap opera to believe that just because Dona Amelinha lived as prisoner in her own body she would understand people who had been in real prison. No way, she would always believe her imprisonment was because of disease, a noble suffering. Was Boni going to tell her that her husband was a prisoner? With two daughters to raise? She couldn't risk it, she had indeed hidden it, and so what? What difference did it make to Dona Amelinha if her husband was a good guy or a crook? She'd just like to see the woman's life without Boni. She had never done anything wrong and, knowing Dona Amelinha as she did—if she had told her, it would have been very bad. And it was.

Today was Monday already, but pain had invaded Boni's soul. She would never forgive.

What did Amélia Lins e Silva think? That Boni was going to show up, make breakfast, take care of everything as if nothing had happened? And bear twenty more years after such ingratitude? Judging Zen? Thinking she was better? That sanctimonious woman, friend of the priest of the Saints Peter and Paul Chapel, which was open only for Mass? The self-styled charitable "good soul"? Dona Amelinha was the one who dissembled and lied! Oh no, it wasn't going to stay that way, not at all.

Boniclaide da Silva Paranhos left the park and entered the neighboring church, also Saints Peter and Paul, but with its doors always open to the people. She sat in a pew, looked God in the eye, and thought for a long time. And narrowed her gaze, as if to better understand Him. And she decided. Let each one do his part. She placed herself in His hands. She went to the baptismal font, took a small vial from her pocket, threw away the pills, and filled it with a bit of holy water. She put it away and walked back to Dona Amelinha's house. The day was lovely, the sun shining brighter than ever.

She entered the house like any normal day. She served breakfast to the orderly, who told her of Dona Amelinha's general condition. He was irritated at her late arrival, even more because she hadn't answered her cell phone all morning. Finally, he handed Boni the device to remove saliva and phlegm, for her to wash and sterilize. As always, he recommended she keep watch so the patient wouldn't suffocate. Of course. Boni witnessed his departure calmly.

She took a deep breath, unhurriedly climbed the stairs to her mistress's room, her uniform impeccable. Her legs were heavy, but a frightful calmness dominated her heart. She said good morning, opened the curtains to let in sunlight. There was already a message on the computer screen, a list of everything she had to do that day. *You witch*, Boni thought, still hoping the old woman would apologize. Of course—to her everything was back to normal. To Boni nothing would ever be the same.

She carefully opened the vial of holy water. She moistened her fingers and traced a cross on Amelinha's forehead, the back of her neck, her chest, on each hand and each foot.

Words began to appear on the computer screen: *What are you doing, Boni? Are you crazy? Blessing me?*

Boni didn't bother to reply. She got a scarf and gently wrapped it around her mistress's head. Amelinha looked at Boni and at the computer, indicating that she wanted to talk, but the time for apology was past.

Boniclaide said aloud: "To you, Lord, I commend an evil soul." She pulled up a chair and sat there, waiting, her eyes locked on Amelinha's eyes, eyes that thrashed about, seeking air. With each gasp, Boni felt more avenged. She even smiled.

It did not take long. Amelinha began to turn blue. Fascinating to see a person's skin change color. Until everything became quiet. Serves her right!

It wasn't she who had killed. It was He who didn't save her.

USELESS DIARY

BY TONY BELLOTTO

Bixiga

December 9

Today John Lennon died. Or maybe yesterday, I don't know. When I came down for breakfast some of the evening papers were already printing the news. At the August Moon, before serving the salami-and-provolone sandwich, a disconsolate Antônio brought me a beer without a word.

"I didn't know you were a Lennon fan," I grunted after an insipid swallow.

"The Beatles changed my life."

On the way to the office I glimpsed through the bus window images of the former Beatle on television sets in bars and appliance stores. The newspaper fluttering on my lap narrated the confused story of an imbecile named Mark Chapman, born in Hawaii, who last night fired five shots into Lennon's back in New York, when the former Beatle was arriving home after a recording session. In the late afternoon, like an ordinary fan, Chapman had approached the musician at the same spot where he would later assassinate him—on the sidewalk outside the Dakota—and asked him to autograph the cover of the *Double Fantasy* album. Lennon had a bit of difficulty writing because the ink in the pen didn't flow smoothly. After signing it and adding a deferential *1980*, John Lennon looked into the eyes of the man who was going to kill him and asked, "Is that all? Do you want anything else?"

* * *

At the office.

Dora Lobo received me with traces of tears and an awkward hug. "Such a good young man, who wanted nothing more than peace in the world."

Just like the waiter at the August Moon, my boss was revealing an unexpected admiration for John Lennon.

"Did the Beatles change your life too?" I asked incredulously. I had always thought Dora's musical idols were a bit disappointing, other than Paganini, Dóris Monteiro, and Dick Farney.

"They changed the world, Bellini," she stated, subtly indignant.

Minutes later, I was in my room facing the client who was waiting for me without disguising an anxiety that was as obvious as her breasts. Her name was Berthe, and she made no comment about Lennon's death.

December 10

Berthe Clemente is looking for her twin brother, Jean Claude, from whom she hasn't heard in more than a year.

"Papa is dying in Araraquara," she said, "and deserves to see his only son before passing."

"Take it easy," I suggested. "Why don't you tell me the story from the beginning?"

"Which beginning?"

"Is there more than one?"

Berthe stared at me a bit offended. There are several, of course. It was on her to choose.

"Jean Claude is gay," she said.

It was a good start.

* * *

Yesterday morning, Mark Chapman left the hotel where he was staying, walked into a bookstore, and bought a copy of *The Catcher in the Rye* by J.D. Salinger. He opened the book and, using the same pen Lennon would autograph the cover of his record with that same afternoon, wrote, *From Holden Caulfield to Holden Caulfield*. Immediately below, he added: *This is my statement*. And underlined the word *this*.

The death of John Lennon suggests "Strawberry Fields Forever," "Across the Universe," or "Mind Games," but the Walkman insists on reverberating in my brain the ethereal voice of Mississippi Fred McDowell: *"Jesus is on that mainline . . . tell him what you want . . ."*

The twins Berthe and Jean Claude Clemente grew up in Araraquara, in the interior of the state. Although Berthe, like their mother Marie Louise, early on perceived the boy's homosexual tendencies, their father only learned of this when Jean Claude, by then living in São Paulo and attending a prep school, revealed his sexual preference to the family one rainy weekend. Jean Claude knew it would be a difficult announcement, but nothing had prepared him for the reaction of his father, who threw him out of the house. According to Berthe, she and Marie Louise made innumerable attempts to bring about a reconciliation between father and son, but time only served to further estrange the two. For several years, Jean Claude maintained sporadic contact with Berthe, who conveyed his messages to their mother. Meetings, however, became increasingly rare.

"One day," said Berthe, "my brother simply disappeared."

I arrived at the Aquarius discotheque on Rui Barbosa, and asked the gay bouncer if Fats was around.

"Fats, at this hour?" I noted the sarcastic smile on his face. "Too early."

I checked my watch. Past midnight. I thought of Berthe and Jean Claude's father dying of cancer in Araraquara.

"Maybe it's too late, " I said.

December 11

Darkness camouflages a wall
By a hair
Real estate lands a punch
On the nose

To kill time at the Speranza, I read a few of Jean Claude Clemente's poetry. They struck me as quite idiotic and devoid of literary merit, but Berthe assured me her brother took poetry seriously: "He had this fantasy of being the Rimbaud of Araraquara, possibly because of our mother's French ancestry. He went around bars in Bixiga selling his photocopied poems. He was a dreamer."

At one thirty, I put the small book of Jean Claude's poems called *Inside Me* in my jacket pocket, killed my third glass of beer, and asked for the check. The escarole pizza had provoked Proustian remembrances in me, but reality took charge and redirected me to more Dante-esque venues: I went back to the Aquarius.

On the dark dance floor, a few skeletons were jerking to the sound of the Bee Gees. I missed Hell. Suspicious eyes followed me as I tried to make my way through the blackness. I ventured down a corridor and opened a door, certain I would enter Fats's office. I was mistaken; it was the bathroom. In order to avoid extended peripheral descriptions, I note merely that the bathroom was much more lively than the dance floor.

At least it was lit. Even so, I refrained from urinating there, believing strongly that urination should be, in principle, a private act. I turned around and went in another door. Fats, who currently manages the joint, was snorting a line of coke. Nothing unusual about that, except for the fact that the drug was lined up on the semierect penis of a naked young mulatto.

"Sorry," I said, and closed the door.

"I don't know any Jean Claude Clemente," Fats affirmed a few minutes later, recomposed and seated calmly at his desk, after waving away the carnal tray of cocaine and hearing my story. "This is a place of refined and Dionysian gay people, not some bar full of phony poets from the countryside," he concluded, smoothing out his stiff mustache.

"I didn't imagine it was," I said. "But your knowledge of the gay universe extends far beyond the confines of Avenida Conselheiro Carrão."

He looked at me for an instant, unsure whether to interpret my statement as praise or insult. "You don't seem like the type who frequents the sophisticated saunas of Vila Mariana. You got a photo of Jean Claude?"

I shook my head.

"You've been better at this in the past, detective."

"He's a handsome man of twenty-five, redheaded, with light skin and a delicate nose like Jack Nicholson's."

"How do you know?"

"I met his twin sister, Berthe."

"A redheaded fairy with a delicate nose isn't much to go on."

"Poet and from Araraquara. A dreamer. His sister has incredible breasts, but that's probably not going to help you much."

"Not at all."

"Well?"

"What'll you give me in exchange for the information?" he asked with a provocative smile.

"A limp dick can't support a line of coke," I answered.

December 12

I sleep late. At the August Moon, Antônio insists on serving me beer before the salami-and-provolone sandwich. I imagine that while the commotion over Lennon's death lasts, hops and barley will continue to initiate my breakfast.

After firing at the former Beatle, Mark Chapman went into a kind of trance. He stood there immobile, clutching the revolver, until José, the Dakota's doorman, grabbed his arm and shook it, forcing him to release the weapon, which José kicked away. Then Chapman took off his coat and sweater, opened *The Catcher in the Rye*, and began reading with intense concentration.

"The maniac said he was obeying voices inside his head," said Antônio, reading the newspaper over my shoulder.

"It's the excuse they always give. The voices should instruct him to fire at themselves, which would've resulted in a providential bullet in Chapman's own head."

"In that case he wouldn't be crazy," Antônio concluded.

"And John Lennon would be alive."

"Have you read that book? *The Catcher in* whatever it is?"

"It doesn't strike me as a good manual for homicide. I've never managed to kill the people I'd like to."

"Yeah. If someday you're told by internal voices to kill somebody, that somebody will probably be you yourself."

"Bring me another beer," I said.

The Persona bar is on 13 de Maio. It's a dark tavern with

psychoanalytic pretensions: in the center of each table there's a small mirror that merges the features of the two diners sitting face to face. It must have something to do with the fragmentation of personalities, quite in fashion these days. I went by there last night. Because I was sitting by myself, I could see in the mirror only my out-of-focus face, which was surprisingly revelatory of my personality's lack of definition. The Persona isn't exactly a gay bar, although homosexual and heterosexual couples are easily confused because they're all equally long-haired. According to the information from Fats, Jean Claude used to frequent the place. After a few beers and two or three questions directed to the waitress—also the bearer of a face very out of focus, framed by uncommonly short hair—I discovered that the redheaded poet had been seen there several times in the company of Danilo, a hippie renowned for supplying pot and acid to the customers from that traditional district of Italian immigrants. Although Jean Claude hadn't appeared lately, the hippie is still in the habit of showing up now and then.

I tried locating Danilo in the vicinity of the Gigetto, Il Cacciatore, and other Italian eateries favored by artists and show-business people, potential consumers of the substances he sold.

"Thursday isn't a good day to find dealers around here," predicted Pajé, a car watcher who works in front of the bar in which a guy with the voice of Djavan was trying to sing "Imagine." "Come back tomorrow."

December 13

Stephen Spiro and Peter Cullen were making their night rounds when they saw the doorman of the Dakota point to the marquee of the building and shout, "That's the guy doing the shooting!" Spiro jumped out of the patrol car, his gun drawn, and approached the man—whose hands were raised—and threw him against the wall. "He shot John Lennon!" shouted José. "He shot John Lennon!"

"What did you do?" Spiro asked the man immobilized against the wall.

"I acted alone," he replied.

Stephen Spiro thought this the strangest statement he'd ever heard.

It was past midnight when I walked under the Bixiga viaduct, switching from Brigadeiro to Rui Barbosa. I've never had any problem walking under ladders, but walking under viaducts has always made me uneasy. Recollection of the collapse of the Paulo Frontin expressway in Rio de Janeiro has haunted me for almost ten years. The viaduct didn't cave in on me, but I was accosted by a strange man, an anachronistic Mohican Indian. The scene would be humorous if the Mohican wasn't poking my jugular with the point of a jackknife.

"You lookin' for me, pig?"

"Don't underestimate me," I said.

"The fuck? What're you gonna say? You a yuppie deciding to try some coke? Or maybe a nickel bag?"

"I'm not very yuppie. Definitely not a cop. No illusions about pot. And I'm taking a break from coke. Would you be the hippie called Danilo?"

"There ain't no more hippies," he said, relieving the pressure of the knife against my throat. "All the hippies died Monday along with John Lennon. The dream is over."

"I understand. And when you woke up on Tuesday you all became Mohicans."

"I am the walrus!" he suddenly shouted, his eyes bulging.

"It must be sad."

"What?"

"To be the walrus."

"Aw, you don't understand shit," he said, putting the knife away in his pocket. "Lennon was murdered. Fuck!"

Before he started to cry, I invited him for a beer.

"I don't drink. What is you want?"

"To find out Jean Claude's whereabouts."

"I don't know him."

"Yes you do."

"Stop busting my balls! I am the walrus!"

At that moment, Danilo really did begin to cry, whether from the ridiculousness of his declaration, the death of John Lennon, the mention of Jean Claude, or because of a hefty dose of LSD, I don't know. Maybe all of it together.

"Let's do it this way: you tell me where Jean Claude is and I swear I won't tell anyone that Mohican Danilo sometimes likes to indulge in a bit of cornholing."

"You bastard," he said.

The building is on Rua Dr. Vila Nova. The address cost me some saliva. I revealed to Danilo that Jean Claude's father is dying in Araraquara and that the old man's final wish is to see his poet son.

"Who said so?"

"Berthe told me."

"Who?"

"Berthe, Jean Claude's twin sister."

"I didn't know Jean Claude had a twin sister."

"It's better for you to focus on what you do know."

Walrus finally confessed to a relationship with Jean Claude, "a relationship of friendship, nonsexual," as he made a point of clarifying. He said he hadn't seen him in over six months. "He vanished."

"People don't just vanish," I said.

"I think he went on a trip," he stated vaguely. "Jean Claude was always saying he wanted to travel. I told him to trip out without leaving where he was, like me. But he wanted to go to Africa, like Rimbaud. He said he needed to experience a grand transformation." Danilo smiled. "He was a weird dude."

"Where'd he travel to?"

"How should I know?"

"Not even a hunch?"

"Somewhere far away, believe me."

The Menotti Del Picchia Building.

Behind the security bars, I saw the doorman sleeping beside a TV tuned to a constellation of black-and-white static. It was almost two a.m., but time flies against everyone, including those who sleep without being aware of this fact.

December 14

"We ran to the trauma ward," said the doctor on duty. "We took off his clothes. There were three wounds in the upper left side of his chest and one in his left arm. No blood pressure, no pulse, no vital signs, no reaction. We knew exactly what to do: intravenous blood transfer, emergency surgical intervention. We opened the chest to look for the source of the hemorrhage. In the process, the nurses took the wallet from the patient's pocket. They said: *This can't be* the *John Lennon*. We realized it was really him when Yoko Ono arrived at the emergency room."

The doorman at the Menotti Del Picchia Building is named

José. Even though the doorman at the Dakota has the same name, the coincidence explains absolutely nothing. I woke him up with the sharp sound of the entrance bell. With the catatonic expression of the recently awakened, he asked via the intercom what I wanted.

"To speak with Jean Claude Clemente," I said.

"He doesn't live here anymore. He moved more than six months ago."

"Moved where?"

"Your name, please."

"Bellini. Remo Bellini. Attorney. And yours?"

"José. José da Silva. Doorman."

For a guy who just woke up, José da Silva demonstrated an admirable sense of humor.

"Excuse me for waking you up at this hour, José, but it's an emergency. Jean Claude's father is very sick. Do you know where he moved to?"

He stared at me in silence.

"Africa?" I ventured, thinking of Rimbaud.

"São Francisco, I think."

"The São Francisco River? São Francisco do Sul?"

"São Francisco with all the queers."

From good-humored, José had transformed into a smartass.

"Did he leave an address?"

"No. But I have something here for you."

I returned home and waited for the day to dawn. I called Berthe. Before she answered the phone, I noticed the heralds of Sunday melancholy through the window: birds singing in the sooty crowns of the trees in Trianon Park. I explained to the Clemente twin that Jean Claude must be living in San Francisco, California, and that the doorman of the building where he used to live had given me a copious amount of mail accumulated in the more than six months since his departure. Confirmation of his whereabouts and the discovery of his current address would require a few more days, or maybe weeks.

"That won't be necessary," she said. "Unfortunately, there's no time, my father is dying. Can you bring me the correspondence? Then we can settle up."

I wrote down her address.

"Be here in an hour," she said before hanging up.

When I arrived at Berthe's apartment—a small studio in Itaim—images of Yoko Ono leaving the hospital emergency room hovered in my brain. I rang the bell and tried to concentrate on my work. It's still an honest way to cross the Sunday desert.

"Come in," Berthe called from inside. "The door's open."

Her living room was small, decorated with Afghan rugs, photos of Tibetan monasteries, and a poster of Farah Fawcett. The place smelled of Indian incense and patchouli. She came down the corridor, smiling.

"Sorry, I was changing . . ."

She was wearing only a blue silk robe with an Oriental design, which revealed much of her electrifying pair of breasts. On second thought, reducing those two round monuments to a "pair" wouldn't do justice to objects so unique and appetizing.

"Don't worry, I can wait," I said, as we exchanged friendly pecks on the cheek.

"I'm anxious," she said, despite not having given the slightest attention to the wad of letters I had deposited on the table in the middle of the room. "Come." She turned her back on me so I could follow. "I need to show you something."

I trailed her down the corridor toward the apartment's

only bedroom. My heart was racing when she slipped out of the robe, revealing a sculpted back that ended in a hypnotic ass.

"Berthe . . ." I said, anticipating the shortness of breath that assailed me as soon as she turned around and I saw the majestic penis oscillating between thighs worthy of a Miss Araraquara.

I had just found Jean Claude Clemente.

December 15

A week after the assassination of John Lennon there began to emerge interpretations about the fact of *The Catcher in the Rye* having been found in the hands of the killer. One writer analyzed:

> *If the person reads the book through an especially distorted lens, he feels sharply Holden's impotence and says, "Yes, I also feel impotent," and fails to make the crucial leap that Holden finally makes, which Salinger always makes at the end of every book and which the imaginative reader is invited to make.*

"I just wanted to see your face," Jean Claude/Berthe said to justify himself. "To analyze your expression when you perceived my transformation."

I finally understood his poetry. "You used me as a guinea pig," I said.

"Right," he agreed with a smile, before leaving for Araraquara to take his dying father to his extreme unction.

"You got me runnin', you got me hidin' . . ." The sound of Jimmy Reed's voice and guitar dissipates with Antônio's approach.

I turn off the Walkman.

After depositing the salami-and-provolone sandwich on the table, he points inquiringly at the notebook open before me.

"Nothing," I say, closing it. "Just a useless diary."

MY NAME IS NICKY NICOLA

BY JÔ SOARES

Mooca

Chapter I
Detective Nicky Nicola's Strange Client

São Paulo, 1960

In the Mooca district, in his beautiful penthouse, actually an extension of the slab on top of Vitorio's bar, Nicky Nicola awoke to the sound of insistent knocking at the door. It was the telephone. Or rather, it was Vitorio advising of a call for Nicola down in the bar. The establishment doubled as the detective's office, jotting down the occasional message. Vitorio owed Nicola a debt of gratitude since the detective had solved the intricate case of the "Stolen Mortadella." Nicky, as the private investigator was known to his friends, leaped from the aged bed and fell headlong onto the floor. He was still unaccustomed to sleeping in the upper bunk. Zé Ferreira, his roommate, had already left for work. Bank employees didn't enjoy the same luxurious schedules as private investigators.

Nicola opened his fine plastic cigarette case with the emblem of the Palmeiras soccer team and lit his first Beverly of the day. He took a long puff, observing the rays of light streaming in through cracks in the window. He was in no hurry to answer the phone call downstairs in the bar. One reason was because he was wearing nothing.

His beautiful blue-and-brown outfit hadn't come yet from

Dona Marlene's laundry across the street: striped blue pants that had once been part of a suit, and a brown coat left over from another, both acquired in the same secondhand clothing store. He went into the bathroom and opened the small mirrored cabinet that functioned as his bar. Using the glass where he kept his toothbrush, he poured himself a stiff dose of Dreher cognac. Nicky kept a bottle in the bathroom cabinet and always carried a flask with him. It was his favorite drink. He wouldn't trade it even for Peterlongo, the delicate domestic champagne. He downed the yellow liquid in a single gulp and shaved using the same blade for the twenty-fifth time. *One of these days I'm gonna have to steal another one of Zé's used razor blades*, he thought.

At that instant, the door began to open slowly. As fast as lightning, calling into play his every reflex, he grabbed his always-near .32 caliber muzzle-loading pistol "Caramuru" with a mother-of-pearl grip, inherited from his grandfather who had been a military policeman in Minas Gerais, and dived under the bed. It was only Dona Marlene from the laundry, bringing his clothes. She hung them in the closet and left as quickly as she had come.

In two minutes Nicky was dressed. He didn't wear undershorts for two reasons. First, because he didn't have any. Second, because he found it useless to spend money on an item of clothing that no one would see. He looked at himself in the large mirror in the closet and liked what he saw: sparse black hair swept across the top of his head in an impeccable "combover" style to cover his premature baldness. In the comb-over style the individual allows the abundant side strands to grow and brushes them over the scalp. That meticulous engineering takes time, patience, and extreme skill. Nicky Nicola didn't look like he was thirty-five. No one would have taken him for less than forty. The flaps and flattened pockets of the chauffeur's shirt pilfered from his uncle were completely hidden by the coat. The black cotton tie didn't show the coffee stains of the same color. Nicky knew how important one's appearance is. He brushed dandruff from his shoulders with an indifferent gesture, donned the wide-brimmed hat that had belonged to his father, lit his second Beverly of the day, and went downstairs to the telephone.

"Hello? Hello?" Nicky Nicola at the phone. "Hello? . . . They hung up. You sure it was for me?"

"Yes, it was, a husky voice, a woman," replied Vitorio.

Strange, thought Nicky, and ordered a mug of coffee with milk along with toasted French bread while ruminating on why a husky-voiced woman who wanted to speak to him had hung up after waiting on the line for forty-five minutes.

Chapter II
The Poisoned Mariola Candy

As soon as Nicky Nicola finished his coffee and toast, he felt like a new man. And that new man wasn't doing well at all. He needed to lose that habit of wolfing down French bread still hot from the oven. So as not to offend Vitorio, owner of the bar and grocery, Nicola, with the consummate ability acquired thanks to years of training, removed the hidden part of his secret ring and stealthily dumped into a glass the sodium bicarbonate he always carried for such an emergency.

Only after downing the glass in a single gulp did Nicola close his ring again, with an almost imperceptible click. He liked that piece of jewelry. He had inherited it from his grandfather, and it bore interlinked initials. Not his, of course, his grandfather's. It was a beautiful imitation ring. Obviously, the secret compartment for holding bicarbonate had been adopted by Nicola after he saw a movie about one Lucrezia Borgia, a prostitute who was the daughter of a pope. While the potion was taking effect against his agita, the telephone rang again. Quick as a flash, Nicola ran to answer it. As soon as he heard the hoarse voice of a woman at the other end of the line, the mystery unraveled: the caller was Creusa, a charming dark-skinned maid who worked in an apartment in Lapa. The hoarseness was due to a strong cold, which she rapidly identified as "a grippe that's going around." Creusa nervously related that the aunt of Dona Mirtes, her mistress, had died mysteriously in the living room of the apartment. She explained that the dead women was Dona Estefânia, a distinguished public servant in Quixeramobim, in the state of Ceará, who was spending a few vacation days with her niece. There wasn't the slightest doubt: this was a case for Nicky Nicola.

Hours later, the famous investigator arrived at the address in Lapa. As he headed toward the elevator, Nicola saw reflected on the wall the shadow of a person approaching him from behind. He turned rapidly, with the swiftness of a panther, clutching his deadly nail clipper. His eyes bulged when he saw who was following him: the building's custodian. Indifferent to the sophisticated appearance of the detective, the custodian made him use the service entrance. Nicola smiled with disdain and showed him his private investigator's ID.

One minute later he was entering the service elevator.

It does no good to argue with the ignorant, he thought.

On his way through the kitchen, the detective kissed Creusa, filched a piece of coconut candy from the pantry, and proceeded to the living room. The scene before him was distressing: Dona Mirtes was crying in one corner, looking at the body of Dona Estefânia lying on the carpet. He kneeled beside her, and with the skill acquired during years of training began to carefully examine her. After two fruitless hours, he found what he was looking for: in the back of the old woman's throat, blocking the passage of food, was a piece of the candy known as a mariola. He examined it with his glass—taken from Zé Ferreira's spectacles while his roommate slept—and his instinct told him the candy was poisoned. To confirm his intuition, he divided the small piece in two and tossed part to the cat that was roaming nearby.

After gobbling it down, the cat jumped violently to one side and fell dead on the floor, its paws sticking up. Nicola congratulated himself for his shrewdness in identifying the poisoned candy, although it brought about a terrible tongue-lashing from Dona Mirtes who, after losing her aunt, had now also lost her pet.

Finally Creusa intervened and succeeded in getting her mistress to hire the investigator to find the killer. Nicola was satisfied. The money would come in handy. It wasn't every day that he got a case paying 2,500 cruzeiros a week, excluding his transportation expenses and snacks, a sum equivalent to a dollar a day.

Nicky said goodbye to Dona Mirtes, apologized again about the cat, and left by the front door, accompanied by Creusa.

"Whaddaya think?" asked the lovely mulatta in her singular way of speaking.

"I don't know, I don't know . . . To me it looks like someone wanted to kill her," Nicky Nicola replied philosophically.

Chapter III
The Treacherous Elevator

Nicky closed the apartment door after him and with remarkable expertise pushed the button to summon the elevator. Really, the candy had been the *causa mortis* of his girlfriend's mistress's aunt. He had been seeing Creusa for a long time, and when she'd phoned to say a crime had been committed in the house where she had worked as a maid for three years, Nicky hadn't hesitated: he'd run from the bar and jumped aboard the 230 bus, the line that linked Mooca and Lapa. Unfortunately, at that hour of the morning it was difficult to find a place to sit, but Nicky Nicola was in excellent physical condition when standing up.

Now, upon leaving Dona Mirtes's apartment, Nicola waited for the elevator that would take him to the routine part of the job: investigating in the bars of the neighborhood to find out in which establishment that lethal delicacy had been acquired.

The elevator finally arrived. Nicola stepped in, turned around to face the door to facilitate exiting, and pushed the button for the ground floor. Some seconds later, the elevator stopped, but there was no door visible. The machine had probably gotten stuck between two floors, and all the detective saw in front of him was an immense concrete wall. His instinct immediately told him that he had fallen into a trap: the killer knew that he intended to take the case and now planned to keep him there, penned in until he starved to death, by placing an *Out of Order* sign on the door below, causing the residents to use the other elevator. What the killer didn't know was that Nicola wasn't easily beaten. There was only one thing to do: scream. Nicky shouted with all the strength of his cigarette-ravaged lungs. He called for help, hammered his fists repeatedly against the elevator. He only stopped when he felt a heavy hand on his shoulder. With his ever-alert reflexes, Nicky turned. It was the custodian.

"No need to be afraid. You're not trapped. This elevator

has two doors. To get in on the upper floors it's there, but the exit is back here," the man said, pointing to a line of people waiting to get on, laughing furtively at the dedicated detective.

Chapter IV
The Noir Series Continues

As soon as Nicola found himself back in the street, he started asking several questions. He didn't have an answer to any of them. Who had an interest in the death of Dona Estefânia? She was probably an unbearable old lady. At least that's what Nicola thought about all old women, except of course his venerable, sweet mother, who had thrown him out of the house thirty years earlier, forcing him to look for work, with a gentle maternal incentive: "Get a job, you bum!"

Would Dona Mirtes, the niece of the deceased, gain anything from her aunt's death? Not unless she wanted to be free of that intolerable pussycat. He immediately removed the idea from his mind. *Ridiculous*, he thought. *After all, she's paying me a fortune to investigate.* Nicola had a dogged loyalty to his few clients. From that point of departure, his thoughts wandered for a few moments as he pondered whether he should have asked for an advance payment for the investigation. He came to the conclusion that it wouldn't go over well and went back to reasoning about the case.

Was Creusa, his girl, involved? Probably. She was easily seduced. She usually let her shapely rear end do the thinking for her. Who then? Nicola relit the butt of his Beverly, which had gone out in the corner of his mouth. *Okay, what matters now is finding out where the candy came from*, he reflected. He walked a bit farther and went into the first bar he encountered. His instinct told him he was on the right track. His instinct and an enormous tray of the same candy he had seen on top of the bar. He went up to the proprietor leaning over the bar, took out his private investigator ID, and said with authority: "Private Investigator Nicky Nicola. You're gonna have to answer some questions."

As he brushed off his clothes, lying on the sidewalk outside the bar, Nicola wondered why bar owners and their ilk harbored such antipathy for private investigators. It wasn't the first time he'd been violently ejected from such an establishment upon stating his noble profession. If not for the years of martial arts he'd learned from movies, watching a Bruce Lee double feature at the Cine Imperial on Rua da Mooca, he could have landed badly and fractured a rib, as had already happened on more than one occasion. But Nicky was not a man to be discouraged by so little. He went back into the bar and warned: "The next time you do something like that, I'm phoning my cousin, who has a brother-in-law who's the nephew of a friend of a cop!"

It was an old trick of Nicola's, and the threat had the usual effect: nothing. Immediately the bar owner, who happened to be from Portugal, responded: "Go eat shit! You can call anybody you want to, but if you stick your elbow in my soup again, I'll toss you out again!"

Nicola examined his jacket at the indicated spot and, seeing the stain, realized what had happened: when he leaned over the counter to show his ID he had inadvertently rested his elbow in the man's bowl of soup. He apologized, saying he would never do it again, and after a brief conversation to defuse the situation, he began his questions.

"Are you Portuguese?"

"From the day I was born, you nitwit!"

Shrugging off the man's vulgarity, Nicola continued the

awkward interrogation: "Did you by any chance notice any-one buying this candy yesterday?"

"No, but funny that you mention it," said the bar owner, who as Nicky suspected was named Manuel.

"Funny why, Mr. Manuel?"

"Well, the only person yesterday buying my candy was a Japanese guy, and you know very well that the Japanese hate that type of candy."

Nicola nodded, despite not knowing that. It was a clue. More than a clue, a lead. Now he needed to find out if there was a Japanese person among Dona Estefânia's relation-ships. He thanked Manuel for the valuable information and before leaving went into the bathroom to see if a little soap and water would remove that greenish stain from his jacket.

As soon as he started scrubbing the sleeve, he heard a click on the outside of the door. The external latch had been locked. Nicola tried to open the door but couldn't. He applied force. The latch resisted. He quickly determined that the enemy must have been following him the whole time. How careless he had been in not searching for a suspicious-looking Japanese guy in his midst. Through the bathroom window he heard a sinister guffaw. He climbed onto the basin to look out onto the street, just in time to see a small Asian man laughing as he pedaled away on a bicycle. He couldn't make out the guy's face, but there was a sign on the bike's frame: *Kiwoshi Dry Cleaners*.

Nicola jumped for joy, which was a pity. When he jumped he smashed the basin, which broke with immense noise and shattered on the floor. The wrecked pipe sent water spewing to all sides. The noise brought Manuel, who im-mediately released the stuck outside latch, leaving Nicola free. Well, almost free, he just had to remain in the bar until midnight washing dishes to pay for the basin he had broken.

Chapter V
An Idiotic Mistake

After washing all the plates in Manuel's bar, Nicola thought it was time to rest. He was wrong. Until he found the address of Kiwoshi Dry Cleaners, he wouldn't be able to sleep. He looked in the bar's telephone directory, but didn't see the dry cleaner listed. He looked, first under *Cleaners*, then under *Laundries*, followed by *Dry Cleaning*. The search yielded no results.

"Strange, very strange," Nicky Nicola thought aloud.

"What's strange?" asked Manuel, who was drying a glass while watching the detective out of the corner of his eye.

Despite the touchy fact of the bar owner having forced him to wash all the dishes to pay for the damage to the bathroom, Nicola was not a man to hold grudges. The only feeling he had in relation to the bar owner was hate. Even so, he explained: "I can't find the name *Kiwoshi Dry Cleaners* in the phone book. But I'm sure that was the name I saw on the bike."

"Of course you can't find it. You're looking in the street listing."

Nicola managed to control himself. His brilliant and agile mind immediately found a way out of that tiny slip: "I know. I was looking name by name, for the simple reason that you can't browse the list of subscribers. I can't imagine how you didn't pick up on that right away. It's obvious."

"And exactly why can't you browse the list of subscribers?" asked Manuel, intrigued.

"Elementary, my dear Manuel . . ." And he let drop the information like a bomb: "The list of subscribers must be poisoned! Whoever browses it dies!"

Manuel refused to argue with that idiotic theory: "Then why don't you look in the Yellow Pages?"

Unwittingly, that ignorant bar owner had given Nicola the correct lead. *The Yellow Pages, of course!* Why hadn't he thought of it before? Yellow Pages—Kiwoshi was Japanese and therefore yellow too! *How impressive the paths of deduction are*, thought Nicola.

He quickly found what he was looking for in the Yellow Pages and left the bar with the address of the dry cleaner carefully noted on the greasy paper napkin that served as his to-do list. There was no time to lose. He jumped into the first car that came by and, making use of his credentials, barked at the driver: "Investigator Nicky Nicola. We're going to this address! Make it quick, it's a matter of life and death."

The driver examined Nicola's business card and immediately threw him out on the street. But the detective wasn't a man so easily discouraged. He got on the first bus going by and continued his journey. The dry cleaner wasn't far away: two transfers until the end of the line. That would give him time to review the main items of the case that he had been able to sketch thus far:

1. Dona Estefânia, a teacher on vacation from the state of Ceará, had been eliminated by a poisoned piece of candy.
2. Her niece, Dona Mirtes, had hired him to solve the case.
3. Without meaning to, he had killed Dona Mirtes's cat to test whether the candy was poisoned.

4. He had been locked in the bathroom of the bar by a Japanese dry cleaner.

Putting all these pieces together, what did he have? The answer was clear: nothing.

To calm himself down, he took from his jacket pocket his special pen with a secret compartment in the ink reservoir where he always carried a good dose of booze. He unscrewed the rear part of the pen and drank it all down in a single gulp to steady his nerves. That was when he tasted ink flooding his throat.

Next chapter: "The Washable Blue Guffaw."

Chapter VI
The Washable Blue Guffaw

As soon as Nicola, installed comfortably in the bus, noticed that, instead of drinking the liquor in his secret compartment, he had gulped down all the ink in his Nogueira (an unknown brand he bought from a street vendor), he pretended nothing was awry and tried to play it off. Futilely. A fat lady seated nearby saw the blue liquid coming from his mouth and began screaming: "Conductor, help! There's a sick man here! He's vomiting blood!"

There was no way Nicola could convince her that his blood wasn't blue. The woman went on bellowing, immediately followed by a chorus of people looking in fright at the investigator's mouth. Several clinical suggestions were offered, the least absurd of which was that the detective was an Indian. Many passengers suggested that it could be contagious and that he ought to be thrown out the window. His sixth sense told him the best solution was to get out then and there. He crossed the vehicle in three agile leaps, crushing the feet of a few passengers, and, pressing his comb against the nape of the driver's neck, said: "Listen, my friend, there's no time to explain. It'd be best for you to stop right here and let me off, or my comb will do some real damage to your head."

For some time Nicola was in doubt about whether the driver had braked because of his threat or because of the co-incidence of coming to an obligatory bus stop. The fact is that two minutes later he was standing on the sidewalk. His next step was a false one: he fell down.

He got up again, now seriously bothered by the sequence of events. He went into a pharmacy, his mouth hidden behind a handkerchief. He requested a bit of alcohol and tried to re-move the traces of ink from his face. In less than half an hour he had managed to clean away those bluish stains and his skin had regained the beautiful greenish hue that had won over so many housemaids. As he was putting the finishing touches on his chin, his eyes chanced upon a large sign on the other side of the street: *Kiwoshi Dry Cleaners*. Incredible. Without meaning to, he had jumped off the bus at exactly the desired address.

He cautiously crossed the street, and from the utility kit that he always carried with him (a cigar box stuck with tape to the lining of his coat) took out his favorite disguise: big fake ears, a mustache, and bucktoothed dentures. He put it on and inspected himself in his pocket mirror. Perfect. With merely one small detail he had managed the impossible: to look even more ridiculous without changing his appearance in the least. That done, he entered the dry cleaning establishment. He im-mediately spotted the Japanese man behind the counter.

"Can I help you?"

"First of all, I wanna settle accounts with you for locking

me in the bathroom." Nicola flew on top of the counter and, with catlike agility, aimed a tremendous karate chop at the man. Instinctively, the guy raised his arm to defend himself. Since he was ironing a pair of pants at the time, he brought the hot iron up simultaneously.

During the next hour, while the Japanese man skillfully wrapped Nicola's burned hand, the detective learned that he had almost committed a fatal mistake. Kiwoshi was the owner of the dry cleaners. The one he'd seen delivering clothes on a bicycle was someone else. Who, by the way, had vanished.

"You'll have to forgive me. It's just that sometimes I confuse one Japanese person with another. You all look so much alike."

"But my deliveryman not Japanese, yes? My deliveryman from Ceará," replied Kiwoshi.

A light suddenly went on in the detective's clever brain: from Ceará! The victim, Dona Estefânia, was a teacher in that state. He felt he was on the right track. He also felt a tremendous pain when, as he was saying goodbye, Kiwoshi shook his bandaged hand.

Chapter VII
The Day of the Pumpkin

Nicola left Kiwoshi Dry Cleaners with his hand bandaged from the karate chop he had inflicted on the steam iron. It was well bandaged and didn't hurt much; the detective's long experience told him that soon he would be back in shape to continue his search.

Two weeks later he was thinking the same way but was still in bed. The comfortable bunk in his penthouse in Mooca aided in his quick recovery. "Quick recovery" in Nicola's case wasn't exactly accurate, for he was not a man to spend money on foolishness like medicine, mainly because he didn't have any. Also, he was a proponent of Eastern medicine and was familiar with all its secrets. For burns, the best remedy was compresses of butter with salt, according to a Hindu guru friend who worked at a gas station. Wisely, Nicola had replaced the butter with cold water, since he hadn't laid eyes on butter for a while and if he did, he would probably eat it before using it as a compress.

"Hey, you any better?" asked his friend Zé Ferreira.

"Yeah," replied the loquacious detective.

"I know a guy who does massages and is a wizard at those things. I don't know why you insist on not dropping by there."

For the tenth time, Nicola explained he had a burn and not a muscle pull. Then he asked whether Zé had seen any mention of the case in the newspapers.

"Nothing."

"I can't understand why nothing's been written about it. Did you do a thorough search? You haven't read my name anywhere this week?"

"Of course I have."

"So why didn't you tell me right away? What paper was it in? The *Folha*? The *Estadão*? The *Última Hora*?" asked Nicola anxiously.

"It wasn't in the paper. I read your name written on the wall of the public urinal in Republic Square. It said, *Nicola burns the donut . . . This seat has a nail in it . . . Plus, his mother—*"

"Enough!" Nicola interrupted, interested only in the relevant facts.

After learning for certain that no news of the case had been published, he pondered the mystery. The death of Dona Estefânia should have at least been cause for comment. Could a powerful international group of traffickers of mariola candy be behind it all? Possibly.

He couldn't stay confined in the bedroom any longer. He had to act fast. With the help of Zé Ferreira, he climbed down from the bed and went into the bathroom to examine his burned hand. He unwound the wrapping paper that served as a bandage and was happy with what he saw: two weeks in bed, along with the cold-water compresses, had yielded miraculous results. The hand was no longer burned. It was swollen. He could go back to the investigation. He wanted to get started right away.

He quickly did his "Bastos Exercises," invented by a friend of his, Marcos Bastos, who lived in the Macuco district in Santos. The exercise consisted of hurling himself from one wall of the room to the other for fifteen minutes. It was inspired by a bus trip from São Paulo to Cubatão. After the exercise, Nicola always felt better. Aching all over, but better. The exercise awoke his appetite and he decided to order something from downstairs. It was two a.m., but he was sure Vitorio's bar was still open. Mentally, he ran through the menu, hesitating between caviar and *pâté de foie gras* but finally opting for refried beans with pumpkin. *Since I'm after someone from Ceará, it'll be a kind of homage*, thought Nicky.

"In the future this day will be remembered as the Day of the Pumpkin," he said aloud, waking up Zé, who had fallen asleep. He then opened the window and, leaning out, placed his order by shouting downstairs, "Vitorio! Send me up some refried beans and pumpkin!"

No answer. Nicola tried again, louder: "Vitorio! Send up my beans and pumpkin!"

Still nothing. *Could two a.m. be an inopportune hour for yelling like that?* Nicola immediately rejected the ridiculous idea and screamed again at the top of his lungs: "Hey, Vitorio! Send me that beans and pumpkin!"

At that instant a lower window in the building across the street opened violently and a man wearing pajamas and looking sleepy shouted in desperation, peering down: "Listen, Vitorio. I don't know who the hell you are, but get him the goddamn beans and pumpkin before I kill the son of a bitch!" Then he nosily shut the window.

Nicola was no longer in doubt: he was dealing with an international gang. That man could only have been put there to provoke him. The Day of the Pumpkin had begun earlier than he'd expected.

Chapter VIII
A Closed Mouth Gathers No Flies, Nor Releases Them

Finally, Nicky Nicola got his plate of refried beans and pumpkin. He was prepared to set out again after the mysterious deliveryman from Ceará who worked for the dry cleaners. He was in good shape. His hand no longer ached. He felt like a new man. Ready and willing. So willing that he fell asleep right there, on top of the plate.

The next day, he rose early. It was only a few minutes past noon. Nicola donned his best (and only) suit, combed his hair, took a shot of his Dreher cognac, and coughed. After verifying in Vitorio's bar—his office—that he had no phone messages, he crossed the street and headed for Dona Marlene's laundry to pick up a handkerchief she was ironing for him.

He went in and saw no one. He found that very odd. Supporting himself against the counter, he leaned his flexible feline body over as far as he could and shouted inside: "Dona Marlene? Dona Marlene?" Nothing. He was becoming worried. His every sense went immediately on full alert. Something shadowy was invading his being. He had felt it before. It was as if the very air were saturated with humidity. Yes, that was it! Where could the humidity be coming from? He ran his practiced gaze over every corner of the room with uncommon care and expertise. After five minutes he made a discovery. Now he knew why the atmosphere was so humid: when he leaned on the counter to call Dona Marlene, he had accidentally stuck both hands in the water-filled basin she used to iron clothes. He didn't let it bother him. He quickly dried them off with a towel and called again, almost shouting: "Dona Marleneeeeee!"

This time the response was clear and immediate: "Coming! I'm just finishing my lunch!"

The detective debated with himself whether he should find a way to participate in that unexpected meal, but before he could decide, Dona Marlene appeared, sucking on an orange.

"Hi there! So it's you, Nickão? What's up?"

"Nothing, Dona Marlene. I just came to pick up the handkerchief I left to be ironed."

"But I already sent it off this morning," she responded, surprised. "My new deliveryman took it with him. Except that he left it to deliver on his way back."

"A new deliveryman?" The words struck the detective's ears like knife blows. "You're using a new deliveryman?"

"Yes. Since yesterday. His name is Severino."

Once again, the name awoke the dormant trail in the detective's unconscious. "By any chance, is he from Ceará and looks Japanese?"

Dona Marlene was absolutely gobsmacked at the private investigator's deductive ability. Where, in her brief utterance, had she mentioned that her new deliveryman was from Ceará and looked Japanese? Her jaw fell in astonishment. That was when a fly went in. Luckily, Dona Marlene kept her mouth open, which allowed the fly to exit, justifying the title of this chapter. Afterward, she confirmed Nicola's suspicion: "That's right! In fact, here he comes now!" She pointed to the door, where the long-sought-after deliveryman was entering. Before the guy could flee or defend himself, Nicola mentally calculated the distance between them and leaped forward. A miscalculation. He landed a few inches from the feet of his adversary. The temptation was too great. Severino cowardly stomped on the defenseless detective's head. But he wasn't counting on the highly technical resources of the private investigator. His big toe exploded when it met the red, round top half of the cheese gourd that Nicky kept hidden in his hat. The vile assailant fell over, howling in pain while the detective finally subdued him. Now they would have plenty to talk about.

Chapter IX
Why? Because

Nicky Nicola was almost shaking with emotion before this opportunity: his rival Severino, the mysterious man from Ceará, the dry cleaners' deliveryman who had probably caused the death of Dona Estefânia with a poisoned candy, lay at his feet. To be more precise, Nicola lay at the other man's feet, as he was still on the floor following his badly judged leap, and the mysterious deliveryman was writhing in pain after having landed a violent kick on the protective cheese gourd under Nicky's hat, the half-gourd covering his skull. In any event, the detective's triumphant laugh did not come easily, because the sharp-edged protective covering and Severino's kick had cut a deep gash in his forehead.

"All right, now it's time for you to talk!" Nicola told Severino, who stared at him in terror. Not because of the private investigator, to tell the truth, but because Dona Marlene was brandishing a menacing broom close to his head.

"I don't know what you want. I got nothing to say."

"Oh no? That's what we're gonna find out now, you coward!" said Nicky, directing a slap at him that went wrong and he ended up twisting his pinky on the countertop.

At that instant, Dona Marlene demanded to know what was going on. Nicky Nicola recounted everything, without omitting a single detail. Six hours later, he finished the narration. Dona Marlene had been sound asleep since the second hour.

It was only then that Nicola thought it might have been better to leave out a few details. When the deliveryman saw he was being accused of murder, he jumped.

"Me? You're crazy! I didn't kill anyone! I'm the new delivery guy for the cleaners here. The only old woman I know is this one." He rudely elbowed Dona Marlene, who awoke, still drowsy.

"I'm a private investigator!" retorted Nicky Nicola. "Just take a look at my badge." He pulled out his credentials with the insouciance he had learned from movies.

"Since when is a beer cap a badge?" the man from Ceará asked.

Nicola realized he was holding one of the rare bottle caps from his famous collection. It was a hobby. Nicola felt that every detective should have one. He kept each cap in its own small plastic bag. The mistake didn't daunt him. He quickly corrected himself: "No matter! It's a code that's part of my professional confidentiality!"

"Maybe, but the truth is that I didn't kill anybody," answered the other man, now on the counterattack: "And just who killed Dona Mirtes's cat?"

"Don't try to change the subject! I'm the one asking the questions! If you didn't kill Dona Estefânia, why'd you lock me in the bathroom?"

"To call the police! When I came back you'd already gone!"

"What about the poisoned candy?"

"I don't know nothing about that! The day she died, I had been by there to take her mariola candy as a gift. I liked her a lot. Dona Estefânia was my son's teacher back in Ceará. The candy I bought was very good. So good that I took a small bite from the edge before giving it to Dona Estefânia, and nothing happened to me! I was surprised. When I heard that uproar I decided to wait and see what it was. After a time, I saw a suspicious-looking guy go into the apartment."

"Who was it?"

"You. I couldn't hear the conversation, but when you opened the door to leave I saw the cat lying beside Dona Estefânia and started following you."

It was only then that Nicky noticed that the brassy man from Ceará was addressing him with excessive intimacy. He was about to call him on it but thought better. *There's no point in being demanding with an uncultured individual.* He resumed his questioning.

"Well, that clarifies a lot of things." The detective knew this was a lie, but he considered it a lovely phrase.

At that moment, Severino burst into tears. "Dona Estefânia always treated my son so well," he sobbed.

While Dona Marlene, visibly moved, dried the deliveryman's tears, Nicola's hypersensitive ears caught the sound of voices coming from the rear of the establishment. He called

at once for silence. He recognized that noise! It was someone arguing in English far off in the rear of the dry cleaners.
His impression that an international gang was tied to the case
wasn't wrong after all! Slowly approaching the curtain that
separated the public area from the room in the back, he heard
an enigmatic exchange.

"Why?"

"Because!"

"Why?"

"Because!"

"Why?"

With a quick, agile movement, Nicola threw open the
curtain with one hand, while taking out his nail clipper with
the other. He was speechless at the scene unfolding before his
eyes. In a large cage he saw two parrots that Dona Marlene
had brought from Manaus. One was biting his own leg, while
the other observed in horror, repeating endlessly, "Oo-aye!
Beak-awes!"

Chapter X
What's That on Your Head, Brother?

After the immense disappointment of his encounter with the
two parrots, Nicola turned back to Severino and Dona Marlene. So as not to stray totally from the topic, he asked Dona
Marlene if the parrots could be trusted. Then he recalled a
phrase he'd read in detective stories: the criminal always returns to the scene of the crime! It was time to head back to
Dona Mirtes's apartment and find out how things were going.
He said goodbye to Severino, apologized to Dona Marlene,
and promised he would keep the man from Ceará informed
about any progress in the investigation.

Two hours later, Nicola was on his way back to the apartment where the crime had been committed. This time he managed to enter through the front door. Not because his standing had increased locally, but because the custodian was on his coffee break. Sweet Creusa opened the door for him, and only then, with backlighting, did Nicola realize how pretty she was. This was because the backlighting hid her face. He gently kissed his girlfriend and suavely said: "How the hell are ya, gal? Your mistress around?"

"What's that on your head, brother?" asked Creusa, looking at the bandage still covering the cut on his forehead. Nicola explained how the deliveryman had kicked him. He omitted mention of the tin half-shell that he always wore in his hat to protect his privileged brain that had led to the cut. The fewer who knew about it, the better. Creusa was trustworthy, but you never know. As he spoke, he noticed that someone was moving on the other side of the door leading to the living room. He immediately leaped and grabbed the intruder. It was the owner of the apartment.

After excusing himself, Nicky presented his bill for expenses during the first two weeks of investigation: 68.20 cruzeiros, minus transportation and bandages. Dona Mirtes paid without blinking. Then she recounted the oddest thing of all: the body of her aunt, Dona Estefânia, had completely disappeared. Nicola asked if she had notified the police and she said no. What was there to tell—that she had lost an aunt and later had *really* lost an aunt? The investigator agreed—because he couldn't come up with a reason for disagreement.

"How was it you realized she disappeared?"

"I went into the living room and she wasn't there spread out on the floor. That's when I thought she must have vanished."

"A brilliant deduction, madam!" chirped Nicola. "Do you

know anyone who might be interested in your aunt's body?"

"Yes."

"Who?"

"My aunt."

Nicola felt this line of interrogation was leading nowhere. He had to find a clue, right there. Seeing that Dona Mirtes was still shocked by the disappearance of Dona Estefânia, he asked: "Would you mind giving me and Creusa a moment alone here in the living room?"

"Greatly."

"That's what I thought. We'll go to the kitchen."

He led Creusa by the arm. As soon as they were near the stove, Nicola asked, "So, you don't remember anything that could be of interest to me?"

"There's some pork roast left over from lunch."

Nicola was about to explain that he wasn't referring to food but postponed clarifying the matter until after eating the pork. Then he extracted the precious information from Creusa's fleshy lips. There had been something suspicious in Dona Estefânia's attitude the entire time: every few minutes she called someone on the phone and spoke in whispers.

"Creusa! Please make an effort to remember his name! Who was she talking to?"

"I know!" she responded after a moment. "His name was João . . . João . . . João . . ."

"João what? C'mon, girl, try to remember!"

"João da Silva!" said Creusa, pleased with herself.

Nicola leaped with joy. At last, a concrete lead! A name! Now all that was left was to look in the phone book and make a call to see which João da Silva knew Dona Estefânia. After all, there couldn't be that many João da Silvas in São Paulo, despite the name being the Brazilian equivalent of John Smith.

Chapter XI
Nicky Nicola's 53,000 Phone Calls

Nicky Nicola decided to call the João da Silva with whom Dona Estefânia had spoken by phone before dying and disappearing. He assumed it would be easy to find the number from the telephone directory. When he realized there were no fewer than 53,000 João da Silvas listed, he wasn't discouraged. The phone was beside him in the kitchen; Creusa could feed him while he worked, and he estimated a mere eight days would suffice for him to call them all.

To his surprise, Dona Mirtes didn't agree with his plan, saying that if he wanted to call he could do so from his own house; she wasn't there to foot the bill for anyone. Nicky wisely ignored that comment. He was accustomed to dealing with clients and knew how nervous they got whenever a victim vanished without a trace. So as to lose no time, he decided to ask Dona Mirtes a few more questions.

"Okay, you say she was here on the floor and suddenly disappeared?"

"I'd appreciate it if you would speak more respectfully about my aunt."

"If you don't answer my questions, she may never reappear."

"If you go on asking questions this way, I may have to hire another detective."

"I was joking."

"So was I."

Something told Nicola that this line of questioning was also going nowhere. He tried another angle.

"Your dear aunt disappeared from the living room?"

"Yes."

"That's very interesting . . ."

"Interesting because it's not *your* aunt."

"How did you realize the body had disappeared?"

"By its absence."

"How so?"

"I left the room. When I returned, no one was here. Only my cat that you killed to test the candy."

Nicola ignored that malicious insinuation. He was going to say that the cat wouldn't bring back her aunt but changed his mind. What he had to do was find the number of that mysterious João da Silva. He asked if there was a notepad near the telephone. Creusa quickly replied: "Yes, there is, sweetheart. Dona Estefânia had the habit of doodling every time she used the phone."

A lightbulb flashed in Nicola's brain; it was Dona Mirtes who had turned on the living room lamp. The private investigator hurried to the notepad and began to search. In the middle of the doodles was a number, faint but still legible, that might have been 27-6478. He dialed it immediately; he tried thirty-two consecutive times but kept getting a busy signal. He called the operator to ask whether the number was out of order. It wasn't.

"Strange," he said aloud.

"What's so strange?" asked Dona Mirtes.

"I'm calling a telephone that I believe may belong to João da Silva and I keep getting a busy signal."

"What's the number?" Dona Mirtes inquired.

"27-6478."

"It doesn't seem strange to me that it's always busy."

"Why not, Dona Mirtes?" asked Nicola, hopeful that the answer might clear everything up.

"Because you're dialing *my* phone number."

Chapter XII
Finding João

After Nicola recovered from his awful mistake, spending almost two hours dialing the same number from which he was calling, he thought it was time to go into action. He cut short Dona Marlene's complaints and asked Creusa to make him a sandwich. Dona Mirtes absolutely forbade the snack. Nicola had to be content with the pork shank he'd already eaten. He lit a Beverly, took a long drag, and coughed. This was when Creusa said: "That João da Silva you're looking for, I know where he lives. I once heard Dona Estefânia repeating his address on the telephone."

"Why didn't you tell me that before?" asked Nicola, rather irritated.

"Because you didn't ask."

Nicola succeeded in getting another ten cruzeiros from Dona Mirtes for transportation, and after giving Creusa a quick kiss, he left in search of the mysterious João da Silva. Instead of hailing a cab, he decided to go on foot. Nicola had more faith in his own shoes, and after all, ten cruzeiros is ten cruzeiros. Besides, João's residence was close by.

Six hours later, he was within two blocks of the address. Another fifteen minutes and he was ringing the doorbell. He was rocked by an electric shock that almost knocked him down. But no one answered. The detective didn't give up—no electrified doorbell could defeat his courage. He asked a young boy passing by to ring the bell again.

He saw with surprise that the kid was unharmed. *Good thing*, he thought. *They must've disconnected the wire.* He sent the boy on his way and, since no one had appeared, rang again and got another shock. Only then did he realize he was standing in a puddle of water and the holes in his shoes allowed the current to run through his body. He stepped aside and decided to knock down the door. Just as he built up speed to break it down with his well-proportioned body, someone opened the door and Nicola passed straight through, unable to stop till he reached the kitchen, where he avoided crashing into the refrigerator only by collapsing in front of the stove.

When he managed to compose himself, he saw beside him an armed man: João da Silva. "I've been expecting this visit for some time," he said. "Stop looking for Estefânia. She's fine where she is."

"You coward! What did you do with her? Why'd you kill the old woman?"

"I don't want to argue. If I catch you around here again, I'll stomp you."

"I doubt it!"

The chair that João da Silva brought down on his head dispelled any remaining doubt on the detective's part. When he regained consciousness, he was bound, his hands tied to the kitchen sink.

João da Silva explained: "I was about to move anyway. I'm gonna leave you tied up here till somebody finds you. So long. Tell Mirtes to let the case of Estefânia go."

Nicola couldn't hold back: "If it weren't for the revolver, I'd have gotten you!"

"What revolver?" said João, looking at his hands. "Oh, this thing? It's plastic. I work as a traveling salesman selling toys." He turned and headed for the door. Five minutes later, his laughter still rang in Nicola's ear.

Very cunning, that João da Silva. Except that he didn't count on the most agile private investigator in the world's utility kit. Flexing his body and using his teeth, the detective pulled the famous cigar box from his coat pocket and hurled it onto the sink. Still using his teeth, he removed a razor blade that he always carried for such occasions. A minute later he was free. He hadn't managed to sever the rope that held him, but his efforts broke the faucet. He rubbed his chafed wrists. If he ran, he would be able to catch up with João da Silva. He leaped like a cat toward the door—and fell into the arms of a policeman who was checking why the front door was wide open.

"Aha! A thief!" said the cop.

"No, a private detective," Nicola replied brusquely, showing the credentials that he'd made for himself in a print shop where his friend Camargo worked.

"A thief and a liar," said the stubborn cop. "You're gonna explain everything down at the precinct."

The handcuffs hurt his already sore wrists.

Chapter XIII
Do You Know Who You're Talking to?

The instant he set foot in the police precinct, Nicola knew he had nothing to fear. He'd been arrested arbitrarily, and as a private investigator he knew several people in the higher echelons of the police. Well, *higher echelons* might be a small exaggeration, but he did know five traffic cops. True, of those five, four detested Nicola, but that left the fifth, the most influential of all: Juca Barbacha—a name feared by everyone who jaywalked, ran stop signs, or committed any infraction of municipal traffic laws. He asked for his friend and was surprised to hear that no one there knew him.

"Move it!" said the cop who had arrested him. He pushed Nicky into a small room.

A plainclothes policeman was sitting on the edge of a table. He read the report and said, "You wanna tell me why you were robbing a house?"

Nicola found the question so ridiculous and offensive that he didn't reply. He limited himself to lighting a Beverly. He took a deep drag and coldly articulated his own question: "Do you know who you're talking to?"

"No, who?"

"I'm the renowned private investigator Nicky Nicola." And he showed his documents.

Apparently, his reputation had yet to make its way to that district. The policeman said he wasn't interested and that he wanted to know what he was doing inside a house that wasn't his. Nicky quickly explained that he was looking for the owner of the house, João da Silva, who had left ahead of him. He omitted the detail of being tied to the faucet, which prevented him from being able to follow João. The police asked several more questions and finally let him go.

On his way out, he passed the cop who had arrested him. Nicola couldn't resist: "Next time, watch out for who you're dealing with."

"Next time, I'll tear up that private investigator card and shove it up your ass."

Nicola didn't want to argue. To his thinking, he had gotten the better of the exchange, and he didn't like to humiliate the defeated. He stealthily descended the stairs of the precinct two at a time, with the result that he fell headfirst onto the sidewalk. An accident can sometimes be of great usefulness. As he fell, a matchbox that he had instinctively picked up at João's house fell out of his pocket. The name of a hotel was written on the cover: *Hotel Prumar*. It was quite possible that João da Silva had moved there! Nicola decided to find out.

He was becoming irritated at the disappearance of Dona Estefânia. He went to a nearby pay phone to call Creusa, planning to inform her that he'd be late picking her up. He deposited a coin and waited for the dial tone. It didn't come. Not that Nicola was miserly, but he couldn't afford to lose that nickel. He punched the telephone hard. The impact brought the concave plastic housing down on his head. While he was recovering from the shock, street kids passing by at that moment dubbed him "Astronaut Graham Bell."

Chapter XIV
Does the Hotel Prumar Face the Sea?

As soon as Nicola freed himself from his uncomfortable headwear, he tried to find Hotel Prumar, the name written on the matchbox found in João da Silva's former residence. It wouldn't be hard to locate: it was the only hotel facing the Tietê River. He had to get there as soon as possible. He decided to walk. By his calculation, if he kept up a good pace he'd be there in less than five hours. But Nicola's pace was erratic at best. He revised his estimate by adding five more hours and saw that really, however much he enjoyed a good stroll, he couldn't afford the luxury of arriving the next day. He jumped on the next bus passing by. He got off at the first opportunity. In his haste he'd gotten on the wrong bus. Finally, the one he wanted came by.

"The Tietê stop, quick!" he told the driver.

"If you're in a hurry, grab a taxi."

Nicola ignored the sarcasm and found a seat in the back. He had time before arriving at his stop at the end of the line and decided to use it to inspect his equipment. After all, he was going to face an unknown person. He took out his utility kit and examined his weapons one by one: Scotch Tape, which had saved him from a hemorrhage of the finger in the Strange Case of Dr. Fonseca; a spool of dental floss, which had already tied the wrists of innumerable criminals; his inseparable nail clipper, sharper than the most dangerous razor; the small bag of talcum powder that he had thrown in the path of pursuers, thus creating a white protective cloud—in short, all the tools that helped keep him alive. He gazed affectionately at the package of peanuts that would be his food should he get lost in the jungle. He was so absorbed in his inventory that at first he didn't hear the tiny voice coming from beside him. Finally he realized it was talking to him.

"Mister, give me a peanut!"

Nicola smiled at the innocence of the little boy sitting to his right. He calmly explained that he couldn't give up even a single nut, since he needed such material for professional purposes. The boy listened attentively before shreiking: "But I want a peanut! My father won't gimme me a peanut!"

Several people on the bus started to interfere, thinking that Nicola should share his peanuts with his son. It was difficult for the detective to explain that the boy wasn't his. It was only when the real father, who was sleeping beside the boy, awoke from the clamor that the detective could rest.

At that moment the vehicle arrived in front of Hotel Prumar. Nicola exited and quickly headed toward the establishment. It was already beginning to get dark. As he was unfamiliar with the neighborhood, he thought it best to proceed with caution. He slowly went up to the hotel door. Just as he was about to enter, he heard a woman's scream that chilled his spine. He didn't hesitate: he made one of his famed karate leaps, smashing the door and landing on top of the reception desk.

"Where'd that scream come from?" he asked.

The receptionist answered with surprising calm: "Here, from the television. I'm watching a soap opera."

Nicola spent the next forty minutes trying to explain why he'd battered down the door.

Chapter XV
A Very Alive Dead Woman

Nicola was not one to waste time with useless arguments. When the owner of Hotel Prumar, whose door he had broken in the search for João da Silva, said he would have to pay for the repair, Nicola limited himself to giving the address to which the bill could be sent. Not his own address, naturally, since he was in no condition to deal with such an expense, but the address of Dona Mirtes. After all, nobody finds an aunt like that for free.

Afterward he was able to discover João da Silva's room number. He couldn't fall into another trap. Or rather, he could but didn't want to. Therefore, upon learning that the room was right there on the ground floor, he opted for going around the back and surprising João by entering through a window. He hurried outside, and as soon as he found the entrance he was seeking, he got a running start and prepared his leap. But a strange coincidence occurred: at the exact moment that Nicola was jumping in through the window, João da Silva was jumping out. The collision knocked both of them down. Nicola was the more agile of the two, and before João realized what had fallen on him, his hands were already firmly tied with the ingenious detective's dental floss. Then Nicola tossed João da Silva back inside the room and followed him in.

"Very well, now we're going to have a little talk."

"I got nothing to say," João replied stubbornly.

Nicola felt he had already wasted enough time with that story and aimed a slap at the malefactor's face. But he misjudged. João ducked and Nicola's hand broke the lamp on the nightstand. The detective didn't let himself worry about such insignificant details. As he blew delicately on his injured hand, he went on with his interrogation: "Are you gonna tell me what you did with Dona Estefânia's body?"

"No."

"That's what I thought."

"Then you thought right."

"Except I've had it with this case. I'm turning you in to the police and that's that."

"You can't prove anything. I'll say you're harassing me."

Nicola saw it was time to bluff. He sat down in a chair facing João, blew smoke from a Beverly in his face, and said, "My boy, I have a lot of friends in the police. If I told you that at this very moment twenty investigators are on their way here to arrest you, would you believe it?"

"No."

"How about five investigators, would you believe that?"

"Also no."

"One cop on a horse?"

"Even less."

Nicola had to convince himself that his bluff hadn't worked. He then pondered why João da Silva had been sneaking out the window.

João explained that it was the quickest way to leave the hotel room. "And I wasn't sneaking out. I was just going for a beer."

The detective regretted not having intercepted João on his way back. At least then he'd have had something to drink.

"Okay, I've got all night. If you don't talk, so much the worse for you."

The door opened suddenly and a woman came in carrying a large paper bag. Her face was hidden behind the bundle, but her feminine voice came out clearly.

"Hi, sweetheart. I brought the goods." As she said this, the woman set the bag down and Nicola could plainly see every detail of her physiognomy: there in flesh and blood, more flesh than blood but more alive than ever, was the sought-after Dona Estefânia.

Final Chapter
The Mystery Solved

As soon as Nicola saw it was Dona Estefânia who had arrived with the shopping bag, he jumped out of his chair. He almost fainted from astonishment. His initial metaphysical reaction was to think he was seeing a ghost, but from Dona Estefânia's rosy countenance he judged her to be in excellent health. Nicola assumed his most intelligent demeanor to say: "Now I understand everything!"

Actually, he didn't understand anything. João da Silva came to his aid.

"That's right, Nicola. That's the case. Estefânia is alive, and we're getting married. The whole story of her death was for show because Mirtes didn't want her to marry me. We were gonna wait a bit longer to break the news. Now we can't hide it anymore."

"But there wasn't any need to frighten everyone."

"It was João's idea," explained Dona Estefânia. "Because I wanted to take advantage of spending more vacation time here. That's why my body disappeared."

"Well, looks like I've solved another case. Now we all go to Dona Mirtes's place," said Nicola.

"To let her know?" asked Dona Estefânia.

"And to receive my money."

Two hours later, they were in Dona Mirtes's living room. Creusa, the gentle domestic, moved about in great contentment. After all, her boyfriend had cracked the case. The only person who appeared furious was Dona Mirtes, who still didn't understand the reason for all that complication. Nicola said that this was par for the course in an investigation, which wasn't true but served as consolation. After receiving the money owed him, Nicola suggested that a round of coffee would be welcome. Dona Mirtes thought otherwise, so the situation remained at square one.

Finally, the famous detective thought it was time to withdraw. He rose, said goodbye to everyone, quickly kissed Creusa's fleshy lips, and headed toward the door. When his hand was on the knob, Dona Mirtes said: "Just a minute. There's something I don't understand. If Estefânia really played dead, if the candy wasn't really poisoned, why did my cat die?"

Nicola had been waiting for this moment. Before going to the apartment he had done some fact-finding and had the answer on the tip of his tongue. "Elementary, my dear Dona Mirtes. By one of those incredible coincidences, the cat didn't die from poison but from a heart attack provoked by fright when it saw the candy. The necropsy of the feline left no uncertainty about it."

"When did you find out the result of that necropsy?" asked Mirtes.

"Shortly before coming here," lied the detective. "Well, good luck to the engaged couple, and now, if you'll excuse me, I must return to my office. Another case awaits me." He opened the door and descended the stairs toward the street. He stopped at the building's front door, breathed deeply, and began the long walk back to Mooca.

A light mist was beginning to envelop the city. Nicky really did have another case to deal with. A case the landlord of his apartment had filed against him for back rent.

Thus Nicky Nicola ended another day of work. Leaves were starting to fall from the trees, signaling the arrival of autumn, and the private investigator hastened his pace for fear that something else might fall on his head from a window.

TERESÃO
BY MARIO PRATA
Vila Carrão

Part One

Teresão is fat. Not as fat as one might imagine, just enough for her husband to spend a lot on spas and endocrinologists in Brazil and abroad. They can afford such luxuries.

Teresão is fat, rich, and does nothing in life but eat, drink, sleep, and other necessities inherent in human beings. Like trying to lose weight.

I would say she's not really fat-fat. Because a fat-fat woman has fat legs. She doesn't. She's short, with a high stomach, as she is wont to define it. High and big enough to break in line in supermarkets, airports, and banks claiming to be pregnant, at least until she was forty. Today she is forty-five and has hit two hundred pounds for the first time.

Teresão has been fat as long as she can remember. In primary school they called her Tubby, Hippo, and other worse fat-words. Much worse.

As for sex, she often says: *Fat women like it too.* Her husband is becoming more and more deaf.

Teresão was in a hammock on the porch of her house, looking at the pool, thinking about not a goddamn thing, when the maid came with the tray holding a heaping breakfast. She placed it on a small table within reach. Teresão thanked her and the maid Dulcineia (extremely slim) grunted. Teresão looked at her. Dulcineia had her mouth shut and her cupped hand covered her lips.

"Cat got your tongue, girl?"

Dulcineia kept laughing, nonstop, until she had to take her hand away from her mouth. That was when Teresão saw. Dulcineia was wearing braces. The kind that bind together all the teeth, the old-fashioned type.

"What new thing is this?"

Dulcineia left almost in a run, laughing, embarrassed, and went into the house. Teresão followed her with her eyes until she disappeared. She lifted her hand to her chin. We can see that Teresão was thinking. And when Teresão decided to think, it was something else!

Dulcineia was picking up eggshells to put in the trash when her mistress came in, drinking chocolate milk.

"Open."

Dulcineia looked at her, startled. "Open what, Dona Terezinha?"

"Your mouth, woman! Let me see it." She approached the maid, concentrating.

"The braces?" She opened her mouth.

Teresão went up very close, looked at the upper part, the lower, and, using both hands, opened and closed her maid's mouth, as if examining a mare. She backed away and stood there looking, pondering.

"You make me feel embarrassed . . . Do I look awfully ugly, Dona Terezinha?"

Teresão sat down and didn't take her eyes off Dulcineia. "Where did you have that done?"

"Is it very ugly?"

"Who was the dentist, Dulcineia? It's pretty."

"A man there in the neighborhood. He opened an office a few months ago. I'm going to pay in eighteen installments. Vila Carrão."

"Call him and make an appointment for me. For today."

"But Dona Terezinha—"

"It has to be today."

"You don't need—"

"Go on, make the call. I'm going to take a bath and we'll go there. I'm going to take control of my life starting today."

She exited and left the maid staring at the phone on the wall.

"You'll excuse me, but I can't do that."

"And just why not? I'm paying, my boy," said Teresão.

Dulcineia didn't understand her employer's request. Joining all her upper teeth to her lower teeth. Practically sewing her mouth shut. Sealing her mouth.

The young dentist: "I could be reported to the Regional Dentistry Board."

Teresão took out her checkbook. "Dr. Peres, your office will look a lot prettier with a chair, one of those that lie flat . . . How much does that gizmo cost? The white ones, you know what I'm talking about, don't you?" She winked at Dulcineia.

After three trips to Vila Carrão, Teresão's teeth were completely fastened together. No food would pass through there. She hummed "It's Now or Never" in the fine, strident tone of a still-young Elvis.

She was sure of it: she was going to lose weight. Nothing but vegetable soup and that's all. She even thought of selling the idea to some spa where she had once been a client.

She said in her tiny voice: "Dulcineia, I've invented the

surest way in the world to lose weight. I might even have a chance to make some money from all this craziness."

You're stark raving mad, the maid didn't say but thought. And she went to make the soup.

Between the front teeth was a small space through which a straw could pass.

After a month, Teresão had lost only 2.2 pounds. At the same time she had discovered that the straw could also convey condensed milk. And whiskey.

Lots of condensed milk. And lots of whiskey.

And her husband, reading *Veja* magazine in bed, declared to his tipsy wife with bad breath from all the steel in her mouth: "It's over, Terezinha! Not the spa, not medicine, not any goddamn thing! This was the final madness. Do you have any idea what that fucking dentist chair cost? Any idea?"

"Dulcineia!!"

She came in running. Teresão was floating in the pool with a buzz on.

"Call Dr. Peres. Now! We're going over there. Today! I'm getting rid of this shit."

One day, because she was afraid of staying home alone (her husband was at a convention in Geneva with their neighbor) and had been having terrible nightmares, she invited Dulcineia to sleep over that night. She said she would pay extra.

Dulcineia thought that rather strange, maybe her boss was one of those women who like women. She had voluntarily wired her teeth shut; anything was possible. But since she needed some extra cash, she called her husband and explained. The guy was somewhat suspicious—what kind of story was that? Teresão went to the phone and he was all, "Yes ma'am, of course, Dona Terezinha."

Teresão liked drinking her whiskey more and more. And since what she wanted was company, she insisted and convinced Dulcineia to drink with her. Teresão didn't know that Dulcineia drank. Not that way. In six hours the pair emptied two bottles of Black Label. And she also didn't know that Dulcineia, when she drank, talked. Talked too much. And because she talked too much, she ended up saying things she shouldn't. That her husband had taken part in the kidnapping of that publicity agent "a few years ago."

"Keep it under your hat, Teresão," said the now-intimate Neia.

Just look at the woman's condition. She was calling her employer by her first name, had vomited in the service area, and wouldn't clean it till the following day while her employer was still sleeping it off. Now she was really, really drunk. She'd never had such good whiskey. Actually, she'd never had whiskey at all.

"Your husband was part of the kidnapping? Your husband?"

"In person, personally. I didn't see 'im for two months. Oh my God, we drank too much . . . I was joking. Imagine."

"Joking my ass! You've already said it. Tomorrow I won't even remember."

The next day: "My God, I talked shit," she thought aloud, like in a TV soap opera.

She prepared a beautiful breakfast for Teresão, which was served just before two o'clock. Dulcineia was very serious, lost in thought, dusting here and there. Teresão was slow to speak.

"What a long night! I'm grateful for your company. If I'd known you were so agreeable I'd have invited you earlier. I sort of tied one on." She leaned back in her chair and looked at Dulcineia through her pince-nez.

Rich folks *tie one on*, noted Dulcineia, who detested those tiny glasses.

"Did I vomit yesterday, Dulcineia?" Teresão asked, conscious of the maid's silence.

"No, no ma'am. It was just tying one on," she answered after a brief silence.

"It's just that there's one hell of a vomit smell," Teresão pressed.

"I don't smell it," the maid pretended.

Teresão served herself the first glass of beer. She didn't offer any.

"Dulcineia, I need to talk to your husband," she told her servant point-blank.

That was what she had feared: her mistress remembered the foolishness that she had never, never told anyone, no one, she didn't talk about the matter even with her own husband. At the time, she became suspicious because Cardim kept speaking half in Spanish and one day ended up telling her. Drunk too.

She still hadn't recovered from the surprise, when Teresão concluded: "Today! And far away from here."

"Dona Terezinha—"

"Exactly! Today! Get ahold of him and let me know."

"Not by phone. It's gotta be done in private."

"Then get moving. Is he at home now?"

"You're going to ruin my marriage, Dona Teresão. He'll kill me, blabbing a secret like that. A kidnap—"

"No I'm not." She removed the pince-nez, placed them on the table. "I'm even going to improve your marriage. Trust me. And the next time you drink here in the house, do your vomiting in the toilet in the service area, okay?" She got up.

"The service area!"

"Yes ma'am."

"Yes ma'am *what?* Meeting your husband or vomiting back there?" Teresão responded, staring directly into Dulcineia's eyes.

"Yes ma'am to both."

"What's his name?"

"Cardim. Ricardim. Ricardo, actually."

After a vast amount of research on Google and having analyzed and studied thirteen Brazilian kidnappings, five Argentinean, two Bolivian, one Portuguese, and one Bulgarian, she understood more about the subject than any antikidnapping officer. She felt like the queen of kidnappings. If she wrote a book someday, she already had the title: *Teresão—the Queen of Kidnapping.* With a self-help subtitle: *How to Lose Sixty-Five Pounds Without Getting Out of Bed.*

She wrote on the screen: Column 1, *gender*; Column 2, *age*; 2-A, *height*; Column 3, *time held*; Column 4, *starting weight*; Column 5, *final weight*; Column 6, *average weight loss per day*.

Teresão was tops at Excel 2013.

There it was, right on the screen—indisputable data: being kidnapped was the best way to lose weight. Kilos better than any diet, tens of kilos better than any spa.

She printed out the table. In the seconds the machine was printing, she thought of the money she could make in the future, after her own kidnapping, with a firm to kidnap fat women and men. Stomach-stapling, who needs it? Why hadn't anybody thought of this before, my God!

Analyzing the table, using a calculator, she rapidly came to a conclusion: a woman, age forty-five, weight 190 pounds (lie!), height 5'3", would with absolute certainty lose a bit more than fifty-eight pounds in fifty-two days.

Almost a model! And with a good pair of heels, Bündchen! Kidnapping!

Cardim had all the trappings of a good scoundrel, even a small scar above his upper lip. A toned mulatto, shaved head, clean sneakers, a smoker. Quite a bit younger than Neia. Thirty-five at most. Had all his teeth.

He didn't take long to understand everything that Teresão wanted. They spoke at a square in Vila Carrão, in the East Zone, at the other end of the city. A far cry from Jardim Europa, where Teresão was neighbor to a former governor of the state.

Teresão asked him to repeat everything.

"You want me and an accomplice—I don't know why you insist on an accomplice. You'll have to forgive me, I don't understand."

She almost got irritated. "Have you ever heard of a kidnapper without an accomplice? Continue, Cardim."

He lowered his head. "Then we—me and another person—kidnap you and treat you the way we did that advertising guy, and the negotiations should last almost two months, and we start out asking for ten million and finally settle for four."

"I know he'll pay four, just to show off at the club. He loves playing the big shot. And what's going to happen with me, Cardim?"

"A small nine-by-three room. A light on twenty-four hours a day, loud music, food once a day. No milk, no sugar, nothing fried, no gluten."

Teresão tapped him on the shoulder. "How many days?"

"Fifty-two!"

"Right. And even if I beg, even if you think I'm dying, you can't change the treatment. Just like it was with him, under-stand? Everything has to be the same! Weren't you the one handling his captivity? No matter what happens, I can't leave that room." Teresão could see that the man understood and was taking everything seriously.

"I was the one who took care of him, yes ma'am. And we didn't go easy on him."

Teresão: "Every three days, we'll meet in the holding room to evaluate the negotiations. Agreed?"

"Right."

And to conclude the pact: "What do we do with the money?"

"Divide it. Me and Dulcineia keep two million and you keep two million." He rose and circled the park bench. "You're not gonna tell me why you wanna put yourself through that ordeal?"

"You'll see. When it's all over, you'll see and understand." She lightly pinched his cheek. "I'm in no hurry, boy. Just one more thing: when it's time to take me out of there, when I fi-nally leave captivity, I want a big goddamn mirror in the bath-room. Full-length. Got it?"

"Leave it to me."

She extended her hand to seal the deal.

"Just a minute. There's going to be some expenses."

"What expenses, man?"

"It's a complex operation. Upkeep of the team. Me, the accomplice, and Neia. Renting a place to put you."

"I hadn't thought of that . . ."

"Yes. Buying a car, weapons, disguises, electronic equipment—"

"That's in advance?"

"Yes ma'am."

"Shit."

The square had a small pond. Teresão began playing with the water, then splashed some on her face. "How much?"

"I calculate about a hundred grand."

"Fuck!"

"My dear lady, you're not dealing with some street mugger. Only kidnappings of vice presidents on up."

"Okay, okay. Tomorrow I'll give Neia the money. I can pay in installments, can't I? Maybe a postdated check?"

"A hundred grand tomorrow, in cash."

She went back to playing with the water. An ice cream vendor passed by.

"Would you like an ice cream?"

"You can get three for me. Does he have vanilla?"

Cardim got the ice cream and took it to Teresão. He stared at her. "Uh, the money?"

She gave him fifty reais. "Keep the change."

He paid, returned the change to her. The ice cream man left.

"What guarantee do I have that you and Neia aren't going to run off with the money? With the hundred thousand."

"None, my good lady! None!"

"I know—"

Silence.

"And when are you going to kidnap me?"

"When you least expect it. You won't know the time or place. It'll have all the surprise of a real kidnapping."

"Yeah, that's probably best. And don't forget an accomplice."

She left with Neia.

She's bonkers, Cardim didn't say but thought.

Part Two

I'm crazy about crime literature.

You must have seen (at least once) the Hitchcock film Vertigo, *known in Brazil as* A Falling Body. *The script is based on the short story "D'entre les morts" by the French writing team Boileau-Narcejac. The incredible thing about them—they wrote nineteen novels between 1952 and 1992—is that one of them lived in Paris and the other away from the city. The first one wrote the initial part and mailed it to the other, who wrote the second and final part without knowing the plans of the other. Then they would reverse the process. And they didn't communicate about it. Total freedom.*

The most incredible part is that each one loved jerking the other's chain. And that's evident in the Hitchcock film. The first one wrote up to the point that Kim Novak leaps from the tower. The second one began writing by saying it wasn't Kim Novak who fell. In other words, he completely changes the direction of the plot and the film becomes even better. So much so—and I'm not making a joke here—that in Portugal the film was called (and is still called) The Woman Who Died Twice *(see Google).*

I told the above story because the one writing now is me, Teresão. Actually, my name isn't Teresão. Prata, the author, changed it. Because it's a true story that involves more people.

He sent me the first part to see what I thought of it. I have to say, right off, that he exaggerated a bit about the weight, lowered my height, and no one ever called me Tubby. The rest was just as he wrote it.

Part Two has to be about the kidnapping itself and I think (without discussing it with Prata) that I ought to be the one to write it. Then he can give some finishing touches (I bet he won't like the phrase "finishing touches").

And I'm in a hurry, because he has a deadline for delivery to the publisher. So let's get started.

* * *

It was late at night (I know that's an awful way to begin a para-graph, Prata). It was raining cats and dogs (you can cut "cats and dogs," because I don't even know what that means). It was raining like hell—there! I was in my pajamas in bed, watching a Swedish-Danish miniseries, when I heard the bomb go off. A very loud sound. (I don't remember if Prata mentioned that we're neighbors and friends of Maluf, the former governor.) I jumped out of bed and ran downstairs where I found my husband Pires. Also a fake name. No one has been called Pires since the playwright Nelson Rodrigues died. We went out into the rain. The security guards were all at the gate to the Maluf residence. The lights of every house on the street were coming on. A security man came out of the house.

"Everyone's okay. The police have been called."

Within three minutes the house was surrounded by that black-and-yellow tape you see in American films, in another seven min-utes the team from the Datena true-crime show arrived as if by magic, traffic was diverted for two blocks.

Someone touched my shoulder, I turned around. It was almost dark under the tree. My husband had gone into their residence. I wasn't going to enter dressed as I was, without makeup, and my hair uncombed. Dona Silvia would notice. I know Arab culture, the Mulaf are descendants. I said I was under a tree where it rained less. Little light, the guy who greeted me was also as wet as could be. About thirty years old, tall, in perfect shape. I was stupefied, people. After the bomb, a candied chestnut.

"I'm the accomplice."

"Who?"

He smiled and then frowned. "The accomplice. For the kid-napping."

I didn't believe him. At that very moment! What a shitty trick! And I was going to miss all the developments? Even the ex-president,

Lula, might show up with his wife. Hebe, the TV star, if she were alive, would already be there. An ambulance arrived. Somebody must be fucked up. A servant, no doubt.

"Let's go, Dona Terezinha. And don't make me ask twice."
The hunk was serious.

"At least let me put on more appropriate clothes, some basic makeup."

He grabbed my arm and pulled me, and I let myself be led. The more we walked, the less pressure he applied. When we got into the car he said: "It was us who threw the bomb . . ." And he giggled.

A lovely plan, I had to admit. I sensed firmness, people. I felt I was working with professionals.

"What did you say your name is?"
"I didn't. You can call me Accomplice."

"Right. You're not going to slap me, handcuff me, nothing? What a lame kidn—"

That was when a hand came from the backseat with a white cloth like a handkerchief and stuck it over my nose. I calculated we were already on the Marginal en route to Castelo Branco Highway. That's all I had time to calculate.

Shit, we had agreed on a meeting every three days and I'm sure I've been here longer than that. A week? I can't take any more. The bucket with pee and poop hasn't been changed a single time. One more piss and it'll overflow. I'm holding it in. The light never goes out, I have no idea whether it's day or night. I reek. And the music? Nothing but Teló. The same CD, nonstop. Loud, very loud. I can't hear my own voice. And it does no good to beat on the walls. They're cork, probably soundproof. There's a small hole above for air to enter. It's my only contact with the outside. I think I'm fucked! And in these goddamn pink polka-dot pajamas! Shit! If it weren't for the cockroaches—

The worst of all, worse than that shitty bucket, the lack of a bath, Teló, the light always on, the worst thing of all is not having Internet. Especially WhatsApp and Facebook. My God, living without Facebook, that's torture! I wasn't counting on that. I should have thought of that . . . Especially now that everyone must know I've been kidnapped—my message box must be exploding. And what about Twitter? Someone must have posted something like #freeteresão. I must be in the top ten, easily. How I miss all those friends of mine, 1,287, to be exact. Loyal, always there giving me strength, greeting me when I wake up, wishing me good night. Those are real friends. I remember that we would talk for hours, organizing demonstrations along Avenida Paulista, discussing where the action was going to start. I miss seeing the avenue all in yellow, the phrase "They should have killed them all in '64" touched me deeply . . . Brazil would have been much better off without the damn Workers Party. How much culture, how much information I learned on Facebook. I love that boy with the complicated name who invented Facebook. You see, if I had my iPad here I'd just use Google to find out his name. Google is another fucker of an invention. The other day, Pires located a very rare part for one of his Mercedes—in reality, mine—on Google, as he said, with two keystrokes. The world advancing out there and me here literally in shit!

People, don't ever wish you were kidnapped. I know every square inch of this cork-lined cubicle, I've measured it with hands, with fingers . . . I know by heart all of Teló's lyrics. I'm even beginning to find some of them interesting. He's no Martinho da Vila, but . . .

My God, the lights just went out. Is it just them or is it a general blackout? Because Teló also shut up and the breeze up there stopped too. Are they going to kill me by suffocation? Have the police arrived? Did everybody run away? Just look at my belly! It's in the dark that you know you're fat. Prodding yourself, without light. By physical contact.

My God, I think they're opening the door. I want Wi-Fi! I don't want to lose weight anymore. Wi-Fi there where the air comes in . . . Simple enough, isn't it?

I can't believe it. I'm in the shower, happy. Neia is sitting on the toilet lid, quite tense.

"You could at least provide toilet paper in the goddamn room. My ass is raw. Do you have any talcum powder?"

"Finish your shower, we've got an important meeting."

"Look at the hair on my snatch, what a discouraging sight. My Portuguese heritage. Has Pires settled for the four million?"

"Cardim's going to talk to you about that."

"You don't have a scale handy, do you? I must've lost seven or eight pounds. What do you think?"

"Put these clothes on. He's waiting for you out there."

Neia left, and I was happy, humming Teló at full volume.

Neia is funny, the scamp. Until the other day I was the employer and she was the maid. Now it seems everything's changed: Get out of there, take off your clothes, get into the shower, Cardim will explain. She's giving me the orders, Dona Terezinha.

As if I were an idiot. Ten minutes ago I was buried in shit, hearing that music, that spotlight in my face. Now I'm taking a shower with hot water, shampoo, etc. and so forth. What happened? Did Pires agree to pay the four million? What shit is this? I ordered the kidnap to last fifty-two days, which is how long I need to lose weight. They're going to take me out of here? Return me? I can't believe it. Pires doesn't love me that much, to pay right off the bat. Something sketchy is going on.

The shower wasn't part of any plan. In none of my research

on kidnappings did anyone ever take a shower. Not even the kid-nappers, I think.

What kind of shit is this?

I'm going to miss Creuza, Edineia, Formigão, Manquinha, Orapronobis . . . There were more than twenty roaches. The first day, when I arrived, there was one. I hate roaches! There wasn't a chair to climb on. But I killed it. I thought: it has to sleep sometime. Every animal sleeps. I don't know how many hours I spent huddled watching it. I sensed it was asleep. Splat! It never woke up again. On the second day, another appeared, which I named Edineia in honor of Neia. I came to think that each day they were introducing another one. I decided to live with them, and them with me. I can guarantee you: they're darlings. I came to cuddle them in the palm of my hand. They were my friends. I talked to them. There were some, the oldest ones, that I called by name, and they would come. Who's going to take care of them now, for God's sake?

Neia took me from the bathroom. I discovered that I was in the upper floor of the house. We went down the stairs. Judging by the sounds of cars in the street, it must be the city. Cardim and Accom-plice were down below.

Cardim opened a drawer, took out a revolver, spun the drum, checked that it had all the bullets.

Accomplice was startled. I thought I was going to faint. No one was giving me any information at all.

Accomplice took a step toward Cardim. "What's this? You're going to kill the woman?"

"For now, no. I've got a hunch I was followed."

I only managed to say: "Oh shit!"

Neia and Cardim were also tense. Cardim gave me a look full of hate.

"The guy laughed in my face!"

"Pires?"

"Yes, I demanded ten million, he laughed like crazy and said, word for word, I won't pay ten thousand for that cow."

"I don't believe it. Pires? Not Pires."

"Fucked!"

"Fucked!"

"We're all fucked. And it won't do any good to call again. I sensed total conviction. He wants to see you dead. He almost thanked me . . ."

That was when I saw the light. Our wealth was all mine. Including our house, which I inherited as the only child of my father, who got rich during the coffee boom. Pires worked at Eucatex, which belonged to Mr. Maluf, because I asked Dona Silvia. The guy didn't have a pot to piss in. He's in charge of the warehouse. Is that a profession to brag about? So, of course, if he didn't pay the ransom they'd kill me and he would end up with everything. Shit!!!

Neia was behind Cardim, massaging his shoulders. He was tense.

"Can you at least take the poop bucket out of the room?"

"First of all, stop doing that shit you call massage on my back. And you, you're not going back to the room. Everything's gone wrong, sister, and you know who we are."

"You're very tense, Cardim! She's not gonna rat anybody out."

"It's your fault! You blabbed about the advertising-exec kidnapping."

"What're you gonna do, Cardim?"

"Don't bust my balls. Fuck!"

Neia went into the bathroom. Cardim gestured for Accomplice to come closer.

"We're going to change to captivity number two. Is everything clean there? I'm almost sure we were followed."

I ventured: "May I make a little suggestion?"

"No fucking way! Is everything clear at captivity number two?"

"Yeah. I went by there early today." Changing the subject, alarmed: "It's probably just your imagination."

"Whatever, we're getting the hell outta here."

Cardim and Accomplice at a table eating finger food and drinking soda. Me sitting in a corner trying to come up with a way of fleeing.

Total silence. Cardim shouted upstairs: "All the doorknobs, Neia! With bleach!"

It was Accomplice who broke the ice: "Every year the turnovers get worse."

Cardim agreed: "Neia's don't crumble. Look at the mess these make. Look at the floor. There's more turnover on the floor than in my stomach."

Cardim took a look: "When we finish eating, we're going to start the cleanup down here. Everybody. Despite us wearing gloves the whole time, you can't be too careful. You hear me, Dona Terezinha? Are you off in space somewhere?"

"No, I'm thinking about my maid."

"Fuck that maid crap! Just look at the shit storm you two stirred up for us."

Accomplice moved to head off the impending fight between the couple. "Are we going to decide what to do? Every wasted minute is a minute we're in danger." I thought I'd heard that in a Mexican crime show, one of the worst.

Cardim went to the window. Neia came down and began gathering up the turnover crumbs. Accomplice picked his teeth.

Before anyone could grab me, I got up and went to help Neia. They didn't even offer me a turnover. Which, by the way, I wouldn't have accepted. A diet is a diet.

Neia tossed the crumbs out the window.

To my surprise and terror, I saw that son of a bitch Cardim pick up the revolver and attach the silencer.

I started praying softly while they did the cleanup of the lower floor. After much discussion they decided it was better for me not to participate because I might leave clues on purpose. So I went back to my corner and began praying by myself, recalling my time at the Sacred Heart of Mary School, when I was just a chubby little angel.

Cardim sent Accomplice out for a newspaper.

"O Jesus, who condemning us to death have hidden its hour and its moment, lead me to live all my days in justice and sanctity, that I may merit the grace of departing this world in Thy holy love, by the worthiness of our Lord Jesus Christ, who lives with us and reigns as one with the Holy Spirit, amen.

"I, a sinner, confess to Almighty God; to the blessed and eternal Virgin Mary; to the blessed Archangel Michael and to the blessed St. John the Baptist: to the Holy Apostles St. Peter and St. Paul and all the saints; and to Thee, Father, that I have sinned greatly in my thoughts, words, and deeds, through my fault, my fault, my maximum fault. I therefore ask and pray to the blessed Virgin Mary; to the blessed St. Michael Archangel and to the blessed St. John the Baptist; to the Holy Apostles St. Peter and St. Paul and all the saints; and to Thee, Father, that You pray for me to God our Lord!"

Neia came near.

"Amen!"

"Come . . . It's all right."

"In the name of the Father, the Son, and the Holy Spirit, amen."

She mocked: "Amen! Saravá."

* * *

Accomplice had just brought the newspaper.

The headline: "Maid Is Suspect in Jardim Europa Kidnapping."

Cardim read: "Since the night of the kidnapping the domestic servant of the Pires couple, Dona Dulcineia Sabina Damasceno, known as Neia, forty, mulatto, has disappeared . . ."

Cardim struck the table with the revolver.

I tried to keep things calm: "You know that banging the gun like that can cause it to go off, don't you?"

"You shut up and listen to me: your fucker of a husband says he won't pay a fucking cent for you. Fucker! Not a cent!"

"You already told me, Mr. Ricardo. I can't believe it . . . Pires . . ." *I put my hand on my cheek and started to cry in earnest. The others even patted me on the back. Except for Cardim.*

"And now where do we stand, my good woman?"

"Shit, here I am in one hell of an effort to lose weight and the son of a bitch refuses to pay anything? Does he want to see me fat and dead?"

Suddenly he understood my plan.

"Fuck! My God! I don't believe that all of this was to lose weight. You're crazier than I thought."

"Yes, to win back that son of a bitch Pires! And he wants to see me fat and dead?"

Neia: "It's not quite like that."

"Yes it is!"

Silence. I looked at the three of them, knew I had to be killed. I couldn't stay alive because I knew the kidnappers.

Cardim pointed the revolver at me as if offering vanilla ice cream. "Forgive me, you have to die."

Neia was desperate: "No, Ricardo, no! For the love of God!"

Cardim slapped Neia, who fell on the floor behind him.

"May I say a prayer first, Mr. Ricardo?"

He pointed with his chin, agreeing.

"Hail O Queen, mother of mercy: our life, sweetness, and hope, hail. To thee do we cry, poor banished children of Eve. To thee we sigh, mourning and weeping in this valley of tears. Turn then, our advocate, those merciful eyes toward us. And Jesus, after our exile, show us." I saw Neia rising silently behind Cardim and approaching where he sat.

Neia brought down a chair on Cardim's head. He turned around and shot her in the chest. Oh Jesus! Blood flew to the ceiling. Accomplice jumped on Cardim's back and they rolled onto the floor, Cardim with the gun in his hand. Accomplice held Cardim's arm. My Virgin Santissima! They rolled on the floor again. I continued my prayer. It was like something out of a Western.

I began to pray more loudly—the final part of the prayer: ". . . Blessed be the fruit of thy womb, O clement, O merciful, O gentle Virgin Mary."

The second gunshot rang out.

"Amen."

Accomplice was under Cardim. Blood ran between the two. Lots of blood. He pushed, and Cardim's body rolled underneath the table. Accomplice stood up.

I was in tears and shouting the prayer: "Pray for us, Holy Mother of God, so we may be worthy of Christ's promises! Amen!"

"Let's get out of here."

The two of us walked in silence. The only words spoken in two blocks: "Neia was good people."

Accomplice put his right arm over my shoulder because I was shaking so badly.

Far away, very far away, the sound of a siren. We pretended not to hear it and said nothing.

I sensed his body, all the affection, the respect.

He asked: "Where are we going?"

The sound of the siren was closer.

"Bauru, are you familiar with it?"

"Yes, in the interior. Why Bauru?"

"It has one fuckin' great sandwich!"

The sound drew nearer. It was at our backs.

"Have you ever been in prison?"

"Twice."

I would lose weight like mad in prison, I thought, and smiled at the men who leaped from the car. Carrying guns and billy clubs to subdue vagrants.

Finally, I was going to lose weight.

Part Three

I resume writing.

Teresão, with illusions of Boileau-Narcejac, only confused me.

I didn't understand the end of the narrative.

What was the function of Accomplice in the whole story?

At one point I even thought he might be with the police. But Cardim wouldn't be that big of an idiot.

And why did they walk away so calmly like someone going to a movie theater to see an Iranian film? To eat a Bauru sandwich?

And why didn't they hide the minute they heard the siren in the distance?

Could it be that Teresão had already had time to imagine losing weight in a torture chamber?

And how could Teresão be so sure she would be found guilty? The ones who set up the fake kidnapping with her were dead. Accomplice had nothing to gain by talking. And it was better to remain friends with the neighbor of Paulo Maluf who was going to get a divorce (Teresão, not Dr. Paulo) and reap a huge reward.

Why would she be arrested?

And why so much blood in the final scene of her captivity (my God!), if up to that point the story was advancing with subtle humor?

Some five years later I met with Teresão. I confess that it was hard to recognize her. She hadn't gotten any thinner, but she had short gray hair and brown lipstick. Almost a hippie. And smiling happily in a robe of every color in the rainbow and a few more.

I hadn't seen her since the trial. She was convicted of forming a gang, extortion, and complicity in a homicide. After four years she got out of prison. Dr. Paulo!

The meeting was a joyful one.

Teresão, with total tranquility, self-assurance, and peace, declared, bringing an end to the story: "My problem wasn't fatness! It was my head! Shall we go have a few drinks and a smoke?"

"Of course! What about Accomplice?"

"That's another story. I'll tell you later. Is your weed good? In prison we had some great weed! Third world stuff, heavy and social at the same time, you get me? How about you, writing much?"

"Trying to sell your story for a miniseries."

"Wonderful. But you gotta show the time I spent inside."

"Let's start in that bar over there. You owe me two stories: *Teresão's Accomplice* and *Teresão in Prison*."

PART II

São Paulo Inc.

AS IF THE WORLD
WERE A GOOD PLACE
BY MARÇAL AQUINO
Canindé

For Mafra Carbonieri

1

With resigned impatience, old Ambrósio was dragging his semiravaged carcass toward eighty when a suburban redhead, whose existence the decennial census had recorded only twice by the period in question, crossed his path. Because of her, Ambrósio, who was already transferring control of his businesses to his son and preparing for a peaceful retirement at the side of his invalid wife, resurfaced. Revived. He had his dentures polished, as people say about old men who get turned on to life once again. He became vain: he got hair implants, dyed his mustache, bought that belt that disguises the belly—not to mention baths, cologne, and lotions.

The man who had previously worn the same clothes for days suddenly took an interest in designer shirts, bespoke pants, and expensive shoes that appeared in magazine ads. I myself accompanied him on various trips to malls from which he emerged happy as a shopaholic, loaded down with colorful boxes and shopping bags. He even hired a gay guy to tutor him on good manners.

An impressive metamorphosis.

All in the futile attempt to gain the favor of someone who, to tell the truth, wasn't worth the effort to clip his toenails. A creature who, if run through a press, wouldn't yield a drop of affection for anyone.

A vulgar and crafty bitch with more tricks than a cruise-ship magician, said Ambrósio Junior. The two detested each other from the first time they met.

Naturally.

The emergence of the woman slowed the ascent of the younger Ambrósio. Reinvigorated, the old man resumed control of the businesses, and the son had no alternative but to suck it up and go back to a supporting role. He didn't like it. No one would.

Once, in the car on the way to a festival in Barretos, he said, "A *galo* to anyone who gets rid of the redhead." (A *galo* equaled fifty thousand in his dialect.)

The driver Silêncio kept his eyes on the road and a firm hand on the steering wheel.

"I want this car," I said. And I turned in the seat to see whether Ambrósio Junior was serious.

(He was extremely possessive when it came to his Mercedes. He didn't like leaving it in the hands of valets and only trusted Silêncio.)

Wearing a hat, shirtless, snorting coke between two hookers dressed as cowgirls, Ambrósio Junior let out his bloated chortle. "Out of the question. I'll give you the money and you buy the car you want, you hear?"

Silêncio reduced speed when we passed by a highway patrol checkpoint. Ambrósio Junior asked one of the women to lower the window, touched the brim of his hat, and formed a gun with his thumb and forefinger, messing with the men monitoring the traffic. The cops must have thought: *Another rich asshole.* But they smiled, taking the joke good-naturedly and waving back. It was a splendid morning.

Just as the morning was splendid when old Ambrósio first laid his cataract-clouded eyes on the redhead. I testify: the old man said he had dreamed about his mother, an ignorant and foul-mouthed Calabrese woman who made money by iron-fisted exploitation of tenements in Canindé. *Dona Gina*. She lived to be over a hundred. It's said she was the origin of the clan's meanness.

"*La bruta della vecchia* whispered some numbers to me, Poet."

Ambrósio called me *Poet* because of my love of books.

He mentioned the story about the numbers right away, when I went to pick him up at home; he said he needed to place some bets. But we didn't have time until the end of the day. Which was a stroke of luck: I stopped the car in front of the first lottery establishment I saw, with greater interest in the bar across the street—it was hot and I was dying for cold water or maybe a beer, depending on Ambrósio's mood after placing his bet.

He entered and ran his gaze over the small mob engaged in spending their change on dreams. Then he leaned over the counter and took from his pocket the piece of paper he'd jotted the numbers down on. I stood beside him with the thought of also taking a chance, although I didn't much believe in it; I've never had any luck with that kind of thing.

Ambrósio rasped: "You're not gonna copy my bet, are you?"

To avoid a scene, I wadded up the slip I had started to fill out and walked away. It wasn't long before the old man asked for help reading one of the numbers. He pointed to a scrawl on the paper. "What do you think that is, a seven?"

"Looks like a two."

"A two my foot, it's a seven! Think I don't understand my own writing?"

"Well, to me it looks like a two," I insisted.

And suddenly I had my doubts: maybe it actually was a seven.

Cazzo.

The girl in a nearby booth overheard our discussion and sang a song of simplicity: "Why don't you fill out *two* slips?"

I've spent several years with old Ambrósio without ever really discovering what pleases him. But I've had time and the good sense enough to learn the list of things that he doesn't tolerate. Cold coffee, for example. A newspaper that's already been read. People who show up late for appointments. The word *no* (perennially first in the ranking). The old man also harbored a special hatred for anyone who butted into the conversation of others, like this young woman, a redhead with white skin and light-colored eyes, had just done.

Gorete, according to the green name tag pinned to the shirt pocket of her uniform.

I watched intently as Ambrósio snorted and raised his head to confront her. The jugular vein pulsed in his neck. An encounter like this could lead to a harsh response. An insult. Or even worse, a slap in the face.

The redhead seemed to capture the powerful wave of energy ready to sweep over her. And she faced it with no sign of fear in her pale eyes. (A small mustache of sweat graced her mouth with its fleshy lips, full of personality.)

The old man's breathing hissed. *Here it comes*, I thought.

But something happened.

Ambrósio turned blue.

He stood there paralyzed and mute from enchantment, with the numbers slip in his hand and his face lit up like I had never seen it. The expression of a saint on the day he discovers he's a saint. He looked at me in search of complicity.

"Why didn't I think of that?"

"Of course," I said.

Ambrósio went up to the ticket window and asked with unexpected delicacy, "Can you do that for me, *please?*"

If she had known how unusual that gentleness was, perhaps Gorete would have smiled. But no. She merely took the slip and went on chewing her gum with an attitude somewhere between arrogance and insolence, as she entered the bets in the machine. Just once did she deign to look in the direction of the old man. To support me: "It's a two."

Ambrósio clapped me on the shoulder, excited. "Didn't I tell you it was a two, Poet?"

I said nothing. Gorete raised her head and afforded me the grace of her attention for a second, if that. She was, in fact, beautiful. More than beautiful, exotic. An unlikely flower. I appreciated how in her expression there was a touch of boredom, a certain impatience with the others of her species.

Ambrósio took the receipt, paid, and told her to keep the change. Gorete thanked him and wished him luck. The old man kissed the paper, folded it, and put it in his shirt pocket. And left the establishment floating on air, his eyes glued to the redhead in the ticket booth. When he landed in the car, he tasked me with a mission: "I wanna know everything about her. And I mean everything, *capisci?*"

I looked at him in the rearview mirror. Ambrósio was still half bluish. His face was bright. A different gleam in his eyes. A dash of adolescent craziness.

2

As soon as I turn on my cell phone it begins to ring, which startles me so much that I almost drop it. I answer because I recognize the number on the screen. Dr. Fontes, *mezzo* lawyer, *mezzo* adviser to Ambrósio.

"The old man's very upset with you," he says. "How could you disappear at a time like this?"

"I had my reasons, I know you understand . . ."

"Where are you?"

"Look, sir, don't take it the wrong way, but I have to hang up. I don't want to be traced."

"Stop being paranoid, man! Ambrósio only wants to talk to you."

"I know."

"He wants to hear directly from you how it happened. I think that's fair."

"With due respect, sir, *data venia*, tell me another."

Dr. Fontes laughs, then coughs. It takes awhile for him to recover his breath. Emphysema. "Listen: the old man is only interested in the black guy."

Silêncio is sleeping facedown, wearing striped trunks. He's sweating profusely. I'm certain the hand hidden under the pillow is grasping his revolver.

"What happened was fate," I say.

"Come and tell the old man that personally."

"The only one to blame in the story is Ambrósio Junior himself."

"Okay, I'm sure he'll understand," lies Dr. Fontes.

The playing cards we used for endless games are scattered on the floor. Silêncio grunts something incomprehensible from the land of sleepers. Laughs. Then opens his eyes and, still without moving, cautiously observes the world around him. He is a bit frustrated by what he sees.

"What guarantee can you give me?"

"He thinks of you as a son . . ."

"That's not much."

Dr. Fontes reflects for a moment. Silêncio sits up in bed and stretches his slim body, cracks his knuckles.

"Hand over the black guy. Then you'll be in good shape. I give you my word."

"I'll think about it."

"You think we don't know where you are?" Dr. Fontes is bluffing. I know his methods. "The underworld talks, you know."

He's right about that: the underworld does talk. And any information is available, all you need is patience.

"Call me," Dr. Fontes says. And he advises, "Careful," before hanging up.

Silêncio gets up to smoke near the window.

"It was Dr. Fontes," I say.

Silêncio considers the information for a second.

"He wanted to know if we needed anything . . ."

Silêncio smiles in his economical way.

The sound of steps in the hallway puts me on alert. Then I hear a key opening the door of the neighboring room and relax. I mean, as far as anyone in my situation can.

3

At the time of this story, Maria Gorete França Cavalcante was renting a room in a less-than-modest house in New World Park, in the most unpaved part of the district, bordering on Fernão Dias. She had just turned eighteen. And she was not at all happy with the life she was leading. She was fed up with everything and everybody, dying to get away.

And I saw no reason to disagree with her.

During the day, at the lottery establishment, for eight hours Gorete handled the bets of strangers for a miserable wage; at night, she shared the poorly lit space of a public school with classmates who did drugs, got pregnant, killed, or died in gang wars. And on the way home she depended on a bus that took forever.

Not that she was in any hurry to arrive.

In the only bedroom in the house, she shared a bed with her mother, a depressed woman incapable of intimacy, with two suicide attempts on her record (gas and razor blade). Marlon, Gorete's brother, slept on the sofa in the living room, although it might be more appropriate to say he *lived* on that dirty sofa, where he spent most of the day fingering a guitar and watching silent images on TV. Averse to work, he used the excuse that someone had to be around to watch over their mother. He took in a few coins by diverting some of the pills she was supposed to take to neighborhood junkies.

Marlon was lame, his right foot deformed from birth, a misfortune that made him the beneficiary of pitying tolerance on most people's part.

At first, he was my main source of information. We became "old friends" at the small grocery on the corner, after I sprang for several rounds of cognac and beer and a few greasy snacks. I didn't need to reveal the nature of my interest in Gorete. Marlon didn't care about that. Just the opposite. He even played the role of go-between without my asking, and informed me about his sister's amorous past.

Apart from the inconsequential flirting with lottery customers, Gorete had had two relationships worth mentioning: the first, with a mechanic from the neighborhood, an adolescent romance; the second, a tumultuous affair with an older guy, a photographer who had a studio downtown.

Marlon pointed out the mechanic: a short guy with kinky hair and oily skin who spent his weekends restoring antique cars in a dilapidated workshop. He figures in Gorete's biography only because he was the man who deflowered her. He would never have the ability to provide her with the luxuries she felt the world owed her.

Gorete considered herself special. And in a certain way, she was. She was lucky, very lucky. She was just waiting for an opportunity to change her life.

There was no reason to condemn her. Lots of people lived like that, awaiting some great event. A turnaround. Nothing wrong with that.

The only problem: it was taking a long time to happen, and that made Gorete impatient and quarrelsome with those around her.

Marlon was waiting too. In a different way than his sister. Him and his twisted foot. It didn't bother him to be the target of others' pity, or even of mockery. Marlon had other preoccupations, a head full of dreams. He wanted to be an artist. He composed romantic songs on his guitar with the hope of one day recording an album and becoming a successful musician. Marlon imagined that music could lift him out of the hole in which he lived.

In case that didn't work out, he had an alternate plan. He knew that if his sister achieved something, he wouldn't be left behind. He therefore rooted for her.

At the end of one afternoon, he coveted my car parked on the dirt road in front of the grocery store: "Can I take it for a spin?"

I don't like offending anyone, I take no pleasure in people's handicaps or suffering, anybody acquainted with me knows that. It was automatic, I was unable to avoid it: my eyes lowered to his foot, a veritable paw encased in a custom-made orthopedic boot.

Marlon showed his overlapping teeth in a sad smile. "Don't worry, I know how to drive."

I apologized. And my penance was to grant him a drive through the neighborhood.

Marlon did in fact know how to drive, even if he had to twist himself in the seat to reach the gas pedal with his heel, a contortion he executed with a joy bordering on vanity. The wind blew through his hair, a residual sun reflecting off his dark glasses. Marlon was happy.

We slowly circulated through the business center, where the stores selling cheap items were lowering their doors, the bus stops filling up. A pair of policemen were drinking coffee at a corner bar and waved when we passed. There on his turf, Marlon was popular on both sides of the law.

Before ending our tour, he took me to the Afro-Dite, a hair salon specializing in African-inspired cuts—the "Black Power" hairdo had returned with a vengeance. In the salon, I was introduced to Luana, a black woman with an easy laugh and alabaster teeth, who Marlon was constantly trying to seduce. The ebony muse of his songs. It was obvious that the woman, flattered, accepted the wooing as a joke, pretending to reciprocate the flirting she received. I saw how she looked at Marlon as he got out of the car dragging his right foot. If they someday got together, the word *compassion* would have to be mentioned.

In any case, there was an obstacle, Marlon later explained to me. Luana had a husband confined to a prison farm in the interior, over four hundred miles from São Paulo. A bank robber who she visited every other week. Sometimes she missed, which, as might be expected, made the guy rather irritated.

Then rumors started that he was about to be released on

parole. Or that he was involved in an escape plan. Marlon was scared to death that the man would suddenly show up at his door. He even made an anonymous call to the CrimeStop line, ratting out a tunnel being constructed at a penitentiary whose location he was unable to specify.

Once, I had the privilege—obligatory—of entering Marlon's club of *preferred* friends, a group of people to whom he pushed a raffle he promoted for his own benefit. It gave the right to a button, one of those sold by street vendors for fifty cents a dozen, that read, *Bosom Friend.* It also gave the right to participate in a drawing for what was perhaps the most valuable item in Marlon's collection of vinyl records: the very first recording made by Roberto Carlos, a 78 rpm from 1959, disavowed by the artist and never reissued. Marlon showed me the rarity wrapped in cheap plastic.

"It's in perfect condition," he guaranteed. "It's priceless."

I bought two numbers. Even though I didn't even have a way to play the record, I was moved when I saw the look in Marlon's eyes at relinquishing something precious to him. I asked what he planned to do with the money he collected from the raffle and the answer was an enigmatic smile.

"It's a secret," he said evasively.

That day, I thought he was planning to buy a car adapted to his physical limitation. I was wrong; the project was much more ambitious. Marlon was letting go of his beloved 78 rpm to pay for an operation to correct his bad foot.

In the end, the vinyl stayed at home: the winner of the drawing was beautiful Gorete.

Of course there were those who contested the result, and some even claimed trickery. I laughed. They were mistaken. The redhead's luck was as uncommon as her ass.

4

I've never been overly tormented by the question of the invisible. We are what we are, it seems to me, nothing beyond some drives and fears. With a little luck, we end up as rose fertilizer. And that's all.

But I must admit, and it's annoying, the bothersome occurrence of signs and warnings that spring up around us with the beauty of trees in a forest.

Ambrósio Junior was taking a long time in the bakery's bathroom, his coffee was getting cold on the counter. I thought something might have happened. Silêncio was smoking outside, distracted by the winter sun. I waved through the glass; he didn't notice. I went into the bathroom.

In one of the stalls, Ambrósio Junior was sitting on the toilet lid, his back resting against the tank, one hand in his lap. With the other, he was holding the Taurus, pointing it at his face. And crying. Sobbing.

"Take it easy," I said.

And I approached slowly, more fearful than confident. I saw the gun was cocked.

He let me take the revolver. Then he got up and, in an unexpected lunge, deposited on me the magnificent weight of his body, wrapping me in an embrace that put my vertebrae at risk. He went on crying, to the point of smearing my shoulder with spittle and mucus. He kept repeating, "I've got feelings too, goddamnit."

Then a man came into the bathroom and witnessed the scene. He also saw the .38 in my hand and retreated, pale as paper. When Ambrósio Junior calmed down and I convinced him to wash his face so we could leave the bathroom, that man was having breakfast at one of the tables, accompanied by a woman with long hair, still quite young, almost a girl, who was nursing a baby at her tiny breast. The two were so pale they appeared washed out. They looked at us sidelong and whispered conspiratorially. Then I saw they weren't just pale, they were albinos.

It had been some time since Ambrósio Junior had suffered one of those attacks. We even came to think he might be cured. A kind of absence that struck him, a lapse during which he forgot who he was, where he was, and what he was doing. Above all, what he was doing.

In the beginning, Ambrósio smelled fraud in his son's disorder. Pretense. He classified them as attention-getting fits. Ambrósio Junior defended himself by saying they were the consequence of the blows to the head he had received from his father from the time he was young.

The duration and the intensity varied. Given Ambrósio Junior's size and temperament, it wasn't unusual for it to veer into some type of brutality. Once, in the period when he was living with a nightclub singer called Lana, Junior sent the woman running in the middle of the night; he chased her with a knife through the streets around the luxury condominium where they resided—both of them naked.

Old Ambrósio forced him to seek pyschiatric help, and for a time Ambrósio Junior took *loco pills*, as he liked to say. The problem was that he mixed them with alcohol and other stimulants.

It was a crazy time.

Over any disagreement, father and son would come to blows. They couldn't be together. Sparks would fly. They would trade punches or head butts or roll on the ground in a bear hug, wrecking everything around them. Large-scale animals.

For third parties, the best thing was to not get involved.

Nor try separating them. Just maintain a cautious distance.

They would finally give up. Either they would grow weary or stop when one of the two suffered a serious injury.

Junior broke his father's nose in one of their encounters and on more than one occasion left his face bruised. His record, however, was inferior to the old man's, who registered several knockouts of his son. In one of them, Ambrósio Junior lost a molar and was unconscious for hours. It caused concern, and emergency medical services were called. The EEG showed what it always did: he suffered from a relatively serious cerebral malfunction and needed constant monitoring and medication. Above all, he needed a different lifestyle. Calmer. But then he wouldn't be Ambrósio Junior, he'd be another person.

Old Ambrósio had been a boxer in his youth, with some degree of success. He was a heavyweight who stood out in amateur tournaments in the meadows of Canindé, famous for his powerful left. Like a mule kick. On the walls of the freight company, yellowed pages from the Sporting Gazette related that promising career in dark photos (you could barely see the boxers' faces) and articles that compared the orthodox style of the husky Italian to that of a great champion from the past, Primo Carnera.

Mancino Ambrósio, as he was known, usually settled his matches in the first few minutes and, by what was said, could have gone further if he'd wished. He abandoned the ring at his wife's request, as soon as they were married. Dona Rosa didn't tolerate violence of any kind. Not even in films or TV. Father and son avoided any "low class" language in her presence. The degenerative disease that had kept her bedridden for years spared her from witnessing the episodes of brawling between the two.

You could bet, with a good chance of making a nice bit of money, that sooner or later they would end up killing one another.

Then, on his own account, Junior stopped taking his medications and, as if by magic, his attacks ceased. He entered a serene phase—serene, that is, for someone with a rap sheet like his. A phase that, for lack of a better word, could be called *mystic*. Ambrósio Junior began to communicate with the dead.

I remember that at the time, a different kind of cocaine appeared in the city, bluish. Extremely potent. Junior would snort long lines, enough to make his feet tingle.

In that state, he would receive messages from people already discarnate. Always souls of opaque light, such as Paulo Sansão, PS, a short, cross guy from Santos, Junior's partner in a used-car business in Boca. What was known was that they'd had a falling out—the reasons were never clear. I heard people speculate that it had to do with Sansão's wife, a former Miss Porchat Island with so much silicone in her body that it was dangerous to smoke near her. It was also said that Junior had discovered his partner's embezzlement in a transaction involving cars with fake documentation.

Both are possible hypotheses. And one doesn't rule out the other. What is undeniable was the event: on a Monday during Carnival, PS was approached by a biker at a traffic light on Anchieta as he was returning home late at night. He was shot five times, all in the face. The shooter fled without taking anything.

As soon as it happened, Ambrósio called to interrogate me about the matter. I told the truth: I only knew what the newspapers had published.

Ambrósio Junior testified twice at the hearing investigating his partner's murder. His phone was tapped, and they tracked the GPS in the Mercedes. (And witnesses were threatened.)

Nothing was ever proven against him. Actually, he emerged from the investigations better than before: it came to light that he had paid Sansão's funeral expenses, something only the widow had known.

However, suspicion and the rumors continued to hover in Canindé's polluted air that were less corrosive to the son's reputation than to his father's projects. Old Ambrósio had been trying for some time to become a member of the Rotary Club, and that desire turned into an obsession and came up against the rigor with which the Rotarians examined the candidate's record. (Having brought Ambrósio Junior into the world, I believed, surely contributed to the veto.)

"A case of patent ill will," opined Dr. Fontes, an illustrious member of the association, who had proposed Ambrósio's name. "They're unaware of the benefactor of the community, the citizen committed to social causes." And, after a short drag on his cigarette holder—he was the only one authorized to smoke on the premises—he turned his lackey's countenance to the old man and added, "They forget the most relevant business leader."

Perhaps in the lawyer's haughty oratory, beyond the habitual affectation, there was more than a little exaggeration. But lie? He didn't lie.

If we consider only legitimate businesses, Ambrósio could be held up as an example of a successful midlevel entrepreneur. Never a leader, to be sure. The problem was his illegal activities: there, the old man occupied a position of prominence, to the point of attracting the attention of the law. It took a lot of work for the emphysemic Dr. Fontes to justify to the authorities the way Ambrósio and his son related to the world. So much so that the lawyer received no fee. He shared in the family's profits.

What I know is that Dr. José Fontes was filthy rich; I was a regular at parties where women squirted champagne onto one another in the pool of the luxurious mansion he kept at the seashore, with a private pier and a fifty-foot vessel. He was a thin and powerful man, used to seeing his will executed without hesitation. I can only imagine how difficult it must have been for him to swallow the Rotary's rejection of someone he'd sponsored. It became a question of honor.

I was at a meeting on the mezzanine of the hauling company when Junior suggested an unorthodox solution to the impasse: coercing the Rotarians. "If not the easy way," he said, "we do it the hard way: beat the shit outta the guys."

Dr. Fontes, who was also the club's counselor, and incidentally the sole vote in the old man's favor, reacted indignantly: "That's a stupid idea."

Ambrósio Junior stared at him. The lawyer turned to Ambrósio for support. And found it. The old man stuck out his tongue in disgust. "*Stronzo.*"

Junior rose from the sofa and dragged himself like a pachyderm to his father's desk. The structure of the mezzanine creaked. I remember thinking: A *lousy place for a fight to break out.* In a strategic move of self-preservation, I relocated to a position near the metal stairs leading to the ground floor. Dr. Fontes wasn't as lucky and found himself penned between the boss's desk and the edge of the mezzanine. Displeased, he estimated the distance to the ground, about nine feet, and looked at me. If I could have, I'd have shown solidarity by reminding him that things like this were why he was so well paid.

Ambrósio rose from his chair and studied his son with half-closed eyes. His body leaned subtly to the left, ready to throw his fearsome punch. Ambrósio Junior knew this—better than anyone, in fact. So much so that he kept his guard low, both hands resting on the desk, in a peaceful—and ultimately false—posture, for he immediately began to challenge his father by a different means. The insult.

"It's a serious club," he commented insidiously. "It doesn't let just anybody in."

Ambrósio observed his son for a time, not saying anything and not relaxing his muscles. His jaw twitched. I knew the terrain to which Junior was taking the assault but couldn't predict how far they would go this time.

The old man's ancestors were shepherds who lived in isolated mountain villages in Calabria. Coarse and ignorant men who "spent more time in the company of their animals than with their wives," in Junior's malicious words. There was a family anecdote, almost a *racconto*, that he always recalled when he wanted to provoke his father.

Ambrósio Junior's uncle came to Brazil in search of "spiritual treatment" for cancer and spent a period lodged at his nephew's home. Junior, who must have been ten or eleven at the time, never forgot the trials his dark-skinned, rough-handed relative confronted in order to adjust to the formalities of civilized life. In his recollection, the man was scarcely more than a barbarian. He refused to enter the bathroom, as if something there—perhaps the shower—threatened him, or to use the toilet, preferring to relieve himself on the balcony of the bedroom where he slept, which wasn't discovered until his return to Italy.

Ambrósio Junior accompanied his mother in the reconquest of the veritable war zone into which the bedroom had been converted. The place reeked of offal, impregnating the sheets, curtains, and rugs. Dona Rosa ordered everything burned, even the mattress. Junior vividly remembered the expression of outrage on his mother's face when she encountered the piles of excrement on the balcony. The gentle and aristocratic Dona Rosa was, that day, still light-years away from the treacherous illness that would transform her into a vegetable.

Dona Rosa descended from a line of mill owners in the interior of the state, rather uncultured people but with resources and the good sense to send their children to study elsewhere. She was a pretty, refined, independent woman who began to fight for her own money as soon as she arrived in São Paulo. It was never clear to me how much she knew about her husband's illicit dealings. They met when they were both still quite young; he was boxing and also took care of matters at the hauling company. All the rest, including activities as loan shark and slumlord and, later, gambling and smuggling, was handled personally by the legendary Dona Gina.

Ambrósio Junior removed his hands from the desk and straightened his body in an abrupt movement that made him pant and served to put the old man en garde.

"Your money doesn't buy everything."

The phrase, though trite, had several consequences. The most important was that old Ambrósio relaxed. He laughed and sat down again, bringing another protest from the structure of the mezzanine. Dr. Fontes replaced the cigarette in his holder and lit it, lofting a puff of gray smoke. I saw sweat exuding from his bald head.

Junior stood in front of his father's desk, not breathing, looking him up and down, as if waiting for retaliation. Ambrósio nodded his head, amused.

"Did you hear that, Fontes? Look how he's talking about money."

Dr. Fontes straightened his tie and flicked away a flake of ash that had fallen onto his six-hundred-dollar Italian cravat, a gift from old Ambrósio to his beloved lawyer, whom he called "the saint of lost causes."

Ambrósio looked at his son and then at his mother in the frame on the desk. Wrapped in shawls in an armchair, in a wintery pose, her white hair like snow, Dona Gina, very near the end, gazed out rancorously at the world with which she was perpetually engaged in battle.

"Know what she used to say?" The old man stopped to kiss his mother in the picture frame. He made the sign of the cross. "She used to say that to be considered a real man, a guy's got to first earn his own money."

Ambrósio studied his son's reaction. Only his skin changed color. It reddened. The old man knew he was winning the fight, easily, on points. Junior let his breath out with the noise of a refrigerator compressor. His father gave no quarter and, in the manner of a left hook, asked: "Have you told Dr. Fontes the story of the widow?"

The lawyer couldn't contain himself and gave an anticipatory laugh. The topic was already circulating among the company's employees. Paulo Sansão's ghost had appeared to Junior and requested help for his unprotected widow, who, according to observations from beyond, was destitute here on earth. When Ambrósio Junior proposed to the old man a monthly amount for the woman, the reaction was almost a whinny: "For what? Services rendered?"

Junior repeated that PS had presented him with that demand and that it wasn't his place to question, only to obey. *Mediumship.* (He said this seriously, a bit contritely; the blue cocaine was really powerful.)

"Do you believe in those things, Fontes?"

The lawyer burped. He was still digesting the copious lunch we had shared at a barbecue restaurant on the Marginal. It was Saturday. "I only believe in what I can see," he explained. "And preferably, touch."

Ambrósio looked at me benevolently: "Poet believes in books."

I confirmed this. He laughed.

"I believe in books too," he said. "Especially in account ledgers."

The old man was given to that type of humor in those days. There was a reason for it, the reason that had him walking on air but also implied an anguish and silent serving of suffering and guilt. Old Ambrósio was in love.

"Why does your partner only appear to *you*? Why the exclusivity? Ask him to communicate with me too," he told his son. "Maybe he'll persuade me to shell out the money."

Junior gave up the fight, left the center of the ring, and took refuge on his side of the sofa. He was trembling, on the verge of having an attack. You could hear him gurgling.

Dr. Fontes went up to the desk and commented to Ambrósio that the donation of a shipment of wheelchairs might be seen as a gesture of good will by the members of the Rotary.

"How many wheelchairs?"

"I don't know. About fifty."

"*Cazzo*. Are there that many cripples around?"

The lawyer mentioned the victims of muggings on the city's public transit lines, which was a constant; whether they resisted or not, they ended up getting shot. According to him, a generation of the handicapped was being created.

Ambrósio scratched a recently implanted tuft of hair. "What's it gonna cost me?"

"I'll have to check."

"Do that."

Dr. Fontes made a notation in his electronic notebook and stored it in his pocket.

Then, as if adjourning office hours after a productive workday, Ambrósio closed the drawer, locked it, and rose. He seemed content with the state of the world at that moment. He got his coat from the hanger and I helped him put it on. His body gave off a pleasant rustic aroma. Ambrósio Junior remained on the sofa, hunched over, seething.

"What about tomorrow, Fontes?"

"I saw in the paper there's a circus in Anhembi. The Mamede Brothers. You know them?"

His wrinkled face lit up—Ambrósio loved circuses. Unconditionally. It didn't matter if it was some shabby suburban amusement park or a superspectacular undertaking with lights and huge computerized screens. He once even traveled to Buenos Aires just to see a Romanian circus. Dr. Fontes said he would check the availability of tickets for the next day.

Ambrósio said goodbye, kissed the lawyer's cheek, and was heading for the stairs when, suddenly, Junior stood up and blocked his path. The old man stopped. I was right behind him, and the possibility of tumbling down the staircase, tangled up with the two of them, immediately made me tense.

For an instant, father and son stood head to head, almost in a clinch. They had precisely the same height and width, except that the son was a bit more flaccid. Impatience could be heard in the old man's breathing.

"What is it now?"

"Why don't you give me my part of the businesses and I'll go away?"

"*Your* part?"

Ambrósio placed his hand on his son's chest and pushed hard, away from the stairs. Junior lost his balance and, to avoid a more drastic fall, had to sit down again on the sofa. The rumble shook the entire mezzanine. The old man was already three steps down the stairs when he turned to apply the final blow of the round. A jab: "Who said you're the owner of anything here? Only after I'm dead."

With that, Junior hit the canvas. And, groggy, fully collapsed on the sofa as Dr. Fontes and I descended the stairs after the old man, leaving the shed to face a cold late-May night. The full moon, of a color possible only thanks to pollution, floated in the Tietê.

As had been happening in the last few weeks, before going home I had to take Ambrósio to a brand-new building with a gourmet terrace and other novelties of the upwardly mobile middle class, located on a quiet street in Sumaré. On the way, we swung by a florist to buy a bouquet of begonias.

"How do I look, Poet?"

I peered at him in the rearview mirror. He was resplendent. "Very good, boss. You look like a kid."

Ambrósio almost believed it. He suggested I come back for him later and got out of the car carrying the flowers.

The gate began sliding open even before the old man made it to the front of the building. The doorman already knew him, knew very well who he was, to which apartment he was heading, and whom he was going to visit. Perhaps he imagined he could even guess to what type of activity the old man was going to dedicate the next few hours. But at this point I'm obliged to introduce myself into the story to affirm that the doorman was mistaken. He would never have guessed the truth.

5

I descend to the reception area as soon as it's dark. In the musty lobby, the TV is showing a variety show to no one. The Sunday paper lies in disarray on the center table.

The man raises his head in satisfaction when he sees me place note after note on the Formica counter, enough money for another week of lodging, with meals served in the room, a change of bed linens, and absolute confidentiality about the identity of guests—towels are extra. On the wall, a handwritten notice advises that the hotel does not provide receipts. A clandestine cave on a dubious street in the heart of the city—let me correct the anatomy: a street that was, in more pleasant times, the heart of the city and is today one of its many sewers.

The man counts the money and opens a drawer, from which he takes a piece of paper. "A message for you."

I know it's impossible even before I touch the note, which doesn't stop me from unfolding the paper and reading the message from a woman called Cida to one Spencer in which she complains of his disappearance and leaves a contact number. And, perhaps to avoid any misunderstanding, adds following her name an irrefutable detail: *Honey pussy.*

"It's not for me," I say, "I'm not lucky enough to be that Spencer."

The man receives the note with the visible ill will and sour expression of someone who had foreseen a tip. I don't trust him. I'm going to hate having him around when it begins to circulate in the underworld that there's a substantial reward for any lead about Silêncio's and my whereabouts.

I go out into the stuffy, noisy, electrically charged night, with insects buzzing around the lights, a racket from the bar on the corner, and people chatting in chairs on the street, something I haven't seen in this part of the city for a long time. I take it as a good sign. I need all the luck in the world from now on. I'm leaving my den for the first time, and that's what my enemies are waiting for.

Signs of heavy rain. A flash of lightning illuminates the sky, a clap of thunder rolls along the sides of Anhangabaú. The smell of decomposition is in the air. There's always something decomposing in these streets, usually something human.

I pass by the Arapiraca Bar, moving along the opposite sidewalk, without stopping. The everyday fauna of Sunday night in a downtown bar: idlers, pimps, whores, small-time con men, people from the boardinghouses in the area, and one or two innocents. No one I know. I return, enter, and go up to the counter near the cash register. Tibério is talking to a couple and it takes him awhile to notice me. When he sees me, his happiness seems genuine.

"You disappeared, huh?"

I fabricate a fishing trip to the interior of Mato Grosso, providing a detail or two. Tibério's smile widens until it shows the metal hooks that anchor his false teeth. I get a curious look from the skinny woman with greenish skin who's drinking standing up, next to the counter. In general, the clientele of the Arapiraca absents itself only in case of death or arrest, never for a vacation. I buy cigarettes, a lighter, and some chocolate bars, a request from Silêncio.

I hand Tibério the money, and he is still smiling when he says: "There was somebody here looking for you."

The information shouldn't affect me. But it's involuntary: I feel a shiver in my spine, the beginning of vertigo. Mazinho, the short-order cook from Ceará, sees me and waves his spatula in greeting. I don't reply. Busy making change at the register, Tibério doesn't notice my uneasiness. He approaches and leans over the counter to clarify in a confidential tone: "A woman."

I was expecting mention of the unpleasant types that Dr. Fontes calls upon to solve Ambrósio's most serious problems. Men from the north who live in the Baixada Santista, real gorillas.

Tibério raises his eyebrows and slyly underlines his report: "A really good-looking woman."

Good-looking. She's not a real blonde; she dyes her hair monthly in a beauty parlor on Augusta. I know this because I took her there several times.

"Did she leave her phone number?"

Tibério doesn't fall for my ploy. "She said you already have it."

The skinny woman finishes her drink and goes out into the street to smoke. I pick up my change and say I'm leaving. Before doing so, I still have time to make a rookie mistake, an unforced error. An instinctive reaction. It happens when Tibério asks about Silêncio.

"I haven't seen him in a long time," I say.

And I regret it instantly. Tibério doesn't say anything, merely observing the pack of cigarettes he just sold me. When he raises his eyes to look directly at me, the smile on his face has turned sad. We've been friends for many years, he knows very well that I've never smoked. I leave the bar before one of us starts to cry. Shitty paranoia.

When I reach Timbiras, near the area dominated by Africans, I hail a taxi. I tell the driver the address and immediately set out talking like a maniac, as if trying to make up for the mutism of days in confinement. Uncontrollable. I speak of everything: the heat, the coming rain, traffic, the football game I saw on TV that afternoon. As if in an eruption, I am draining the words accumulated inside me during the last week. I don't give the driver a chance to comment. From time to time he glances at me in the mirror. He must think I'm high.

The street where I live starts in a small cramped square that during the day serves as a latrine for all the dogs in the nearby buildings and at night as a poorly lit refuge for the needle people. Then it snakes its narrow way uphill until it ends at the dirty wall at the rear of a defunct textile factory. A dead end.

I tell the driver to stop a little before the low building with green tiles on its facade and, while waiting for the taxi to turn around at the end of the street, cautiously analyze the scene. My car is still where I left it last week, with two wheels on the sidewalk and its rear against a pole. I have the key with me, but it would be unwise to use it without a careful examination of the vehicle; I read recently of a guy who was blown up when he turned his key in the ignition.

I enter through the garage and slowly ascend the stairs to the third floor. My movement activates the security lights, and to be on the safe side, I wait till they go out before resuming my climb. In the still air of the corridor hovers a mixture of food and disinfectant. A child is crying somewhere in the building.

I establish that the door to my apartment hasn't been forced open; the key turns easily in the lock. A sign there was no unwanted visitor during my absence.

This impression lasts only until I turn on the living room light.

Immediately I see that the intruder had ample time to carry out his task. And that he was meticulous, a professional. Not a single thing is in its place, everything was searched and turned inside out.

My books were painstakingly removed from their shelves and scattered through every room, even the bathroom, as also happened with magazines, photos, documents, and other papers. He poured the contents of the liquor bottles onto the sofa and the living room carpet. The TV is facedown on the floor. In the bedroom, he ripped open the mattress and emptied the closets, leaving the clothes piled in a corner. He removed the pictures from the walls, without damaging any of them. He urinated and defecated in the toilet but didn't bother to flush.

Despite the diligence with which the visitor executed his mission, I know he wasn't looking for anything specific in my apartment. The invasion was just meant to intimidate. The time-honored tactic of keeping the enemy under constant pressure, to incite him to make a mistake. Didn't I already say I know my gang?

In the kitchen, more disorder and damage: the cupboards wide open, the floor covered with scattered provisions and broken glass—lots of broken glass. Not a single dish appears to have been left in one piece. Over the sink, pizza wrappings reveal the intruder's fondness for Calabrese sausage and hide a cockroach that scampers away when it sees me, then climbs down the wall and takes refuge behind the stove. I contemplate killing it and even move the stove aside. But I lose interest in the roach when I discover the message the invader has left me. More than a message, a declaration of principles.

The old tea can where I hide money for emergencies is open in the middle of the table. Around it, carefully arranged, the money itself—or what's left of it, every bill rendered useless by a hole in the center, methodically burned by the flame of a lighter. As if to tell me that he found my dough but he's not a thief.

At this point my visit is over—there's no more reason to stay there. I've already taken a big risk by entering the apartment, where someone could have been waiting, because of that money. The strategy of strangling the enemy is starting to work: soon, Silêncio and I won't have the resources to remain in hiding. We'll be forced to move, making things easier for them.

I'm on my way out, with the key in the door, when I turn back, attracted by one of the photos my visitor left on the living room floor. It's a picture in which the woman Tibério described as good-looking appears smiling at the camera. Her hair, its roots a darker color than the rest, is uncombed, her face flushed, and her shoulders bare. Although it can't be seen in the photo, I know she is wearing nothing but earrings. I also know she is happy. We had just made love. And at the time of the photo there was not yet any poison between us.

Rain decides to fall just as I leave the building. Warm, thick drops begin to come down sluggishly onto the ground and rattle against the metal of my car, the only one parked on the street. I touch the keys in my pocket, but I don't even need to get very close to see that the apartment invader did a complete job: the air has been let out of all four tires.

The rain picks up. All I can do is go down to the square and look for a taxi. A bit before the first curve, I cross the street, intending to seek the protection of the trees planted at regular intervals along the opposite sidewalk. And it is this that saves me.

The headlights emerge from the curtain of water and the car slows to make the curve. Though the driver doesn't see me, I have time to observe him. I can see that, despite the heat, he is wearing a brown leather jacket, an almost new jacket, coming slightly unstitched at the right underarm, but a good jacket. I know because it belongs to me.

The car moves away, I pick up my pace. Soon I am running down the street under a summer cloudburst. I run as fast as I can, to the limit of my strength. Only my heart is faster than my legs.

(This is an excerpt from the novel
As If the World Were a Good Place.)

MARGOT

BY DRAUZIO VARELLA

República

Early that morning Margot was happier than ever. "I should have been suspicious. Happiness like that, in my life?"

Born in a wooden shack precariously perched over the waters of a riverbank, built by her father to shelter his wife and their five children, she had experienced the trials of poverty since early childhood, on the outskirts of Iranduba, a small town on the banks of the Rio Negro opposite the Manaus side.

She was barely twelve when her father left Iranduba to try his luck at prospecting in Santa Isabel, on the central Rio Negro, to which thousands of Brazilians and Colombians flocked, attracted by news of abundant gold in the depths of the waters and fortunes made overnight.

To support the family, her mother found a job as a kitchen helper on the *Asa Branca*, a boat that went up and down the Rio Negro, taking and bringing back merchandise, construction materials, and passengers to the riverside communities. In the dry season, when navigation was dangerous, she would spend two weeks or more on those journeys that afforded her less than the minimum wage and no worker's benefits.

To Margot, the oldest daughter, fell the role of heading the family and abandoning her studies. She cooked, cleaned the house, took her older siblings to school, kept an eye on the younger ones so they wouldn't venture out onto the loose

boards of the footbridge that linked the stilt houses to one another, and she still found time to wash and iron the neighbors'
clothes to supplement the household budget.

At the end of the afternoon she would fill the bucket with
water from the river for the little ones' baths, serve supper,
and set up the hammocks. She held out against fatigue until
all were asleep. Then she would take her teddy bear from the
shelf and lie down embracing it in the hammock beside the door.

Leaving the house occurred only two or three times a
month, to help their mother with shopping for provisions that
had to last until her return from the next journey.

On those occasions, Margot would take a leisurely bath
in the river, put on some perfume, slip on the necklace of açaí
beads that her father had given her, and don the only clothes
she considered nice. It was her favorite day. They would return
with bagfuls of lumpy flour, beans, rice, noodles, potatoes, dried
beef, and a two-liter bottle of *guaraná* to share on Sunday.

She followed this routine for four years, until her mother
found work in the home of a family in a condominium in Ponta
Negra, a district of Manaus where the population with the
highest purchasing power was concentrated.

Life at the edge of the river improved. They had more
money for expenses, the younger children were in school, and
their mother came home every Sunday.

At sixteen, Margot fell in love with Edinaldo, a muscular youth who worked as a stevedore at the port of São Raimundo, from which the barges linking Manaus to Iranduba
departed. To avoid malicious gossip, they would meet in the
most deserted places in the neighborhood.

One Sunday, she waited for her mother to fall asleep and
quietly left to meet her boyfriend. Fuinha, the grandson of
Baré Indians, who at fifteen roamed around the area drunk,

caught them in a dark corner, she with her mouth on Edinaldo's sex.

The couple hoped that the meddler's state of intoxication wouldn't allow him to discern or remember the scene he had witnessed. They were wrong. The next day, she awoke to shouts of "Cocksucker!" coming from three boys not yet ten years old.

Life became hell. When they saw her, neighborhood women would whisper and laugh, men would make gestures alluding to the scene in the alley, street urchins would grab her rear and run away. She was given the nickname Catfish Mouth. Her mother, a fervent evangelical, accused her of disgracing the family.

Intimidated, Margot locked herself in the house. The few times she needed to go to the store, she heard insults and provocations that she bore in silence. The afternoon she lost patience with a group at the door of a bar and replied that the cocksuckers were their mothers, she went home with the taste of blood in her mouth and her face swollen. Her mother blamed her for having provoked the men.

The aggression caused such revolt in her spirit that she decided to carry a sharp knife in her waistband, hidden under her T-shirt.

For weeks she avoided passing by the bar, until she was forced to do so one afternoon in the Amazonian heat. Two of the aggressors were drinking beer at the counter. Her precaution of changing to the opposite sidewalk was futile: they crossed the street, wanting to know if the little whore was happy with the beating she had received.

Her head lowered, she tried to move around them and continue on her way, but they blocked her path.

The shorter one laughed when he saw the knife. He was

the first to fall. The fatter one tried to run but was overtaken in the middle of the street.

She ran home, put her clothes and hammock in her backpack, got the money she had saved up as a washerwoman, and left without saying where she was going.

At the port of Iranduba she caught the barge, crossed the Rio Negro, and disembarked at São Raimundo, where Edinaldo found her a spot on a small fishing boat that took her to the port of Manaus, next to the market. There, she bought a second-class ticket on one of the boats that travel the Amazon as far as Belém do Pará.

On the deck, a painted sign indicated the different sides for women and men, some of whom were blond and were speaking unfamiliar languages. She walked past them without anyone bothering her, and went behind a corner to set up her hammock in the women's wing. She needed the help of a crew member to find a spot on the overloaded vessel.

She was enchanted to see the muddy waters of the Solimões travel for kilometers side by side with the Negro, without mixing. And for the first time in her life, she saw a river that didn't have dark waters.

Four days' journey crossing the jungle, to the sound of *forró* music on deck, voices from transistor radios, and endless conversations between passengers in colorful hammocks, docking in isolated communities and larger cities. In each port, the commotion of cargo, boxes and more boxes of soft drinks, men, women, and children descending with packages, plastic shopping bags with red and blue stripes, television sets in crates, bags of flour on their backs, and cans of paint, while another wave quickly boarded in search of nooks in the wooden ceiling from which to hang their hammocks and mark off their personal space.

In Óbidos and Santarém, the federal police came on board to inspect the baggage, looking for the cocaine paste that goes down the Negro and the Solimões toward Manaus and then follows the Amazon to Belém. One of them stopped in front of her.

"You got drugs in that backpack?"

She didn't answer, she simply opened the zipper and began to remove her belongings. The policeman interrupted: "You can close it. You look like a good girl."

The journey, which had begun Wednesday afternoon, ended in Belém on Sunday morning under a merciless sun.

Alone in an unknown city, she looked for the cheapest boardinghouse she could find. After walking for hours, following directions given by passersby, she stopped before a place in Terra Firme, the most populous district in Belém, formed thanks to an invasion of federal lands on the banks of the Tucunduba River.

In the small, stuffy room, she did the arithmetic: her money would last five days, if she didn't eat.

The next morning, there was a knock at the door. It was Kézia Giselle, the tenant in the room next door. Almost six feet tall, Kézia empathized with her neighbor's story and was willing to help her.

"Dear, you have the body and the age that men like. I'll arrange some clothes for you. My part is 30 percent."

At the hands of her companion, at sixteen years of age, Margot debuted as a street prostitute.

Kézia taught her to get paid before performing her services, to refuse drunks, not to do drugs, to charge extra for unusual sexual favors, and to identify by their eyes the perverts who might beat her. According to the agreement, of the thirty reais she usually charged, nine went to her companion.

On good nights she would have five or six dates. At the end of the night, she would sit at the counter of the bakery, order a coffee with bread and butter from the grill, buy a chocolate bar, and go home with money in her purse and the certainty that she was getting ahead in life.

The exceptions were the nights when the police showed up to extort. She was outraged at having to give them the money earned through so much sacrifice, but what was the alternative? To be hauled to the precinct as a dealer of the cocaine they put in your bag so they can claim they caught you red-handed?

One night an older man with gray hair pulled up to the curb in a sports car. Unlike her usual clientele, he was well dressed, cultivated, and polite, which made her feel safe.

Instead of stopping the car on a side street, as was the norm, they went to a motel. En route, he asked if she knew Rio de Janeiro, spoke of Sugar Loaf, Corcovado, Copacabana, the bars and restaurants along the beach, Carnival, and the samba schools. Margot listened eagerly to the description of that world she knew only from soap operas.

The client went into the room carrying a bag. He took out a small envelope of cocaine, which she refused, meticulously divided it into lines with the sharp blade of a red pocketknife, and took a long snort.

The drug left him with an agitated look in his eyes. He opened the bag and took out a pair of red patent-leather shoes with high heels. He removed his shirt and pants. Instead of undershorts he was wearing black lace panties, triangular, that barely concealed his sex. He put on the shiny shoes and paraded back and forth in front of her as she lay on the bed.

Then he lay down on his stomach, handed her the belt from his trousers, and ordered her to whip him. With each stroke he asked for more force, in an authoritarian tone that intimidated her. With his back marked, he opened the bag again, took out a plastic penis, and handed it to her. She hesitated; it was large and thick and would hurt him, but he begged her, almost in tears.

Reluctantly, Margot stuck the plastic penis in her client, who screamingly implored her to use more force. Blood ran from his butt and stained the sheet. He asked her to whip him again.

In the midst of the whipping, with the dildo rammed as far as it would go, the client came.

She dropped the belt, rose from the bed, and went into the bathroom. When she returned, he was snorting another line of coke. Seeing her ready to leave, he said: "Where do you think you're going? The best part of the party comes now."

"What do you mean?"

"Now you lie down and I'm going to stick this dildo in *you*."

She replied that she wouldn't do such a thing for any amount of money. The man insisted, he'd pay double, promised he wouldn't hit her, he just wanted to see the penetration. Adamant, Margot moved toward the door.

She already had her hand on the knob when she was grabbed from behind, the knife blade against her throat. Forced back onto the bed, she felt the heat of blood descending between her breasts, there was no way to resist; she thought he would cut her throat.

She smiled and said she'd charge an extra fifty, with the condition that he use Vaseline. Dry, she wouldn't do it. Without taking the knife from her wounded neck, he allowed her to reach for her purse on the nightstand.

Margot handed him the tube and asked him to let her take off her shorts and panties. Busy opening the tube while his companion undressed, the man committed the indiscretion of setting the knife down on top of the pillow.

The thrust caught him in the middle of the chest.

Margot opened the door, descended the stairs, climbed on the hood of the car with her shoes in her hand, reached the top of the wall, and jumped into the vacant lot on the other side.

The following week, two armed men appeared at the boardinghouse. They were searching Margot's room when Kézia arrived. They wanted to know the whereabouts of her neighbor who had knifed an entrepreneur from the duty-free zone. When she said she didn't get involved in the other girls' lives, she took a blow to the chin that sent her reeling.

Lying on the floor, she heard that the man had barely escaped with his life and had hired them to wreak his revenge on the assailant; they would go to the gates of hell after her. With a revolver against her head, Kézia confessed that, after the incident, her friend had changed her post to an avenue on the other side of the city.

They had been gone only a few minutes when Margot arrived. With an ice-filled plastic bag against her chin, her friend recounted what had happened and advised her to disappear.

She closed out her accounts and fled to Salvador—in her backpack, clothes thrown together in haste and the address of Vanessa, from the same area as Kézia, who worked in a nightclub in the Lower City.

The two got along very well. Without asking anything in return, Vanessa arranged a vacancy in the rooming house where she lived, introduced Margot to her friends, to Soft Finger, owner of the drug site next door, to Raimundo, responsible for the safety of the girls whose post was the Largo de Roma, and to the madam who came by every Friday to collect the eighty reais owed for the right to that post.

It was with Vanessa that she learned the badger game, a con in which the client is led to a tenement room, where the couple is surprised in the middle of sex by one of Raimundo's henchmen, claiming to be a vice squad policeman charged with cracking down on prostitution in the district. The amount of the extortion was divided equally.

The badger game brought in a good profit until it was used against a state prosecutor. Margot was sentenced to three years and eight months; Vanessa, a recidivist, to five years and two months.

In the crowded cells of the prison, Margot met Mindinha do Pó, a trafficker in Soft Finger's gang, caught in the act with five kilos of marijuana and three hundred grams of cocaine she was transporting to Porto Seguro, on the coast of Bahia.

She left prison convinced she should start working in drug trafficking. Better to take chances in that millionaire world than to risk dying at the hands of some pervert in the poverty of prostitution.

Soft Finger read the note signed by Mindinha: "Okay. There's just one thing. If you're caught, you take the rap by yourself. If you rat on any of us, you die; if you try to play us, you die sooner. Crime has its rules."

She was taken into the team of dealers who distributed cocaine in the Lower City bars. Loyal and able to keep a promise, she quickly won the confidence of customers and her bosses and was promoted to group coordinator. It was her job to weigh and distribute the drugs to the street dealers, check the money from sales, and serve as go-between with the police, an activity that won her a reputation as a skilled negotiator.

She interacted so well with the cops that heads of other drug gangs hired her services to achieve less extortionary financial agreements.

"Even the police trusted me."

The converse, however, was not true.

"They're the worst kind of people. They don't invest money in purchasing, they don't go to the trouble of selling, they're never harassed, and they don't end up in jail. They don't risk anything, they only show up to collect the dough. When they don't get paid, they arrest everybody."

She never imagined she would one day get her hands on so much money. She earned more in a night than prostitution paid in a month. She could buy dresses, jeans, designer sneakers, sunglasses, yogurt and cheese at the supermarket, imported cosmetics. She had her hair done at the best salon in the district. Twice a week she ate at a steakhouse. She took taxis. She had more pairs of shoes than would fit in her closet.

"From a hooker, I became one of those spoiled daddy's girls."

Her social rise was interrupted when Soft Finger went to war to take over one of his competitor's territories, and he lost his head, severed to serve as an example. Margot was arrested as a trafficker, sentenced this time to eight years, of which she served four.

Upon being set free, she had no trouble returning to trafficking, but the police wouldn't leave her alone.

"I was a marked woman, it was raid after raid. One time, they took the cocaine and the dough I was carrying. I went hungry to pay the supplier."

Weary of persecution, she decided to come to São Paulo. A stranger in such a large city could relaunch her life without the permanent threat of the police. As she packed her bags, she concluded that, despite the setbacks, she had in fact improved her life: "I left Manaus with three T-shirts, an old pair of pants, and two pairs of cheap shorts; from Belém, a little better. I left Salvador with two suitcases full of shoes and pretty clothes. I was proud of myself."

She rented a room at a small hotel near the Estação da Luz, recommended by a friend who ran crack from São Paulo to Feira de Santana in the backlands of Bahia.

Swearing to never again set foot in a jail cell, she went back to street prostitution.

"Sure, it pays less than trafficking, but the chances of staying alive and free are much better."

Months later, she was invited to work in a house in Baixo Augusta, an area close to downtown and its concentration of bars and nightclubs with heavy nocturnal activity.

"It was a chic place, a select atmosphere, lots of big spenders. I charged eighty per trick, sometimes more, depending on the person. There weren't those gross, stupid men like in the Lower City."

Between the percentage she received from the customers' bar tab and what she earned going up to the rooms on the second floor, she made more than two thousand a month.

"Plus, it was all inside the house, without the dangers of the street."

In the anonymity of the city, she experienced the freedom she'd never had. She succeeded in renting a studio apartment to live in on her own, on Rua Dr. Teodoro Baima, near Avenida Ipiranga.

"For the first time in my life, I had my own place, cramped but arranged to my personal taste."

She made friends with a group of clients from the club. On Saturdays she would go with them for *feijoada* at a restaurant close to Paissandu Square. Now and then, at the end of the night, they would have dinner at Boi na Brasa, a traditional steakhouse that survived the disappearance of the dive bars near Rua General Jardim. One bright Sunday she was introduced to and fell in love with Ibirapuera Park: the ducks on the lake, the trees, attractive men and women on bicycles wearing colorful clothes, couples with their children in baby carriages, joggers in shorts and tank tops.

"I walked among those people like a respectable woman. Nobody knew who I was or how I made my living."

She always avoided romantic involvement. In her years in the profession, she had witnessed the suffering of others like her, in love with men of low character interested only in exploiting them. The two or three boyfriends she'd had in Bahia hadn't really touched her heart.

"I stayed with them more out of need, I didn't expect anything in return. When they went away, I missed them a bit, but I didn't suffer."

With her more relaxed life in São Paulo, she let down her guard a little.

Edu was five years younger. He was so delicate the first night when they went up to the bedroom that she found it odd.

"I thought he was gay."

Two days later, he returned. The waiter served him whiskey and her a fruit cocktail. They talked and laughed. When Margot asked if he wanted to go upstairs, the young man said no, he was there just to invite her to go to a movie the following afternoon.

After the movie and a sandwich, he accompanied her to the door of her building. She didn't invite him in—it was her habit to avoid problems with the neighbors and maintain the intimacy of the home she had always dreamed of.

They went out several other times. They traded confidences. He revealed he had been hooked on cocaine but had been clean for six months. Because of his drug use, he had been kicked out of his parents' house and lost his job. Abstinence had brought back his self-esteem and a return to the parental home.

"Before I realized it, I was in love. I never would have believed it. Since Edinaldo, in my adolescence back in Iranduba, it was the first time."

Edu promised to take her out of that life as soon as he found work. He didn't want to see her with all those men and was consumed by jealousy at the mere thought of her in bed with someone else.

The nights when he went to pick her up, they would have dinner at the Planeta on the corner of Rua Augusta, which stayed open late, and end the night in her small apartment on Teodoro Baima. At the nightclub, she prayed for the time when she could go home and watch a film on TV, holding hands with her boyfriend on her new sofa.

After two months, they were practically living together. She took care of the household bills, as well as his expenses— only until he got a job, he insisted.

One night Edu showed up agitated, extremely talkative, his eyes bloodshot and his nose itching from cocaine. She removed her makeup and went to bed without saying a word.

The next day he apologized, wept, said he was depressed about not having work and being obliged to live off his companion, like a gigolo. This was why he'd snorted the line his friend gave him. He asked her to trust him, swore he wouldn't disappoint her.

"A false promise—in reality he was already doing crack."

She did everything to get him off the drug, even tracking him down among the crackheads on the sidewalk at the Estação da Luz. When she managed to bring him back, he would sleep for two days and two nights, waking up well-behaved,

affectionate, committed to kicking the curse that was destroy-
ing him so they could live in peace . . . promises kept until the
next time he disappeared.

It was raining the night that Margot screamed in horror
when she opened the door to the studio apartment. Everything had been stolen—the TV, the sound system, the clock
on the wall, silverware, pots and pans, clothes, sneakers, and
the transistor radio from the night table.

"He even took my açaí necklace. So cruel! How much
could that be worth?"

In desperation, she wandered around Cracolândia until
daybreak. No sign of the thief. At home, she sat down on the
sofa and cried as she hadn't since childhood.

Night after night, she searched among the crackheads
sleeping under the marquees at the Estação da Luz and among
the groups who gathered in the vicinity where Rua Helvetia
crossed Dino Bueno, near Coração de Jesus Square, asking
about her boyfriend. But she wasn't seeking revenge.

"I was so in love that all I could think about was pulling
him out of the gutter, bathing him, making him hot soup, and
putting him to bed."

Time took on the task of consoling her.

"People like me are born to be alone. It does no good to
dream."

Her work at the nightclub helped her overcome the pain
of disillusionment. She was popular among the regulars and
enjoyed a good relationship with Mr. Gino, the Italian who
owned the house. The difficulties began when Mr. Gino hired
the services of a new bouncer, Bentão 45, thrown out of the
civil police after a scandal involving the extortion of a bank
robber whose young son was held hostage until his father paid
the ransom.

Bentão was pushing fifty. He circulated among the brothels, to which he provided protection, wearing a black coat over an abdomen that spilled over his belt. On his wrist gleamed a gold watch, around his neck a chain with thick links visible under his half-open shirt; three rings of wrought silver adorned the three middle fingers of his right hand.

The arrogant and authoritative posture that he made a point of displaying since his time on the police force, the reputation acquired from deaths he was rumored to have caused, his uncertain relationship with the police, and the inseparable .45 pistol he carried imposed respect among the rowdy customers who tried to hit on women, and those who refused to pay for services rendered or started fights with rivals, upsetting the calm atmosphere. A phone call from the proprietor was all it took for him to be there in five minutes.

Burned by her earlier experiences with the police, Margot kept a prudent distance after meeting him. She would greet him with a lowered head when they crossed paths at the entrance and would find a reason to move away every time he approached.

The antipathy was mutual.

"He wouldn't look me in the eye. When I said good evening, he almost didn't answer. He would walk right by me on the floor of the club like I didn't exist."

Upon entering the house, Bentão would drag his massive body to the bar, grab the glass with a double shot of cognac served before he even asked for it, and run his gaze over the customers. When he was irritated with someone, he would set down his glass, walk over to the table, and whisper a few words into the person's ear—the customer would immediately ask for the check and leave.

It was said that in the houses under his protection, he only admitted the traffickers who bribed him; those who dared to act on their own were gently invited to vanish, unless they preferred falling into the hands of the drug enforcement agency.

After a few weeks, the disdain that Bentão demonstrated toward Margot changed its form: he continued not looking at her when they crossed paths and didn't respond to any timid greeting she gave, but at the end of the night, invariably drunk: "He would look at me as if tearing off my clothes with his eyes."

Like the majority of women, she could recognize libidinous male gazes a hundred yards away. Despite her years in prostitution, she still felt intimidated when she encountered them in the street, the supermarket, at Sunday Mass, and other settings alien to the exercise of her profession. The fact that they were now coming from a violent former cop frightened her.

The fear that took control of her made Margot lose her natural rapport with clients and work companions. She spent nights awake, anxious and constantly looking at the door.

"He could appear at any moment, and I didn't know in what state of mind: looking at me with hate or with lust."

At five one morning, as she was retouching her makeup in preparation to leave, Bentão blocked the bathroom door.

"He grabbed me and kissed me on the lips before I could resist. He had a drunk's tongue, tasting of cigarettes, forcing its way into my mouth. I started to scream. He pushed me hard, I hit my head on the mirror, and glass went everywhere."

The next night, he went back to his routine of ignoring her and not responding to her dispirited good evening.

"It was as if he was ashamed and sorry. He never looked at me that way again."

Free from police harassment, Margot recovered her spontaneity. She became increasingly calm. "Freedom tastes different when oppression stops."

One night, Mr. Gino called her into his office.

"You're the only one in the house who doesn't do cocaine or cause trouble—just the opposite. I want to offer you a job as manager. You'll control the coming and going of the employees, the percentage charged by the girls when they go to the rooms, drinks at the bar, the cleaning staff, and you'll resolve any disputes the women are always creating. In exchange, I'll give you a room, a salary of 1,800 a month, and a signed work card."

It was less than she made as a prostitute, but she went away jubilant. She wouldn't have to sell her body, wouldn't have to go to bed anymore with stupid, unpleasant, ugly, pot-bellied men who suggested the most extravagant sexual acts. Finally, she had succeeded in life.

"A professional work card, manager of the business, and a room with a desk full of drawers, just for me."

She bought a bouquet of roses from an itinerant vendor who hung out by the door, and she went down the street singing. When she entered Roosevelt Square, two buzzed adolescents crossed the square beside her, repeating the refrain of a popular samba in slurred voices.

Entering her studio apartment, she placed the roses in the vase of the small center table, glanced around, and felt proud of herself. The place was prettier and more orderly than before the robbery: flat-screen TV, picture holder on the bookcase, two little angels with open wings on the wall, the statue of St. Sebastian with pious eyes, riddled with arrows, on top of the dressing table.

She opened and closed the refrigerator. She went down to the corner bar, sat on a stool at the end of the counter, and ordered a sirloin, rare, with two fried eggs, mashed potatoes, and rice—her favorite dish.

She was waiting to be served when Bentão appeared at the door and ordered a cognac. He was drunk, as was usual at that late hour. At the other end of the counter, she lowered her head in an effort to remain unnoticed.

She had barely begun to eat when he came her way. She kept her head down. The ex-policeman stopped beside her, silent.

After a few interminable seconds, he grabbed her by the chin. "Listen here, you cross-dressing son of a bitch. You goddamn degenerate. I never did like your cocksucking face, you low-life faggot."

The punch came with such force that blood from an eyebrow spattered onto the counter.

Even stunned, she managed to turn her face away from the next blow and dash outside.

At home, she got a towel to stanch the blood, sat down in bed, and fell into convulsive sobbing.

"I should have anticipated it. Precisely today, when I was so happy."

Absorbed in his glass of cognac, Bentão only realized what was happening when the knife penetrated his back for the first time.

24-HOUR SERVICE

BY FERNANDO BONASSI

Morumbi

> **Adviser** is a masculine noun with its origin in the Latin
> assessore, *which signifies helper, assistant, counselor, be-*
> *cause he is someone who* **advises** *an individual or organi-*
> *zation in a certain area or task. An adviser's function is to*
> *offer his knowledge, orienting and clarifying issues related*
> *to his specialization. There is a common error as regards*
> *the spelling of the word: the preferred form is adviser and*
> *not* advisor.

It begins at two a.m.

The senator in question here is a man respected throughout
the national ideological spectrum: democratic, religious, advocate for growth; concerned by the political threat repre-
sented by his youngest son calling at this hour of the night—
Daddy, I fucked up!

The senator immediately calls the governor of the state
and appeals to their mutual family sentiments, of their party
and *whatever the fuck!* He relates what he heard from "his" little boy, passes along an address, and hangs up. It's well known
that the governor of this state wouldn't be worth a crap without this senator, to whom he owes his first nomination to a
post bringing visibility and money: director of public works.
A civil engineer from a for-profit university, lousy at math, he
was incapable of building the smallest project that wouldn't

collapse. Still, he did know finance and percentages and trends. Uncomfortable with the possible politico-financial re-percussions of what was happening, the governor immediately calls the secretary of government (whom he calls "his," like his wife, free of all awkwardness), reiterating the commitment they have to the others, what they all owe to the administra-tion, to governability—*and my, your, our future, goddamnit!* He relays what he heard from the senator, gives the name of the son, the address, and hangs up, panting.

It's one of the hottest October months since they started keeping records. Secretary of government is a position enjoying the governor's confidence. The absolute greatest confidence. Without the governor, in fact, "his" secretary of government would likewise not be the big shit he is, whether naturally or by his own efforts, all of them erratic and worthy of limits: a jail-house lawyer in the most violent area of the northeast, he paid 1,500 US dollars for a competent man to take the bar exam in his place. He passed with flying colors. He was elected presi-dent. Startled, lacking intellectual resources or the power to formulate answers on his own, he doesn't hesitate to call the deputy secretary of government, his person of course, whom he personally appointed when he was nominated by the peo-ple of some other somebody . . . The deputy secretary of gov-ernment didn't have a pot to piss in when he went to work for the secretary of government, it's good to remember. It was said he was a violent man who had lost prestige in the area of security thanks to an incident involving the sale of transfers and promotions of civil service employees followed by deaths, many deaths, about whose well-known culpabil-ity nothing was ever proven, nor were there living witnesses to testify against him. The secretary of government relates to the deputy secretary of government the case of the senator's son: *Spoiled-rotten little queer! And son of that tremendous whore! What did he say?! He said, "Listen to me, listen to me"!* And he repeats what was narrated by the boy's father to the governor and came to his knowledge through these tortuous calls with cordless telephones, in a dialogue of the blind, the deaf, and the cowardly, and he dictates to him the address he noted down without asking questions. He hangs up not believing he has rid himself of the problem. *Fucking ass-kisser like me!* That's what— without saying it to anyone, not even to himself, officially— the deputy secretary of government thinks too, understanding the gravity of the facts, calling at once "his" private adviser, a man selected, nominated, and controlled by him. *Somebody under me will take care of it!*

3:10 a.m.

When the telephone rings, the adviser to the deputy secretary is actually already awake. *It's those guys' number . . .* Lying on his back, water drips off his belly. His desiccated scrotum glued to his legs. The mattress is soaked. It'll lead to mycosis. Nothing good happens at 3:10. He needs to write himself a reminder to buy cream. For his sunburned thighs. In this heat. What can you expect? That telephone never brings good news either. Besides which, it's an election year. He answers the phone. *I need you.* Is it urgent? *It's a fuck-up! What do you think?* No room for argument. *Write down the address.* He leaves his wife grumbling, sleeping naked from the waist down. A beautiful married woman's ass. *Oh, my cazzo.* He sticks his hand down his undershorts. His dick responds to the contact, but it's contained. The couple has a schedule for screwing. *Shit . . .* Adviser grabs the following day's clothing, set out in an orderly fashion on a chair. Through the blinds, a sliver of dark night. He leaves before he forgets. He gets dressed in the living room. Still half-asleep, he almost falls. Trips. Jumps. *Fuck me!* He survives with a bruised shin. The gun, on top of the empty bookcase, he puts in his waistband. The window covers the living room wall, with no view. A few meters away is the neighboring building, and looking, without even wanting to, looking, he sees that behind the curtains several rooms are lit. There is no movement. Many are sleeping. Others are quietly dying. It's a neighborhood of old people. Retired Italians and Brazilians. *A bunch of bums, perverts! They spend the day jerking off and dreaming about what they never were, the pathetic losers . . .* Adviser of all trades, he washes his face in the guest bathroom. He's on his way out. He looks at the door from the outside with his family (a wife and two kids) sleeping inside and runs down the stairs to avoid the hateful creaking of the elevator. He has chills and is sweating when he arrives in the basement. The smell of cement from the remodeled garage is more suffocating than the smoke that lodges in the irregular ceiling. *Everyone's going to die from that, from breathing it. One of these days, at the condo owners' meeting*—his car, at least, didn't get cold. That helps. And it starts on the first try. It turns out, though, that the battery for the remote control to open the gate is dead and it takes him awhile to wake up the doorman. *Bum! Illiterate! Foreigner!* The tires squeal on the slippery ramp. He manages to leave. A cry accompanies him: *Concha tu madre!*

Four o'clock / Sleep, wake up again . . .
His eye continues to burn. When he stops at the traffic light, a few birds are already singing as if it were dawn. *What the hell is that?* It's way ahead of time, as if the animals are in a hurry for the night to end. *What do they know that I don't?* Adviser is melancholic. *Tonight's going to last a hundred years, I think.* This is more or less what he feels, or thinks, when he thinks

however fleetingly of the service he provides, or doesn't provide . . . It's confusing, but obscure, certainly. He ponders this while waiting at the green light, waits at the green light, at the green light he waits . . . *Fils de pute!* Someone honks behind him. He awakens with a start, vulnerable. Then he becomes frightened of the emptiness in which he was plunged at that moment. He accelerates, alarmed, pulls out in third gear. The car chokes and lurches along the road. It's ridiculous. When he enters the lane for the center of the Radial, en route to the West Zone, he nips the median that separates the lanes. He slaps his face—he'll have to be careful not to do something stupid. On the radio, neosermons (*Repent, asshole!*) and slow black music ("*Let's blow, baby, let's blow*"). To keep from falling asleep, he drives draped across the steering wheel, his neck stiff and stuck out ahead, both shoulders folded back like a chicken. Suddenly, just past the whorehouse area, the air-conditioning sputters and conks out. He rolls down the windows to the sweetish and nauseating exhalation of the Higienópolis district. He foresees that the lack of sleep is going to catch up with him tomorrow morning. *The whole day's going to be shit, of course.* He thinks the car's AC is still under warranty, maybe, but nowadays it's really hard to set up an appointment that works with his schedule. The little that he manages to sleep is *between the problems that have to be solved.* At this time of morning, at least, driving is easy. The road is unoccupied. He steps on the gas. *Best to get there fast.* He arrives at Rebouças like someone trying to get a dying man to the emergency room, but it's nothing like that. He goes straight through. Radar hidden in an unlit lamppost under a viaduct in the Butantã registers a fine at 4:43 on this new day. Speeding, six points on his license. *At this rate I'm going to reach my limit before vacation!!*

A few minutes past five
It's still dark. *Continue for three hundred meters* . . . It's a hidden favela of black earth that winds its way down that side of Morumbi. *Sharp turn to the left* . . . A place that belongs to who knows who, but it faces the Marginal. *Sharp turn to the right* . . . Down below, waters stagnant for many decades reflect the intelligent, ecologically sound buildings, sold with subsidized financing. *Sharp turn to the left* . . . The country is experiencing a historic moment of prosperity. Everyone can buy like never before in this land of the needy. It'll end soon, but who cares for now? *Sharp turn to the right* . . . The river is dying too, but who worries about something reaching its end? *Sharp turn to the left* . . . A dog crosses from one side to the other, on top of the water, as if it were a miracle of Christ, placidly leaping over garbage. *He's even pretty!* And lame in one leg. *Continue for 124 meters and*—suddenly it's dawn. Before the sun appears, brightness emerges on the horizon like a blind lifted for spying. It becomes golden amid the detritus. All of that is democratic. Even if no one wants to see it. And from there rises the stench of a living being rotting slowly, slowly, slo—*turn left*. The pavement stops. It's inside the city, but everything is as precarious as if it was the back of something that came to an end. An old earthquake too. The buildings, the parked cars, the trees, everything turns its back on his transit. *Continue fifty meters and turn right* . . . Up there the hum of traffic long past, a braying of protest from the population, suspended in air, surely. And the street of black earth, greasy, that fades away in a square where light doesn't enter. The place belongs to the rats. Calmly, promenading. *Disgusting animal!* Twenty-five of them died and forty-seven more were seriously injured by the approach of the vehicle. Adviser does it on purpose, driving in a zigzag

pattern, increasing the contact surface and death by crushing. *Damned rodents!* Brute force, however, isn't enough to defeat the quantity of animals available to die until they exhaust the genocidal motorist: *You fulfilled your destiny.*

6:15, more or less

The senator's official car is locked, its windows fogged, and inside the boy sobbing. The fragile sound can be heard from outside. *Open this door, open this piece of shit, boy!* Adviser shakes the senator's car, but the lock doesn't yield. *Goddamn faggot!* He returns to his car. He opens the trunk and, in it, the toolbox. He finds a piece of wire, which he twists into a hook. He tries to use it on the door of the senator's official car, but now he sees that the doors are impervious to his cheap trick. *I'm getting too old for this.* Many would agree. It happens that Adviser has bills, obligations, desires, and vices to sustain despite the final decadence that is already showing signs of having installed itself in his middle-aged body. *My knee! My kidneys! My stomach! Hell . . .* Everybody knows the frying pan in which he lives, but it shouldn't be this hot. This summer, after four years of suffocating weather, will still be the worst of the decade, marked by a volcano out of control in the Andes. *At least I'm not Paraguayan or Panamanian or Peruvian!* It's a consolation that vanishes in an instant: here, the pollution and humidity are greater, the rain is acidic, and the tomatoes and onions are full of pesticides. *Us spaghetti-lovers are gonna get fucked, that's for sure!* Down below a speeding ambulance turns on its siren, but nothing happens. No one moves. *I'm gonna have to break this window.* Adviser doesn't want to damage government property. An automobile means a lot in the culture of movement of these people. Especially a luxury vehicle. *And even more the official car of a senator.* He calls his immediate boss, the deputy secretary of government. The official answers, but paralyzed with doubt, with any doubt that presents itself, he decides not to take responsibility and calls his superior, the secretary of government. The secretary of government doesn't know how to answer either, also doesn't like to make decisions, and much less wishes to risk making his situation worse: *I don't want to get involved, my Father in Heaven, I don't want to get involved!* And so he consults the governor: *I should be taking care of our public interest, colleague!* The governor, really, is the one who has the most assets and bank deposits abroad to lose through denunciations. There is, of course, the authority of the representative position, but the authority doesn't belong any longer to the man elected. It's like a modern soccer player: 29 percent of his passes are as stockholder, 20 percent belong to another minority partner, and the majority are of that "friend of his," the godfather, the boss, the nervous senator there in his official residence, in the living room, on his third whiskey, in a robe, with his wife yakking hysterically from the living room to the kitchen, from the kitchen to the living room, to the kitchen, to the living room, to the kitchen: *Use the hammer on the door of my official car, Governor, everyone's worried about this son of a hooker!* And he hangs up. The senator's wife asks for respect from her husband. The husband tells his wife to fuck herself and her need for respect. He says he pays her bills for her to keep quiet. The woman cries a little and goes up to the bedroom. It is not a generation of statesmen. The governor doesn't even hear the end of the conversation, but the necessary information, urgent to convey, delays in getting back to the private adviser, to them all, three calls on the congested telephone system later.

And so it's only 7:30

Not with a hammer but with the South African stainless steel tip of a German screwdriver, in the corner of the door of the Japanese vehicle, a small twist, a sharp blow, and that does it. Everything shatters. The pieces of glass fall on the boy, the urchin, the—they're in the backseat. There are two. Mucus is coming from the nose of one of them, the senator's son. Beside him, someone of the same size. Black. *Fainted?* The unconscious youth's pants are open, his penis out, large, flaccid, fallen on his thigh. There's a lot of glass, and cocaine. *The effect of the drug depends on user, quantity, concentration, method of use, ambient conditions, and the activity exercised (wake, party, sports, etc.).* Did he vomit? *I'm also not Colombian or Romanian or Estonian . . .* and they're not the most violent people in the world. Only the most hypocritical. Yes, he vomited, on his chest. *A pig. And a queer. What did you say? Nothing, my boy.* The low flight of a helicopter that continues to the dead river, broadcasting news of traffic along its banks. Toxic dust that has settled onto the muddy ground rises. *We were talking and . . . he stopped. Suddenly. It happens.* Adviser checks the unconscious youth's heartbeat, first the wrists, then the throat. He quickly understands that his immobility and languor are merely the beginning of rigor mortis. *Died of a heart attack. Poor guy.* The city is waking up, believing it is just another day, but many will be laid off when they arrive at work. *My father is going to kill me.* Adviser is there also to calm things down. *There's no sickness without remedy. Or pain without end.* Someone is coming down the hill on the other side of the field and pretends not to see the nakedness of a corpse lying on the backseat of an official car. *My mother is going to kill me. Dona Iolanda doesn't have to know everything that happens to you. Do you think so? I'm sure.* The telephone rings. In the photo on the screen, Adviser's daughters at the beach, without his wife. But it's she who wants to know why he left. *I can't now, dear. Ah, is that so? I call because of love and this is how you treat me!* She hangs up on him. *In itself, love is a second family to provide for*, he philosophizes. *And cowardice too . . . But it's good, who can understand?* So, without anyone below and less important to appeal to, Adviser turns to the senator's son: *Give me a hand with your*—Adviser grabs the body by the hands, the senator's son by the legs, to move the cadaver to the other vehicle. It's not easy. The head dangles grotesquely. The dead man's pants descend to his feet. His penis shakes in view of a bystander. *What're you looking at?! You're still gonna be president of the republic someday, so listen to what I'm telling you, boy!* Adviser is there also to instill confidence, self-confidence, distrust . . . *You think so? For sure, every indication's there.* The body must be folded and turned on its side to fit into the trunk. *Three hundred liters, huh? So skinny, so dead . . .* It appears the senator's son is praying. *O Lord God . . . no.* And God doesn't appear either. The toolbox spilled its contents into the space where the spare tire sits. *It's gonna be one helluva job to reorganize that shit. How?* Adviser points to the dead man: *What's his name? Now you got me. I don't know, but they always use the same name, don't they?* Adviser is sorry he asked: *I understand, you little son of a bitch. What did you say, hireling? You're young and I understand your behavior, you're somebody rich*, was what I said, boss. Adviser has to guide the senator's son to the steering wheel of the official car in which he was found. The youth is bewildered. The official car is switched every other year by the same senator for more than six congresses. *My father is a success. True, you can go home now, there's a football game tomorrow. I don't know how to thank you, I'm going to talk to my father.* Money wouldn't be too bad, thinks Adviser. They say the economic situation is going to worsen at any moment, and his job, though one of trust, doesn't offer great stability. *Thank you, young man (you faggot, for the opportunity to help you, and do recommend me!), yes (I want money, goddamnit!), to your father (that infernally powerful cuckold)! See you later (fucker, see you never!).*

Almost 9

When the boy, the senator's son, virtual heir to his father's democratic vote (it's predicted it'll be two congresses before he's recruited for the first time), descends the hillside in the late-model official car, man and machine disappear in the traffic along the Marginal highway, headed for the old South Zone. Something stirs with fear and haste, but it's invisible. No one breathes the contaminated air. They speed by, armed, with their fingers raised and their noses upright. *For sale. For rent . . . Free!* Even the most recent initiatives are abandoning the place. *I'm not from Ecuador, or the Dominican Republic, or from Paraíba. Glory, Lord!*

10 o'clock

Adviser takes the road back. Accelerates. He remembers he hasn't had breakfast, then begins to feel hungry. His vision darkens. It's rapid. *Hypoglycemia? That's all I need!* The sun beating down on the viscous river delivers a slap in the face to anyone who looks at it. *I don't have health insurance.* What will he say when his daughter asks again, in English, *What the fuck did you do, Daddy?!* He thinks about his cargo, the cadaver: *No one has "health insurance"* . . . And laughs. At the sadness of the thing, of course: *a War with capital "W"!* He retraces his route over the dry asphalt, now from south to west and from west to east. *There's a bakery in Mooca that makes* grilled bread pressed flat and covered with melted butter, so greasy it smells bad! That's where I'm going! Traffic and lost time. Two delivery boys on scooters on 23. They're all cheap. What do you want to eat? Your mother, you Portagee! What'd you say, asshole?! A grilled sandwich, brother, a grilled sandwich, that's all. Besides, the orange juice and the special treatment are both sugary. Afterward he accepts a chicken thigh. On the house . . . Two. Toasted and crispy. This crap is from last week and there's a lot of flour in it, you tightfisted Portagee. Go fuck your mother's twat, nigger! It's very good, thank you! Both he and the owner of the bakery are going to die from heart attacks. But it won't be from love or hard drugs like the cadaver in Adviser's trunk. It'll be from those truncated curses and bad cholesterol, the LDL that clogs veins and arteries, leading to heart attacks and vascular accidents with high fatality rates. And it's not easy to get rid of a dead body nowadays! That's the truth. The exploding city eliminated vacant lots and the walls came down, replaced by iron bars (safer), exposing to the indiscreet gaze of passersby areas formerly used for dumping the victims of vigilantes. The sites now are in locations more and more distant from the center of the city and hidden, increasing the costs of transportation and the logistical necessities. Also, there are lots of cameras spread out in the streets, people pretending to be speaking on their cell phones when in reality they're filming everything that goes on: Smile, you're being caught in the act.

Between 11 and 12, he's in the middle of the East Radial
Telephone: Forgive me, but the girls drive me crazy! They left now, thank God, for the van to school that will keep them far from me for a while, amen! I love you. I love you too. Me too-too . . . One, two, three! Hang up! You hang up. One, two, three. Go . . . One, two—line dead. He hangs up. Since parking is more

expensive than gasoline, vehicles remain in perpetual motion. It's not that, properly speaking, they move about in space, in the congested streets. The "elevated highway," for example, is at a standstill at the moment. The drivers spy upon the intimacy of the new apartments. *There's nothing you can do to get away from it!* And Adviser racks his brain, racks his brain, the cadaver in the trunk getting stiff *(best answer I: rigidity of the body occurs close to seven hours after death)*, and him racking his brain, racking his brain until he remembers a doctor be-ginning his career, a resident in psychiatry, if he's not mistaken, the son of a cousin of a seamstress who once asked him for a favor, a recommendation for a position as an aide at the Tat-uapé Municipal Hospital, a sad memory, since most of those who enter there half-alive end up dead, like a death camp for the poor, given the gravity of everything that happens in the region, the difficulty of being attended to, the unavail-ability of doctors, medicine, plasma, and replacement organs. The telephone rings: his wife wants to know if he's coming for lunch: *Don't bother me! What did you say? I'm sorry, sweet*—she hangs up.

12:45

A Korean beggar mistaken for a Bolivian panhandler was lynched on Avenida Liberdade. Many cars ran over the body. Ahead, the East Radial is bloody. Isn't there a rush hour any-more in this shithole inferno? And Adviser misses those days when things that went wrong had known languages, scheduled days, and set hours to happen. *We could escape ahead of time!* And now we have highway police roadblocks on top of everything else. *I'm gonna die of sunstroke!* Police cars machine-gunned by private militias and by the mafia of private security syndicates. The smell of burned metal and flesh. He shows his membership card for a gun club and quickly passes through the check-point, accelerating, closing his eyes: *Have a good day, sir!*

Only 1 p.m.
He arrives at Avenida Celso Garcia, where the businesses show signs of failing once again: doors closed by legal deci-sions, walls covered with socialist protest graffiti, private buildings without maintenance, mustn't-be-missed clearances, idlers, drunks, cripples, and unattended buses occupying the sidewalks and passageways, blocking even ambulances from approaching. Many die from being run over, others involved in far-off accidents waiting for some driver heading in the op-posite direction (*Penha/Lapa right-hand lane*) to yield to the rescue vehicle (*Lapa/Penha left-hand lane*).

Police presence is common to guarantee the right of pas-sage for citizens with special needs, doctors, and patients.

The Dr. Carmino Caricchio Municipal Hospital has beau-tiful photos on its apps, but in reality its state of preservation is deplorable—the outside plaster cracking; tiles on the in-side coming loose, trying to flee from the walls at the ear-liest opportunity, preferring suicide, disemboweling from the concrete, the hardware eaten away by obscene infiltrations; windows fracturing under the weight of toxic dust from the Sapopemba district; and the niches in the facade, which now serve to merely collect corrosive materials, bird fleas, and young pigeons. Adviser goes to the old PBX, asks the oper-ator to page the doctor he names: *Celso . . . or Carlos . . .* He doesn't remember. *Attention, Dr. Celso . . . or Carlos . . . The person looking for you is at the entrance to the ER and wants something . . .* Adviser takes out his small notepad. *At least I'm not some stable hand from Jardim Pantanal or Recife . . .* He consults the notepad, which lists on one side (front, normal, in blue) those he helps, and on the other (back, upside down, in red) those who help him, in a systematic network of suspicion, with feedback resulting from small influences at various levels. *I don't like owing anyone, but I can't help it, I need to take care of this, so fuck it.* Adviser waits, in the resigned silence characteristic of his generation, standing in a line of kidney patients (transplants, dialysis, etc.), only to urinate in one of the most fetid bathrooms of the public hospital system: the one for the cleaning staff.

2:50 p.m.

In the hospital parking lot the cars are more or less new but already rundown, with patches of plastic putty, stickers, and compulsory safety items fastened with wire, beneath a thick coating of soot. *Neglect . . .* Gray from the ashes of some volcano, perhaps. Or faulty engines. Many vehicles are covered with tickets, past-due bills, and police notices, some of them involved in kidnappings, skirmishes, and obscene incidents, among other criminal activities, and they remain there abandoned until the Department of Transportation tows them away. In the meantime, the car watchers hired by the city (the most stable in their career) rent a reclining bench for thirty reais a night and an entire stall for eighty, to the foreigners who live in the vicinity. There's no bathroom—businesses only allow paying customers to use them—and bottles of urine and bags of feces are deposited on the ground. Where they ferment—*like cadavers!* A guy in a lab coat approaches. *Remember me? More or less. Son of a bitch! What?* Adviser adjusts his shirt inside his pants, allowing the butt of the gun to show. *You don't remember that you owe me?* The doctor is a coward, and he decides to stay alive: *Maybe I do remember you, yes. But what can I do for you?* While this is going on, the dead and wounded from daily combat, with all the difficulties of the drug trade and locomotion, are arriving at the emergency room, many of them half dead, the way the ER doctors like, grotesque and hunchbacked with twisted members, bones exposed through the flesh, snorting: *Is there a rush hour anymore in this shithole inferno or isn't there?* The telephone again: *Who are you talking to? He's . . . "a friend," dear. Someone I recommended. I'll call you later. You bastard*—he hangs up.

3:30 p.m.
Adviser looks around, makes sure they're not being observed, that the surveillance cameras in the parking lot are broken, or missing, or were never activated, and with repeated gestures, silently, motions Dr. Celso *(or Carlos?)* to come closer. He opens the car's trunk. The seminude body of the young black man remains doubled up, however much space there was for it to relax and expand near the toolbox. The tension in the fibers of the upper members is evident. And screwdrivers. And scattered screws. Glass, cocaine. His penis down there is still wilted and inert *(best answer II: rigidity occurs owing to muscular hardening, which disappears in a period of one to six days, when decomposition begins)*. The physician, Dr. Celso or Carlos, takes a used surgical glove from the pocket of his lab coat, reluctantly pulls it onto one hand, and pokes the corpse with his fingertips, visibly disgusted, looking for signs of life. *But this man is dead!* Adviser reminds him (he shows the gun again) that time of death is in itself a matter of dispute: *even among doctors!* And what may have happened is so-called "brain death," and therefore a "lesser death."

The doctor is sponsored by someone, that's certain, he was one of the worst students in his class, his diploma was bought in a for-profit school, but even he knows that *brain death happens when blood ceases to flow to the brain and the individual perishes, suffocated. Which is death, beyond any dispute, and can occur as the result of heart stoppage through an overdose of cocaine, "for example"* . . . The main thing is that Adviser would like his "doctor friend" to receive that stiff in private as if it were some unknown indigent, so the suspicious death can be given a clinical pretext, an official place in the government statistics; cause unknown but correct for the medical records . . . It should be submerged among the many cadavers of the city of São Paulo: *He needs to disappear . . . But—the entire body?* Impasse on Rua Santo Elias.

Nearing 4:20 p.m.

The doctor is reflecting. He's not good at that (*"reflecting"?!*), with a diploma bought from a for-profit school. *Have you tried funeral parlors? I don't know anyone who owes me favors like you do.* Adviser wants to go home in time to help his wife bathe their daughters. *Otherwise they all get irritated!* The doctor doesn't know whether to repay the favor the other says he owes him . . . *What did he do that I didn't do myself?* He can't recall anything specific but knows that he owes everything to someone or something. *Maybe I should ask for a new car? A plasma TV? A small laboratory for clinical analyses!* Yes, Dr. Celso . . . or Carlos . . . also thinks about asking Adviser for money to cover up the corpus delicti. *But how much is it worth, for God's sake? Is twenty or thirty thousand enough?* This god, duly named, keeps quiet, as always. And the doctor finds himself obliged to ask directly whether he should risk his position, which is insignificant, virtually nothing, but solid: *Should I? Or shouldn't I? Speak to me!* The phone rings: *You said you were going to call and you didn't. What's going on? Now it doesn't matter anymore, you jerk. My lo*—she hangs up.

And they remain in that indecision until 5 o'clock . . .

. . . alternating between drinking hot water and cold coffee
sold by wandering vendors camouflaged in the soot of the
parking lot, when the doctor decides the best thing to do—in
the manner of the wise who make it to old age—is nothing. *Yes,
nothing! And you know why? I owe. I don't deny it . . .* But it happens that his supervisor, the holder of the opening for which
he is currently the first alternate psychoanalyst member of the
society, had been appointed by an enemy: *a top-level qualifier,
above any suspicion!* And in addition, the director of the unit,
an experimental psychologist appointed by a deputy of the federal police, was opposed to all the previous appointments and
was concerned now with recruiting *his own gang—that is, "his
team."* He wasn't going to help others who were trying to cut
corners. All of it under the patronage of the pharmaceutical
industry that, through gastronomic conventions and sexual
events, encourages the quarrel among the diverse clinical spe-
cialties, to improve the sale of medicines to all. *Our boss's boss
can take advantage of this body, you understand? I understand,
of course, you ratshit! What did you say? I said I understand and
that's it!* There are so many living-dead awaiting their turn in
the cars that no one suspects that Adviser and the doctor are
talking about a cadaver. *Where's that sickly sweet smell coming
from? It's the stands selling Indonesian food!* All Adviser required
was a signature on a medical report, but the problem was that
it was precisely the signature of that other man that he needed,
the other man who saw all the advantages of not committing
himself to anything, from his position, so compromised: *the
process of decomposition of proteins is highly fetid.* Adviser finally
gives up on attempting to rid himself of a simple dead man
among the many peculiar cadavers in Tatuapé Hospital. *How*

much time do I have before that—before he—causes me more problems than I already have? The smell, for example . . . The doctor was weak, but he was interested in the matter and had encyclopedic knowledge: *The first phase of putrefaction is the chromatic period, or the period of blotches. In general, it begins eighteen to twenty-four hours after death and lasts approximately seven to twelve days.* Around him, attendants faint beside relatives and friends, frail and needing assistance, none of them receiving any help. The sun melts the plastic roof tiles, which drip and scorch the skin of the people. As if that vision of hell weren't enough, the other man, the sponsored doctor, has the gall to add, as if delivering a judgment: *It has been demonstrated that putrefaction can accelerate under certain conditions of pressure* . . . *and temperature. Am I fucked? Of course you are. Thanks. You're welcome.*

6 p.m.

Night falls as if someone was turning off the damned light. Suddenly, just as it came into the world, this miserable day goes away. The sun disappears hurriedly for the other side of the planet, better and more peaceful than this half. *Each one takes care of what is his.* That's what you always hear. Along with *the whore that bore you*—against black foreigners in general and Latin Americans of any color in particular. *The body won't be as hot, less rotten now, I suppose,* thinks Adviser. *What am I gonna do with that—with him—my God?* As is customary, the divinity doesn't lift a finger to help rid Adviser of the cadaver, and vice versa. In spite of everything, he still remains, like others, very spiritual.

The daytime car watchers are departing for the outskirts of the city and taking their firearms with them. The nighttime watchers haven't yet arrived in the parks and alleyways. The residents have their own nightmares, as they doze in front of the TV. The news is bad and the examples worse. As for those still stuck in traffic, soon they'll all be home. The trip will be long and exasperating today, by decree of the priests and ultra-Catholic congressmen; the recording of our parents and grandparents is back on the radio: *hailmary,fullofgrace,thelordis-withthee;blessedartthouamongstwomen,andblessedisthefruitofthy-womb,jesus,holymary,motherofgod,prayforussinners,nowandat-thehourofdeath,amen.*

7 p.m.
These are the saddest and most invisible hours in the unhappy city. Everyone is on his way out of here; quick, out of here! *I didn't have lunch and I'm going to try to have dinner before it's too late and I'm devoured by my own hunger!* He stops in a semiabandoned bar that he calls by name, near the Juventus playing field. He orders a chunk of fatty meat, grilled red onions, greasy french fries, a lot of salt, and a cheap alcoholic drink, preferably strong to forget the wasted hours: *A meal like that means three or four fewer days of living!* That was the warning in some self-important magazine. And two cans of Coca-Cola bubbling in the middle of all that must be worth three or four fewer hours, for sure. *Sugar and starch, less complex in their makeup, stink less in the process of putrefaction.* Seven buses caught on fire this afternoon, which the authorities attributed to "electrical malfunctions"—but no one believes it: this was the day for the 10 percent payoff to the highway traffickers, and whoever is late pays with his life, or the destruction of material or moral values . . . His wife calls, in a panic because the school van hasn't dropped off their children, his two little girls; the driver's telephone is busy. *Is he phoning and driving at the same time, the perverse bastard? Why doesn't that pothead talk*

to me, huh? Do you have any way of knowing? The cadaver, to be clear, is liquefying back there, the blood decanting inside the young half-naked black's folds of skin, forming a red pool, leaking out his ass, or out the ears maybe, but in any case completely melting there in the trunk, and him here having to calm this woman wed to the fury of her own elements: *What? I don't think I'm hear—Believe me, the connection is awful. Really terr—I have to hang up so as not to hear you better . . . Eh? Me too . . . I'm not—Hea—Ciao!* He hangs up.

The 8 o'clock news
TRAFFIC: *Since Sunday, thoroughfares in the West Zone have been closed off for work on the flood control reservoir and for a coordinated army blitz to apprehend explosives and illegal weapons.*

WEATHER FORECAST: *A high-pressure system is influencing atmospheric conditions in the city. Cloudy skies and scattered storms. Tomorrow, if there is a tomorrow, temperatures will be higher, with a predicted maximum of thirty-seven degrees Celsius.*

ECONOMY: *With the publication of the balance of payments, the relevance of remission of profits from our prostitutes working abroad to the gross domestic product is greater than ever. It's a question of total credits generated in markets throughout the world, whose value grows and remains a reliable source of income for the treasury even when a consumer crisis affects the importing countries, leading to reduced demand for our commodities and services.*

HEALTH: *According to the metalworkers union in São Bernardo, insistence on the theme of class struggle on the part of the owners and provocateurs depresses the morale of workers and harms the efficiency of the chain of production.*

MIGRATION: *A network of passport counterfeiters has been discovered, along with the sale of visas and permits for slave labor in which Argentineans and Chileans subcontract Peruvians who* exploit Bolivians—who normally utilize Paraguayans and Brazilians for the more menial services, but are now using Haitians to save money. Scum! Scum!! Scum!!!

Nine p.m.
The woman, the wife, calls again: the girls got home from school, finally. The van is old. Slower, less safe, and cheaper. The driver was a replacement and got lost en route. Retard! He apologized with that humble demeanor taught in the service unions' training sessions. Excuses false but accepted, because he's false but no one cares, or demands honesty in anything. You're forgiven, retard. It's all rather fraudulent. And disorganized. To make things worse, a police van was bombed at an intersection on Avenida Paes de Barro, it seems. It was parked sideways on the median between lanes, with the wounded men moaning while they waited for their friends to act, which took some time and was twice rebuffed by the adversaries, but thank God everything is all right now . . . When are you coming back? I don't know. Why not? The temperature of the conversation is rising rapidly, very rapidly, despite the late hour! What have I done? Adviser knows where it will end. I still have a package to deliver. His wife hangs up again, but this time she calls back almost at once, immediately regretful, to say: Sorry, the girls went to bed and I get crazy when they're not around. Thank God we have your job. I love you. Amen. My cazzolino! Me too. The Lord is our father. Bagascia mia. Saravá! Kiss/baccio.

Ten p.m.
I'm not Guatemalan, or Mexican, much less Nigerian . . . Finally it rains as it cools off, which is no longer necessary for those who spent the day sick from heat, or dying from suffocation: sons of bitches, all of us. All who survived, however, are desperate for

that brackish, dirty, slimy water. They open their water tanks wide, put buckets and basins in their yards. The government's reservoirs are empty, on full-scale alert, and equally thirsty for it. They drink everything that falls from the sky, dirty as mud and acidic as vinegar. *I need a new car.* Adviser remembers the condition of his imported vehicle in the first years after 2000: leakproof then, but now . . . The trunk's going to be soaked, he knows. *The guy's flesh is gonna melt inside there. The smell is gonna get into the carpet, the floor I walk on when I leave there, in the garage in my building, the living room of my apartment, my daughters' bedrooms! No!* Adviser even starts to pray, but his divinity fails to declare itself, even now, when he has reached the peak of his ability to believe in superhuman forces. *Where am I gonna stick this fucking dead man, Lord? That's all I wanna know . . . You there! Tell me! Any of you!* No one is going to get involved. People move away, their heads lowered (*best answer III: it's a logistics problem, and a police problem!*). That thought stays in his head . . . He's unaccustomed to thinking in frankly abstract terms. He thinks only about concrete data of assistance given, calculating: amounts of money, favors, stabbings leading to death . . . And he brakes in the left lane of Avenida Aricanduva. In the ugliest stretch in the most desolate place in a city most indifferent to beauty, where no one has the courage, the stomach, or the displeasure to park in front of these blots of paint, rust, and assorted filth. There, isolated from any of the world's aesthetic intelligence, Adviser opens the trunk and observes the twisted corpse. He laughs like someone in a Tim Burton film, and he, the seminude black youth, were he to awake, would sit up on the deflated spare tire and explain how to get rid of his own remains . . . *But* . . . But it's then that a somewhat daring but efficient idea occurs to Adviser (*Wow! Wow!! Wow!!!*). Lacking an appropriate place to dump "his" cadaver, he will do the opposite—denounce it in order to get rid of it! *The poor guy is still black and probably indigent, that makes everything easier, thank God! Eureka! Eureka!!*

11, 11:30, about

Come home, love, I miss you here . . . Here . . . Here . . . And here . . . Kisses . . . Me too . . . And here . . . Goddamn! Nobody below him can do this job: it's a burden. He hangs up. *Right at the time the best films start on TV and I'm not at home . . .* Adviser decides to leave the cadaver in Bela Vista itself, near that samba school, on the steep descent that ends at 14 Bis. He parks on Marques Leão, takes the body from the trunk. Drags it along the ground in full view of anyone leaving or arriving home before or after prostituting themselves in the streets, government offices, or private businesses. Nothing any longer causes suspicion or embarrassment in these people. *It's full of the poor . . . and actresses . . .* Adviser sets the body of the young seminude black man on the driver's side with his hands on the steering wheel, as if he were the owner of the car. He buttons the shirt over the vomit, using the tips of his fingers. He doesn't have the heart to touch the flaccid penis, but he notes that even in that condition, flopping and softened like a severed tail, stuck to the dead man's thigh, it's larger than his own penis at its full erection: *which my wife wouldn't have the courage to say—the boy . . .* Anger, envy, pettiness cloud the remnant of thought. Furthermore, Adviser is no better than those he serves. *However . . .* Therefore, he takes the gun from the rusty toolbox, a Taurus pistol with the serial number filed off, wipes the butt and the breech with a flannel cloth, places it in the youth's hand, vigorously rubs the youth's hand against the metal to transfer DNA. Adviser lifts the man's hand holding the gun and points it outside the car and upward. He fires at random. The gunpowder burns the dead man's hand at once. He fired in the direction of the TV Paulista antennae but hit the last working mercury-vapor streetlamp on Veloso Guerra. It dims for a moment and blacks out. Total darkness. *Carai! Taxi, please!*

Zero hour

Adviser enters the precinct with a nonchalant air. The three cops on duty (two detectives and a scribe, hired without competitive examination and appointed by the deputy mayor of the area), who were sleeping on the sofas and swivel chairs of the establishment, alerted by the Chinese ding-dong bell, leap behind the reception counter, protecting themselves and pulling their unregistered private guns, expecting the worst. The precinct chief runs toward the rear, where a wagon with a permanently running engine awaits, ready for departure. Adviser has to show his ID from someone in the government before the men relax from their combat positions and come forward for congratulations. *Is this any time to lodge a complaint, partner?!* The police recommend that you call them during normal business hours, in sunlight, with your hands up. Adviser apologizes for the urgency and for the inconvenience but it's a matter coming from above, way above. *I have to report the theft of my vehicle to save the reputation of a federal senator.* They all understood that things *from above* could very well affect everybody there below, on the ground floor of a precinct house. *Right away, my friend.* A task force is rounded up of everyone who can write a report of a certain cultural level for the blotter. The precinct chief, for example, who bought his law diploma for the state qualifying exam but knew quite well how to draft a public document: *THAT a young black perpetrator had accosted Adviser at an intersection; THAT he had exposed his penis and stolen the car; THAT the assailant appeared to be under the influence of drugs; THAT the victim barely had time to recognize him* . . . One hundred and eighty reais were quickly distributed in appreciation, although not mentioned in the text: forty for each of the investigators and the scribe, and sixty for the precinct chief. Everyone saw that the chief, more cowardly and higher ranking, received 50 percent more than the others, but no one complained. They respected the hierarchy: *for practical purposes.* Adviser considers picking up some phony receipts—gasoline, pharmacy, meals—to offset his operational costs.

1:40, 1:45, whatever

That was when Adviser called the deputy secretary of government to confirm that the mission had been completed: *by the grace of the Lord.* That information was relayed by the deputy secretary of government to the secretary of government, overjoyed that those below him had resolved the whole thing; he didn't even want to know how: *Spare me the details, for the love of God!* The senator is awakened by the governor with the news, considered a blessing by both: *Our congratulations! By every indication, all evidence of the recent incident that took place with His Excellency's son has vanished from the face of the earth!*

At 2:20 sharp

Adviser arrives at his apartment. Late night is covered in silence. His daughters sleep with open arms, enveloped. Melancholy takes hold of him: the ineluctable solitude of the provider, the paterfamilias. Adviser goes to the bedroom, sits on the double bed, begins to undress. His flaccid penis on his thigh. Then comes the surprise that matrimony holds for him (they are monogamous, from fear and laziness): his wife's hand grips his member. Moves. His penis reacts, becomes tumescent. She runs her fingers up and down, and each time she runs her fingers up and down, it grows and expands in the caressing hand. Then it's the mouth: *Good night.* And his wife's blessed mouth sucks the sweaty dick of Adviser, her most worthy husband, with a knowledge and dedication that make him think at the end of that workday: *What whorehouses were you in before you met me? Speak softly, dear! We don't want to wake up the children! It's good to be back. Amen.*

THE FINAL TABLE

BY MARCELO RUBENS PAIVA

Baixo Augusta

One truth for those who live at night: where there's amusement, there's blood. Where there are excesses, everything can be expected. Where there's happiness, there's pain, there's death. Hedonism is deceptive, it's a fantasy: that's why everything is fake in Las Vegas and Disneyland. That's why on the most bohemian and merrymaking street in Brazil, Rua Augusta, pain is too close to happiness and entertainment.

Chief Detective Marcelo Santana couldn't believe that a heinous crime had been committed right under his nose. The girl, without any clothes or ID, had already been there in the thicket of the gigantic plot, 24,000 square meters, across from the 4th Precinct, for four days, according to forensics. A plot in dispute because activists wanted to make it into a park, and the owner into high-rises, signed and sealed by the courts to be known as Augusta Park.

The detective descended the ramp leading to the precinct, through the gate forced open by his assistants, into the thicket, and lamented seeing such a young girl naked and dead. No one had witnessed anything. It was the strong smell of the decomposing body that drew attention. Detective Santana was furious: not only had a homicide been committed, the girl barely even out of her adolescence, but they hadn't even buried or burned her. Left her to the elements. Like a warning!

"Right across from my precinct!" he shouted on Marquês de Paranaguá. "On this shitty, controversial piece of land, just to attract the press! To challenge me!"

His highly esteemed team of investigators didn't know how the body in such an advanced stage of putrefaction had ended up there either, and they were as outraged as their boss.

She was a dark-skinned girl, pretty. Painted fingernails and toenails. She had been strangled. Had anyone reported a missing young woman in recent days? Nothing. It was as if she had fallen from the sky, though if her dental records or prints were in some file in some system, it wouldn't be hard to identify her.

"Check street vendors, residents, whores, gas station attendants."

"We did, sir. Nothing."

"Check again! Do the buildings have security cameras? Get the tapes."

"Yes. We found nothing."

"Trash collectors?"

"They didn't see anything."

"Doormen."

"No sir, no one saw anything."

It wasn't possible to determine if she was a resident or just a night worker in the area. The activists who sometimes staged protests and occupied the park that was not yet a park and, depending on the size of the bribes distributed by the construction firm that owned the land and its lobbyists, never would be, didn't recognize the girl, didn't see anything, didn't know anything. The most perturbing part was that, despite it being the busiest area in the city, despite the comings and go-ings of a precinct that dealt with the confusion of a conflict-filled district, no one saw anything.

The girl paid a severe price. She was where she shouldn't have been. She saw what she shouldn't have seen. And they had been merciless: it's not a region for amateurs or the adventurous. If every city has an arterial thoroughfare that summarizes and unabashedly exposes its disorder, from glamour to the darkness of the saddest dive, I doubt anyone in São Paulo would disagree we're referring to this feminine street of unstable moods, ever in transformation and conflict, Rua Augusta, which cuts the city from downtown to the districts, the Jardins, begins at the intersection of Martins Fontes and Martinho Prado—an homage to the Prados, a billionaire family that amassed its fortune in the nineteenth century, through coffee of course, and brought the railroad to the state. It is a street that crosses Franklin Roosevelt Square, or just Roosevelt Square, ascends, passes by nightclubs, whorehouses, dives, cantinas, ethnic restaurants (Greek, Spanish, Italian, Bahian), hotels, theaters, colleges, art-film houses, record stores, street vendors selling pirated DVDs of classic films, street vendors selling pirated DVDs of films that haven't yet been released or have just appeared in theaters (including the theater in front of them), street vendors selling pirated software, another selling T-shirts, incense, handicrafts, a street vendor selling pirated copies of gay films, another selling pirated DVDs of leftist films, and bookstores; the street crosses Avenida Paulista, the most important avenue in the city, the Brazilian Fifth Avenue, and begins to descend to what was once known as the Cordilheira da Paulista, the high part of the city that houses radio and TV antennae, data transmission, cell towers, then descends again, leaving behind the sourness, another art-film house, more restaurants, traditional stores like Casa Tody, which has sold footwear to the São Paulo middle class for over seventy years; it goes past Americanized luncheonettes, luxury supermarkets, a French restaurant, crosses Rua Oscar Freire which once had luxury designers like Ermenegildo Zegna, H. Stern, Gucci, Chanel, Bulgari, Rolex, Cartier, to emerge in the Jardins, as if from a turbulent polluted sea with a countercurrent that becomes a calm and prosperous delta, which begins at Rua Estados Unidos, a neighborhood of houses worth millions, where the wealthiest people in the country live, a country that is home to both the richest on the continent and the poorest.

At the intersection of Augusta and Paulista, playboys of the rebel-without-a-cause stripe from a 1960s-style "gang that knew no fear" ran red lights at high speeds. They called it "São Paulo roulette." I don't know how, but they laughed at this. And the homage in an ingenuous rock song by the Young Guard, that even the Os Mutantes recorded: *"I raced up Rua Augusta at seventy-five miles an hour, scattered the pedestrians, took the curve on two wheels without honking, stopped inches from the show window. Cool . . ."*

Cool, really, is the sensitive and cultured samba, not at all ingenuous, that the Bahian Tom Zé of the Tropicália movement would perform: *"Augusta, how I miss you. You were vain, how I miss you, and I spent my money, how I miss you, on imported clothes and other foolishness . . ."* Much other foolishness. And what other foolishness . . . In the rotten part, the central region, anything can be bought: expensive sex, cheap sex, same-sex sex, sex you think is with the opposite sex but holds a surprise between the legs, pure cocaine, adulterated, cheap, false, marijuana, crack, Ecstasy, weapons, fights, watered-down wine and amusement, if the customer's liver holds up. In an American city it would be known as the red-light district. In São Paulo, it's Baixo Augusta.

It's not known with any certainty when the street's prostitution began to spread to the south side of Avenida Paulista. The girls did well, while on the other side of Paulista, the luxury boutiques also did well. A portion of the population of the city contaminated with AIDS in the 1980s contracted the virus in those alleys, saunas, and nightclubs. The trail from 1875, bearing the well-behaved and pious name of Maria Augusta, which crossed the lands of the Chácara do Capão belonging to the Portuguese Manuel Antônio Vieira, saw the arrival in 1890 of horse- and mule-drawn streetcars. In 1891 they changed to electric. Division into parcels brought houses, commerce, small residential buildings, small hotels, large ones, flophouses, fitness centers, a traditional Italian confectioner, even ice-skating rinks, workout and aerobic centers, all under the vigilance of the 4th Precinct at 246 Marquês de Parana-guá, responsible for combating and investigating lawlessness and serious crimes in the region, especially focused on the al-ways tense relationship between transvestites, prostitutes, and their customers, drug traffic, and robbery, sometimes followed by death, death that always left Chief Detective Marcelo San-tana furious. Not to mention the perennial cunning of drunk customers and nightclub bouncers with no notion that they almost invariably overstepped the rules of behavior and the ethics of professionals of the night by using excessive brute force against the perfect jaws and teeth of their rich young clientele.

It was in the decade of the seventies that Augusta began to lose its glamour. Shopping centers came on the scene, and the stores moved there. Prostitution, previously limited to be-low Roosevelt Square, began to rise and spread. Houses and hotels profited from the new market. Nightclubs in the 1960s featured the cream of MPB, Brazilian popular music, even Elis Regina, and catered to young men looking for strippers with

Americanized names like Shirley, Brooke, and Daisy. Congestion took over the street, from Paulista to the city center. Wretched losers in search of amusement, like humiliating girls and cross-dressers, caused confusion that Chief Detective Marcelo Santana didn't know how to handle, and sometimes abusing his authority, he simply blocked off the street with sawhorses and police cars, a blockade that lasted for hours and infuriated the nightclub owners.

Starting with the new millennium in 2000, flouting the rigid laws of silence passed by conservative administrations who wished to "clean up" the city, some professionals of the night began opening nightclubs with shows in an area where everyone was accustomed to the commotion, noise, lack of control, and the insanity of bohemian life. From this came the nickname Baixo Augusta, or Lower Augusta, an allusion to those spots most often associated with Rio de Janeiro— Baixo Leblon and Baixo Gávea. Venues with English names opened, such as Vegas Club and Studio SP, coming from Vila Madalena, repressed by corrupt city officials, the Pub, Club Noir, Inferno, Play, Fire. They were "ballads," as the spaces for dance, shows, and amusement came to be known, which attracted a more elite public and students to the moral chaos. On parallel or perpendicular streets, excitement also became professionalized. Some whorehouses closed. Their neon lights disappeared. They were bought by the owner of the Vegas, who opened a bar called Neon. The press celebrated the revitalization of Rua Augusta.

A detail known to few: a guy is partner in a club, which has another guy as partner, who has participation in another club, forming a domino effect with influence in high spheres of power. The first clubs were founded by friends. Friends who would win or lose money at night basically because they liked the night. They won or lost money on Mondays, the day the clubs were closed, in a poker game in which few knew the rules, which began at the home of Plínio, a journalist specializing in music, a bohemian, a bachelor, a former addict, former alcoholic, who hosted the game of poker dice with male and female friends, married, single, fathers, mothers with nannies, idlers, those less interested in betting than in gossiping, seeing friends, drinking, snorting a few lines, witnessing some drag races, and having a few laughs. Nights that became the stuff of legend.

Poker dice would earn its winner at most fifty bucks. To participate, players threw five thousand reais on the table. Gradually it turned into poker with cards, first the traditional exclusive game, later a sloppy open session, until it adopted all the rules and principles of Texas Hold'em, in which there is room for ten players (as many as twenty-two can play), which some knew and taught to the others. Amateurs, little by little, became familiar with terms like *blind*, popularly known as *pingo* until that decade, *small blind, big blind, all-in*. *Cacife* became buy-in. *The pot. To pass, check.*

New residents moved into the apartment next to Plínio, which had been vacant for a while. They were a weird family, not at all trustworthy, who seemed modern, made friends with everyone in the building, but deep down were hypocrites: they detested noise after the ten p.m. limit established in the condo regulations. A couple with two small children. The wife dressed like a punk: torn fishnet stockings, heavy makeup, leather skirts, and T-shirts featuring hardcore bands. The husband had the face of a psychopath: he would go downstairs in a Speedo to pick up the pizza and lock his unruly son in the hall as punishment. Beyond a doubt, it must have been the wife who started calling the doorman's desk on Mondays to complain that the poker game was exceeding the limit of forty-five decibels allowable in residential zones after ten at night, quieter than a crying baby (fifty decibels), which under Article 42 of federal law governing penalties for infraction (Law No. 3.688, of October 3, 1941) carries a fine or a sentence of two weeks to three months—disturbing the peace of others with shouting and racket.

After the third night in which "a neighbor" complained of noise, according to the doorman speaking over the intercom, Turquinho, an owner of Fire, one of the first nightclubs on the "new" Augusta, dedicated to fans of Brazilian music—a place that Plínio and his friends frequented, where they knew all the employees' names, and routinely skipped ahead in line— suggested they move the game there. On Mondays the nightclub was closed for the workers' day off; on Mondays only Amaral, a combination of doorman, bouncer, and amiable manager, who lived on the second floor of the club, monitored the place. The area was semideserted. A perfect solution. It wouldn't be a meeting at a friend's home, whose purpose in reality was seeing one another and badmouthing friends who happened to be absent that Monday. It had bathrooms, space, a wet bar, even a VIP room with sofas, a parking lot where you could hold onto your car key, and Amaral to keep watch on comings and goings. Not to mention the numerous restaurants for sandwiches, health food, vegetarian fare, pizza, and cocaine dealers who delivered.

There, the following Monday, playing over a plank resting on sawhorses that Plínio helped to get from the storeroom and cover with an old tarpaulin, was the same group. A group that had known one another for years. And were familiar with the tricks of each player: the heavy hand, the bluffer, the methodical kind, the wild man. Plínio almost always won. Because

Plínio, on doctor's orders and not from personal choice, had stopped smoking and given up marijuana, stopped drinking hard liquor, and gave a wide berth to the sink where the lines of cocaine were, sticking to the classic and stimulating Coca-Cola. While his friends went crazy, Plínio, more sober than ever, raked in the chips.

On leaving, he would see hookers unhappy at a slow Monday leaning against lampposts, walls, gates, on the stairs of two-story houses, where who knows what transpired on the second floor: most of them were quite young, fake blondes, biracial women recently arrived in the big city. That kind of boredom is more depressing than arousing. Prostitution was one leisure activity that held no attraction for Plínio. He felt sorry for the girls, despite knowing, as did every denizen of the night, that many of them were not there by choice but because of the urgent need to earn some money.

The Monday-night table was a delight. The smell of an old "ballad," of past drink. The club they went to was packed from Tuesday to Sunday. The smell of happiness, of craziness. Sweating walls. Leaks. All dark with artificial light. A well-decorated nightclub. Mondays, it was all theirs. And a very fun poker game.

They would spend the week trashing the losers on social media, reliving the unusual plays, the near victories, the bluffs. Nicknames emerged, Carnival music was sung in mockery, like *"Grandpa's pipe just won't rise, for all his effort, Grandpa can only agonize!"* Almost always the same players lost. But amateur poker follows the rules of horseracing: sometimes a beginner hits the jackpot. Often because he does crazy things that an experienced player wouldn't do and unexpectedly claims the pot. The losers were the ones who drank too much and lost concentration. As in football, the winner is the one in best condition physically. If the player tires toward the end, if he keeps checking his watch, if he needs to get up early and the game drags on, he does mad things, commits suicide like a kamikaze, blows everything in a play that resembles a counterattack by a country that has already lost the war and goes for all or nothing. Ted, a photographer who worked with Plínio on the newspaper, was one of those. With two small children and a bossy wife who was constantly phoning him, at the end he would invariably go all or nothing. Drunk. And usually he went bust.

The problem was that the game that started for small stakes began to have an impact on the losers' pockets. The buy-in was fifty, with the right to two or three rebuys. A big loser could drop two hundred. Four hundred if he was unwise. Everyone there was a grown-up. If he wanted to lose five hundred, he did. If he couldn't decide when to quit, he would wake up the next morning with a spiritual hangover worse than the alcoholic one. And poorer.

Deal the cards, shuffle, remember whose turn it was to ante, or who was the small and big blind, cover the bet . . . It was no longer just a poker game. It demanded attention, some sobriety—*go, your bet, go*—it changed, required a professional dealer. So they hired one who, it was said, had even dealt cards in Ronaldo's home. A phenomenon, himself a football player addicted to Texas Hold'em who became the spokesman for the Poker Stars site. With the pro dealer, the game picked up its pace. Someone was finally controlling the anarchy. And with the dealer, they bought a professional table. The dealer made a good bit of money during the night, plus a tip from the winner. More people wanted to get in the game, which was becoming known to friends of friends. Plínio was outvoted—*No, let's keep it among friends. But he's so-and-so's cousin, and the guy who owns the bar is a friend of mine since childhood* . . . No problem. They hired another dealer, bought another professional table, and started charging money beforehand for pizza and drinks.

Plínio and Ted noticed it right away. More expressions in English came to be part of the gambling, like *bet*. The verb *betar* acquired a conjugation (*eu betei, ele betou, eles betaram*), as did *foldar*, from fold, *flopar* (from flop), *showdown, turn* . . . Plínio was supremely irritated when *flush draw* entered the player's vocabulary to stay, an expression he had to google to understand. To increase the bet became *raisar* (to raise). And, surprisingly, betting followed a pattern. If someone bet two, the next one bet four, always double. A guy only bet holding an ace if he was well positioned, after the big blind. The pattern was noticed. Something changed.

Plínio lost once, twice, three times . . . Unbelievable. He was always the guy who finished in the top three. Ted rarely made it that far, but now he was the first to bust, and he left pissed. It was no longer a game among friends. There were people there studying. There were people with private teachers. There was a kid who spent all day training on the Internet. The amateur table of friends looking for a good time was turning into a business.

Plínio complained: "This isn't fun anymore. You all have perverted our friendly poker game."

"You have to read, practice, study," replied Turquinho. He recommended books. Websites. Shit, Plínio didn't have time for that. Ted didn't have the time either. The journalism market was tense, massive layoffs were announced every week, he was working twice as much for half the pay and collaborated with whoever paid, however poorly. A freelance job was worth four hundred, which could be lost in one night with these nerds! So that was it. The game that went back so many years, with so much history, such friendship won and lost, so many laughs, became a plaything in the hands of nerds. Cunning, bluffs, a stern expression no longer ruled. It was mathematics, statistics, rules, manuals, a logic that transformed a game of trickery into a game of strategy.

Ted stopped going. Sergião stopped going. There were now four professional tables spread out on the dance floor of the Fire, with waiters, four pro dealers, a chronometer running. About fifty people were playing. The games began at 10:30 on the dot. If someone arrived late, he paid a fine. A kid once sat in front of Plínio wearing a beret and an earphone. He just played four hands. He only stayed in if he was 100 percent sure. He lost all four and left without saying goodbye.

"This is a joke, it's like something on ESPN," complained Plínio aloud. No one paid attention.

We're dealing with someone whose pride is wounded, beaten by youth and by fad and who doesn't like to see traditions dishonored. Someone who learned to play poker with his father and who was accustomed to winning before Colombian cocaine arrived in Brazil (he snorted only the pure, crystalline, expensive Peruvian coke) in the eighties. Speaking of which, no one there was snorting, smoking, or drinking hard liquor. That Monday was a drag!

Plínio started playing on the Internet, practicing, studying when he had time, watching championships on ESPN. He upped the level of his game. He didn't do badly the following week. He broke even. The next week, he was prepared to raise his place in the rankings and teach those young kids a lesson. He got there early. He had brought five hundred bucks with him, carefully counted out. It was enough for two buyins. He remained focused. Coca-Cola and coffee. He had eaten earlier. He started out well. He won two small pots, but at least he won. The others began to respect the old guy, until a latecomer sat down beside him and "discreetly" put the keys to a BMW i8 on the table. He never stopped talking, bragging about being hired by a famous law firm. All the strangers at the table had seen Plínio win twice. The talkative guy hadn't. Holding an ace-queen, Plínio played correctly. Mr. Chatterbox called. Son of a bitch. He had a pair, for sure. Must be a pair of sixes. Everyone else folded. Plínio raised. He wanted him out of the pot. But the guy stayed in. He was going along well, ace and queen; the guy had a pair and believed in it. The cards were dealt. First, second, third—no ace or queen. But a king. Plínio made a heavy bet. *Get out, man. Believe I've got the nuts.* The son of a bitch called. He won with a pair of nines, against Plínio's "nothing." That was all the guy had. He didn't celebrate and went on relating details about the new law firm that gave him a BMW just like 007's. Plínio was fuming. Not only did the guy never stop talking, he also invaded Plínio's space with his arms, a bowl of peanuts, and lit a cigarette!!! Plínio hated cigarettes.

"Cards dealt. Let's play."

The son of a bitch blew smoke over the table. Plínio had been a smoker. *I'm going to get this guy out of the pot.* He had nothing but was in the best position. *I'm chasing him out right now. All in. Everything or nothing.* The guy didn't even hesitate. He called. They both showed their cards. Neither had anything. Not even cards of the same suit. Both with a jack as their high card. Plínio held jack-nine, the son of a bitch jack-six. He would win if nothing showed up. A six appeared. The guy won with the pair.

"Jeez, that went badly," Plínio said. *I lost everything in less than fifteen minutes of play,* he thought. *I could do another buy-in.* He still had 250. But it wouldn't work. Playing beside that guy wouldn't work. The guy did everything just right: the chattering, the cigarette, the arms, the peanuts. Maybe he hadn't even gotten a job in some law firm.

Plínio decided to get out. He said goodbye to his old friends at the next table. He mentioned that the son of a bitch wouldn't stop talking. Turquinho took a look. "Goddamn, that guy won a tournament in Miami. What shit . . ."

Plínio drank a Coca-Cola, sighed dejectedly, told Turquinho the table had been spoiled, looked at the chips for the next rebuys, a pile of fifties beside them, thought of returning to the table, but desisted. *I have more to do.*

A dark-skinned whore in a red miniskirt was leaning against the stairs of the neighboring club. She was arguing with a drunk junkie who was harassing her. She was hot. The most stunning legs he'd seen in a while. He stood there, torn between calling a taxi or an Uber. Amaral, the doorman at Fire, who also moonlighted as security for the whorehouse next door, initiated a conversation.

"Like her? She's sensational. Got here last week. She says she's from Minas Gerais. Two hundred. Want her? Turquinho doesn't mind. Take her back there, to the dressing room. It's VIP. There's a sofa. Want her? She's worth it . . ."

Plínio spoke with her. It was true—her soft accent and her congeniality left no doubt: from Minas. Two hundred bucks. Half an hour. She doesn't do everything. Fine, but can you make the others jealous? She didn't understand the question.

"How old are you?"

Twenty.

"Have any children?"

No, she lied.

"Two hundred?"

Two hundred.

Plínio gave her the money he would have spent that night and returned to Fire with his arms around her.

Amaral opened the door. They went past the empty ticket counter, past the storage area, and entered the dance floor where the four poker tables were. Turquinho's eyes widened. Everyone halted their play. Even the dealers were paralyzed. Plínio and the girl from Minas paraded around in an embrace in full view of everyone. Not even the ice in mixed drinks melted, nor did the pizza get cold. They crossed the counter, went into the back, the dressing room in the VIP area. They didn't close the door. Plínio offered her a drink. Nothing. Whores don't drink. They sat down, he caressed those legs like a gambler patting a pair of aces. He saw that his companions in the gambling area continued, speechless. Plínio had half an hour. They chatted, kissed, laughed, embraced until she removed her panties. He did nothing. He caressed that skin and those delicate legs like a touch screen, kissed her neck and whispered in her ear: "Don't cry out aloud, but moan in great pleasure, so they can hear, like it's the best sex of your life." For the full half hour, she played her role, laughing, murmuring, moaning softly; they hugged, talked softly.

Then he instructed: "I'll go first. You wait a few minutes, then leave, okay?" And he left. He crossed the large room. Said nothing. He didn't even glance at his fellow poker players. At the last table, he saw the pile of money that grew with every round, thanked Turquinho, and said that the girl was available to anyone willing to spend a buy-in. He went into the storage area without being noticed, pocketed a copy of the door key, and left.

Through the social media group he found out who won, who lost. No one mentioned the girl. He exchanged messages with Turquinho, who said the girl left two minutes later. And that no one had wanted her. And that Plínio deserved to be congratulated: a sensational girl. Sensational, but no one paid to see. Hatred for the group swelled. He thought rapidly. He stealthily appropriated an old revolver that once belonged to his grandfather and had no ammunition. He bought a used yellow Dafra Speed 150 motor scooter with a carrying case for 1,600 reais, including a helmet. He bought a ninja hood and protective clothing from the *motoboy* who had sold him the scooter for a song. He stuck it in a black backpack with four pieces of cardboard, placed it in the carrying case, and waited till Sunday.

Plínio descended Augusta on the scooter, stopping two blocks from Fire. He entered the club in light clothing, happy, crazy, just as the venue was about to close. He took the heavy backpack and the helmet to the storage area. He was given a ticket. He drank, danced, went wild. He collapsed onto a sofa. He was awakened by his good friend Amaral.

"We're closing, my friend."

"Of course, of course . . . just need to use the bathroom."

He got up. The sound system was turned off. He went around the counter, entered the deejay booth like one who has nothing to hide, and waited behind the turntables. He stayed there, curled up among the equipment. The final people in the club finally headed out. The lights were turned off. Silence began to dominate the place. Doors were locked. A dry-ice cloud, sweat, spilled drinks, and wasted adrenaline dissipated in the air. Plínio remained hidden in the same position for several more minutes. When he felt safe, he came out. He went directly to the locked storage area and opened it with the stolen key. Nothing. Nobody. He entered. His backpack, helmet, three coats, a raincoat, an umbrella, and a purse were there, on a plywood board that had once served as the first poker table. Those sons of bitches in the storage area locked up and left without worrying whether someone would be coming back to pick up what they'd forgotten. They didn't want to miss the last subway.

Plínio quietly picked up his backpack. He wandered about the place. He checked all the doors. He knew the space by heart. He went to the VIP dressing room, put on the biker's clothing over his own, looked in the mirror; with the four pieces of cardboard, he made the backpack into a trunk. He stuck an ad from a delivery pizzeria on it. And went to sleep on the sofa where a week earlier he had been with the sensational girl from Minas whom no one wanted.

Monday morning he woke to the noise of a cleanup taking place and rap music. A two-man cleaning crew had arrived. They turned on the lights and began mopping the floor, sweeping, emptying the trash cans, cleaning the bathrooms with long-handled brushes, lots of Lysol, and a noisy high-pressure water jet. As he had imagined, the cleanup was done from the inside to the outside. Plínio went around, entered the main area from the opposite side, ducked into the storage room, locked it, and hid in the corner. He had two health bars, an energy drink, stretched his legs, and opened a book. He read and waited.

In the afternoon he sent a message saying he had a hangover and wouldn't be playing that night. He slept. He woke up to the sound of the tables already in action. He heard the dealers, the laughter, the usual arguments. He recognized the voices of his friends and the wretched nerds. Heard the voice of the talkative son of a bitch who had humiliated him a week earlier. His excitement at what was about to happen was an antidote against his watch: the time passed more slowly. Relax, meditate, stay calm, breathe, think about song lyrics, the books you've read in your life, the films . . .

Two a.m. Tuesday morning. He knew there was only one table still in operation. Dealers and waiters had already gone. It was the final table. They were down to four or five. The winner would come from there. *Now!* Plínio donned the ninja hood, zipped up his biker outfit, closed up, left the backpack, which was now square like a pizza box, and the helmet in the corner. Holding the gun at arm's length, he entered the playing area and announced the holdup: "Hands on the table, nobody say a word, cell phones and wallets on the table, shut up, you son of a bitch, the first one to peep gets a bullet." It took less than a minute. He forced the dealer to put the money in a bag along with watches, cell phones, wallets. It was pleasing to see the yapping son of a bitch among them, and the keys to the BMW on the table. Everything was going according to plan. If he were caught, he'd pull off the mask and say, *It's me! It was all a joke, to show how precarious security is here! It was funny, wasn't it? This museum piece doesn't even have bullets!*

But the men were paralyzed. The dealer, who might have caused problems, was the most solicitous—after all, it wasn't his money. No one moved. Plínio grabbed the bag, backed away still pointing the gun at them, left the room, tossed the bag in the backpack, adjusted it on his shoulders, went to the entrance, opened the circuit breaker controlling the lights, put on his helmet, and left.

He ran into a sleepy Amaral on the sidewalk; the man neither recognized him nor seemed to wonder what the pizza deliveryman was doing there at that hour. Plínio went into the parking garage, easily located a brand-new BMW, clicked the keyless entry button, unlocked the doors, got in, and drove off.

When he reached Rua Augusta, he removed the ninja hood. He stopped at the traffic light two blocks down. His friend—the girl from Minas, the one with a red miniskirt and sensational legs—was standing by the pedestrian crosswalk and smiled at him. He pretended it wasn't him and didn't return the smile. The light changed. He took off. Descended Augusta to 9 de Julho and headed toward the Pinheiros River.

The robbery was not reported. After all, gambling was illegal under Decree No. 9.215, of April 30, 1946, signed by then president Eurico Gaspar Dutra, which outlawed casinos and games of chance throughout the entire country:

The President of the Republic, using the power conferred by Article 180 of the Constitution, and considering that suppression of games of chance is an imperative of universal conscience; considering that the penal legislation of all enlightened peoples contains precepts conducive to this end; considering that the moral, juridical, and religious tradition of the Brazilian people is contrary to the practice of and exploitation of games of chance; considering that from exceptions to the general law there have resulted abuses harmful to morality and good customs; considering that the licenses and concessions for the practice of and exploitation of games of chance in the Federal Capital, hydrotherapeutic spas, or seaside resorts were given under revocable conditions, and could be rescinded at any moment. Article 1: There is restored in all the territory of the nation the validity of Article 50 and its paragraphs of the Law of Penal Infractions. Any licenses, concessions, or

*authorizations given by federal, state, or local authorities,
based on the now revoked laws, or those that in any way
contain authorization counter to the provision of Article
50 and its Paragraphs of the Law of Penal Infractions, are
hereby declared null and void.*

Days went by, and nothing. The body of an unidentified dark-skinned woman was found two blocks from Fire, on the land known as Augusta Park. She was nude. She had been strangled. A red miniskirt was found thirty feet from the body. Chief Detective Marcelo Santana was unable to determine whether the clothing belonged to the victim. Newspapers reported that no relative claimed the body at the morgue, there was no wake, and she was buried as an indigent in the cemetery in Vila Alpina, on Avenida Francisco Falconi. Santana angrily closed off all access to Rua Augusta for two nights, claiming a "routine" operation. A stolen BMW sports car was also found in the Pinheiros River, but that didn't make the papers, and neither did the theft of an old yellow Dafra Speed on Rua Augusta.

It's not known if it was a coincidence, but with the unprecedented increase in the number of young people infected with HIV—precisely among those who frequented the Baixo Augusta houses and the Largo do Arouche—the Vegas, the Play, and Studio SP closed. Fire went under shortly afterward. Plínio didn't know if the guys continued to play poker, as he was no longer invited. He never again saw Turquinho, who avoided him. Especially after he learned that Plínio had invited Ted for a trip to Vegas, where they blew a small fortune at the Bellagio Casino.

PART III

Discreet Inelegance

THE FORCE IS WITH ME

BY Beatriz Bracher & Maria S. Carvalhosa

Panamericana

Miranda, my sixteen-year-old niece who lives in Rio, is spending her January vacation with me. She preferred coming here to spending the month at a friend's house in Rio, or traveling with her parents to the northeast. Spending the holidays in São Paulo, without friends, during an especially stuffy summer, in a district with nothing nearby and full of mosquitoes, was an easy decision for her.

Aunt Flora lives by herself. The district is full of trees, and birds sing before daybreak. I can read all day long if I want to.

I'm fifty years old and have three adult children who have moved away from São Paulo. I live alone in a large, empty house that belonged to my parents; I moved here when they died. It was enjoyable when the children were young; the calmness in the neighborhood, nearby schools, spending the afternoon in the small square with its ironwoods and eucalyptus, running in Villa-Lobos Park, and being able to greet the people passing by on weekends were luxuries that did me good.

I read on the tablet, with huge letters, read more than before the accident. I think it's to make up for lost time. I think it's because

I like reading even more. I think it's because I don't want to have anything else to do.

Vacation.

It's the district of tipu trees with their long horizontal branches spotted with light green parasites, smooth, that resemble ferns, only more delicate. In spring the streets and squares turn completely yellow with their tiny blossoms.

I read at home and on the subway. I spend three hours in the same car, reading and soaking up the air-conditioning. The noise of the engine and the murmur make me feel good. As if I'm living without having to do anything, just living.

I gave furniture to each child when they moved out and didn't buy anything new. The house became empty and too large for me, but I can't manage to sell it for a reasonable price. It's located on a wide tree-lined avenue that today is very busy. The district is residential, not even bakeries are permitted, which is why no one is interested in buying. I don't have the money to maintain it; the house is black from bus exhaust. Lately I haven't had the energy to take care of it; mold has begun growing in the closed-off rooms.

Vacation from everything. Vacation from everyone.

The lot is more than a thousand meters, with pitangas, avocados, guava, *ipê-rosa*, and a silk-cotton tree, and cannot be subdivided. It's the law. The trees grew, I stopped trimming them, then stopped raking up the leaves and gathering the ripe fruit rotting on the ground.

* * *

I lived with Aunt Flora for six months to stay closer to the treatment I had to have. She took care of me the whole time. Roberta, my cousin, moved to London during this period. Sometimes Mom would go to Rio to stay with my sister, and it would be just Aunt Flora and me. Besides taking me to vision therapy and training me in using my fingers, she would tell me stories and read to me every night. My going from fantasy books to Salinger, Cortázar, Kafka, and Murakami was her doing.

I get home at five thirty in the afternoon, and at night watch American television shows with Miranda; from time to time we have dinner at a pizzeria near here. In the mornings she sleeps, in the afternoons she catches the train on the Marginal, almost two kilometers from here, and visits the subway stations.

It used to not make much difference being in a dark bedroom or out in the sun. Now that I'm better it seems that the light hurts my eyes, not a lot but a little. That's why I like to spend the day resting and go out at night, after Aunt Flora goes to sleep.

When I arrive home Miranda is reading on the sofa in the empty living room, in T-shirt and underpants, with the ceiling fan on high.

I try reading in the garden, but the smell of flowers and rotting fruit is kind of sickening, like wine, and there the mosquitoes are even worse than in the house.

I know we love each other, but for a while now we've barely spoken. Sometimes she tells me stories, most of them made up I think, despite her saying they're real.

* * *

I go out after Aunt Flora falls asleep in front of the TV. I leave my bedroom door closed so she'll think I'm sleeping. I wear a light jacket to protect me from the mosquitoes; I stroll through the neighborhood streets with Legião Urbana playing loudly in my headphones.

Walking around here at night reminds me of the times I would walk around during the day and not see anything. I can still smell the different scents of the flowers, not as well as before, but better than other people.

I wake up on the sofa facing the TV, still playing. Miranda has already gone to her room. I switch off the living room lights, spray insecticide in my bedroom, flick on the fan, and toss and turn in bed, unable to sleep. I'm a bit nauseous.

After midnight the streets are deserted and full of watchmen. In front of some of the houses spotlights come on as I pass, in others dogs bark and other dogs, hearing them, start barking too. I go on a little farther—one after another, bright lights snap on. The watchmen in the streets and sentry boxes wave and the electrified tennis rackets that electrocute mosquitoes go bzz-bzz, I smell them burning as I go by. Small red lights of surveillance cameras blink in the low foliage of trees. The storms and lightning of late evening have brought down large branches onto the sidewalks and streets. Swaying branches at the top of trees lash against exposed wires that crackle to the rhythm of the gentle wind, tlec-tlec. I dance to the sound of Legião Urbana, to the barking, the tlec-tlec, the bzz-bzz, illuminated by the spotlights of the surveillance cameras.

The motors of buses, the cracking of branches hitting bare wires, the noise of the persistent frying of mosquitoes against the rackets of the watchmen in the streets, along with dogs barking, keep me in a state of relentless exhaustion. I get up, have some chamomile tea. It works, I sleep, but after an hour I wake up even more nauseated.

I walk, walk, walk, and continue walking. The watchmen know me. I bump into things and stumble—I'm still not fully recovered, there's still a fog in my brain. Maybe they think, There goes the little drunk. I go on. I stop at the gas station.

Miranda is pretty, she seems to float, the owner of the space in which she moves. When she walks, without realizing it she dances, spins, and goes back to walking. Her beauty, her smile, and the attention with which she listens to us are irresistible. Sometimes I get home and, instead of finding her reading, she's dancing and singing in the living room with her headphones on; I am hypnotized.

Faces are still a problem for me. If I don't know the person, he seems very much like anyone else, especially if he's immobile or silent, like passengers on a subway car. But if the person speaks, moves his cheekbones, opens and closes his mouth, his head leans a little, his hair stirs. These small things begin to form a face in my mind and then he becomes a unique person, never again will I confuse him with another. That's why I recognize the street watchmen, the workers at the gas station, the cashier at the store, and some of the customers whom I've seen around here more than once.

I had such fears about her eyesight that her treatment came to be my North Star.

An adolescent in darkness seemed too cruel a solitude. Estela, my sister, dedicated herself completely to all possible treatments and instruments to keep Miranda in our world, even during the years in which she could see almost nothing. Estela was successful; Miranda never lost her light or her sweetness.

Perhaps only now is she seeking, of her own free will, a bit of calm in the dark. I don't know. I don't know if it's me or her. Maybe it's what she's looking for in me. Or in this abandoned house that belonged to her grandparents—they were always happy and festive, like Estela. Whether in the district filled with silence, or in São Paulo.

Next to the gas station there's a supermarket. They're both in a place called Panamericana Square, which is actually just an immense traffic circle. The station is right beside where the trucks unload their merchandise for the supermarket. While the stevedores unload, the drivers have a sandwich in the station's store. Or they just have a coffee and stay there in the air-conditioning that cools them and keeps the mosquitoes away. Most of them are old and fat. Today there's one who's good-looking.

Three months ago the first cases of dengue showed up here in Alto de Pinheiros. Yesterday, at the supermarket, people were talking about zika. There's no way to avoid mosquitoes. As recently as two years ago they could be shooed away with repellent, but now they seem to have developed a resistance. People living on the block by the river say that it's even worse there, but I don't know how it could be any worse than here, six blocks away. There are niches of mosquitoes in every dark corner, underneath the table, behind the curtains, inside the closet. The thing to do is close all the windows in the TV room and the bedrooms—the only spaces we live in, or in which I live when I am home—spray insecticide, and turn on the fan. It gets hot, because the air that circulates is the same, but it's the only way to keep the mosquitoes from biting us. You can't use the bathroom during the night; when I open the door a swarm of mosquitoes invades the bedroom. Then I have to spray again and cover myself completely until the poison and the wind repel the insects.

Before the accident I believed in a magical world. Peter Pan, Harry Potter, The Chronicles of Narnia, The Lord of the Rings, Divergent, *Percy Jackson,* Star Wars. *It wasn't just that I read, I truly believed it. It wasn't actually the existence of a magical "world" that I believed in but the logic of magical thinking. It's hard to explain—I've always had the Force with me, me and my country. It seems silly, but that's how I thought of the world. To tell the truth, even now I don't completely disbelieve in the Force. It's something that helps me do good; if I'm doing that—good—I know that nothing bad will happen to me.*

I walk, dance, and eat a ham-and-cheese sandwich late at night and nothing bad is going to happen to me. That's a little bit of what I think, and I want to test it by walking at night like this. I'm a little afraid, of course, but I want to put it to the test. To see if I'm good, that nothing bad will happen to me. To be happy, to think cool things about people, about everybody.

Having Miranda here with me at night is making me think about how nice it would be to have friends, to go out to the movies, to be interested in what I read in the newspaper. I don't know when I stopped being interested. I'm lazy, the house is far away from everything, too large and too empty. Suddenly, with Miranda, it makes more sense. I want to believe it's the house that's empty and not my life. And I think I'm right. I don't need to occupy spaces I don't use, but they still exist in their emptiness. When Miranda is here, and I occupy them, the house becomes less heavy. I don't have the feeling that I must drag bedrooms, living rooms, and bathrooms with me every day like I do when I'm alone and wake up and intuit, more than see, its many unused areas.

I also go into the station to escape the mosquitoes. I order a ham-and-cheese sandwich, and the good-looking guy laughs at my Rio accent and invites me to sit with him and a friend. He speaks of a flower festival in Ceasa, close to there, five minutes by car. It starts late at night.

"Want to go with me?" he asks.

His friend gets kind of peeved; it's going to get in the way of their job. But the good-looking one is the boss and I go with them to the flower festival.

I fear I'm not a good companion for her—we barely speak, because I don't have much to say. Even quiet, she is so alive.

Their vehicle isn't a truck and has nothing to do with the super-market. It's a dilapidated pickup parked in front of the gas station. It has a bunch of trash bags in the bed.

"What's that—garbage?"

"More or less," he says, "it's material for recycling."

The mosquitoes are a tiresome subject. They remain, but there's not much to be said about them, and you can't say the same thing day after day.

I sit between the two of them, kind of crowded, and it's only then, when the good-looking one, whose name is Diego, starts the en-gine, that I realize my blunder. I'm very afraid, feel like vomiting. I suck it up, keep quiet, and try not to imagine the worst things in the world. I look at Diego and think I may not have read his face correctly. I start to panic. What if I'm not seeing the person he really is? What else is there in his face? Does he have a weird way of laughing? I can't tell—the more nervous I get, the less I see.

Three a.m., the nausea increases, a headache begins.

He turns on the Marginal highway and accelerates. The taillights of the cars become red lines flowing like a river of fire. Diego switches on the turn signal, a small red light inside the cabin, blink-blink, and he cuts rather sharply to the right, the movement throwing me into his friend, who holds onto my thigh. "No, no," I say softly.

I can't help but go to the bathroom, I think I drank too much water, it's too hot, everything is too much, including my sleepiness, but I can't sleep. I wasn't able to vomit, I return to my bedroom, the headache gets worse. I remember I forgot to spray Miranda's room with insecticide. I'm sleepy and decide she'll know how to get by; actually, she prefers to use repellent cream on her skin, says it works better. I lie down, sleep doesn't come, the mosquitoes attack, I'm sweating a lot. My head throbs in a way that's never happened before. I get up again, the room spins. I sit down on the bed, everything aches, and I think I'm not going to make it to the kitchen. I need water, my mouth is dry. It's not possible for zika to be so immediate, but I think it must be that, or dengue, every bone in my body aches. I knock on Miranda's door to ask for help. I don't know what she can do, but I'm afraid I'm dying. She doesn't answer, I knock harder, she doesn't answer. I try opening the door, it's not locked. Miranda isn't in bed, she's not in the room or in the bath. I support myself along the walls till I make it to the kitchen. Miranda's not in the kitchen. I'm burning up with fever, I can't think straight.

Diego stops the pickup in a parking area full of trucks. He and I get out. His friend says he'll stay right there. I have to figure out how to run away. Diego pulls me by the hand and we go between tall trucks. The first thing I smell is diesel, then I see we really are in a place filled with flowers, flowers I'm not familiar with, scents I've never smelled. It's half dark and bright at the same time. The lights on the Ceasa lampposts are strong but tightly focused, here and there I make out trucks full of flowers and, in the middle of them, dark spaces with tall shapes, only from close up do I see they're more trucks. We go through those narrow passageways. A few boys are wheeling plants on wooden carts, which they drag without looking out for anyone, almost running into one another. Inside a large shed, stands are already set up with many different kinds of flowers. Here inside I manage to see better and distinguish between the various flowers and foliage. Diego's face is handsome and I think he's good, that I wasn't mistaken.

Where is Miranda? What have I gotten myself into? I fell, I fall. When am I going to get up? How? What can I use for support? Metaphorically and really, where are we? Everything gets foggy and I can't see well, my eyes are swollen and teary.

Diego knows, or makes up, the names of all the flowers. I find it funny because I think he's making them up, but I like the names he says as we quickly pass through more and more stands. We stop at one with strange and pretty flowers, and he buys a super bouquet of "moon purple," a lilac-colored flower with pink stripes. Moon purple! The bouquet is wrapped in thick paper lined with aluminum foil so the flowers can survive the trip to the florists. He takes that enormous bouquet of moon purple, there must be five dozen, and gives it all to an old legless lady who begs around there. But first he removes one and gives it to me: "The most beautiful and most purple moon purple, to the most lunar and luminous girl I've ever known."

His voice is deep, he's joking but speaking seriously, he likes me, his face is full of light. We return to the pickup and his friend is smoking a joint. He offers it; Diego takes a drag and tries to pass it to me. I've never smoked marijuana. I'm curious but I didn't want it to be like this. Diego offers it to me again, looks deep into my eyes, the joint has a strong smell, I take a deep drag and choke—I've never even smoked a cigarette. Naturally they laugh, and I decide to take another puff just to show them I know how. I hold the smoke in my mouth and let it out, proud of myself.

I have to buy medicine, the Panamericana Pharmacy should be open. I can't even walk as far as the door, but I need to get to the pharmacy. Miranda went out for a walk, that's all. What do I mean, that's all? Four in the morning and Miranda went out for a walk? That's crazy! I have to go after her. I have to survive to find her. I can't think, I'm burning up with fever and shivering from cold.

We get in the pickup, I ask him to take me back to the station. His friend says no way, they're already behind on their delivery and the boss is going to be mad.

"Boss?" *I ask.* "Delivery?" *I think,* This late at night, who can be in a hurry to receive garbage for recycling?

We get back on the Marginal, continue a bit more in the opposite direction from the station; the trip takes time, becomes a journey, I've lost my sense of time, it stretches out like chewing gum in a small space, a second and an hour get mixed together in my head.

We cross a bridge over a large river and continue until we stop in front of the gate of a very big lot—everything is big around here. A boy about twelve opens the gate. He's carrying a weapon, and that makes no sense to me. The weapon becomes a green plastic machine gun with which a boy dressed like an American soldier plays at firing by making noise with his mouth, Bang-bang, then it goes back to being a real gun in the hand of a real boy. Diego waves; the boy gets out of the way and lets the pickup enter.

I open the gate to the house and go to the street watchman at the closest corner.

"Mr. Expedito, can you help me get to the pharmacy?" I lean against him and we go together. "Have you seen Miranda?" I ask.

He replies, "She dances every night in the streets." I don't have the strength to ask what he's saying. Something scary that I can't deal with right now.

Diego parks in a cement courtyard in front of a half-abandoned warehouse. There are piles of crates made of cheap wood everywhere. I see people wrapped in blankets sleeping in the middle of the crates, a baby's cry that seems endless enters my head and won't stop. Afterward, either it already stopped long ago, or didn't even exist. Maybe they're not people but dark sacks and wolf cubs howling. Diego's friend gets out of the pickup, Diego kisses me on the lips, caresses my cheek, brushes against my chest, it's enjoyable, he gets out and I stay behind. I don't feel like moving, I sit there on the front seat of the pickup. I don't know where I am. Sometimes I don't know where I am in the most absolute sense, like when you wake up in a hotel room without any idea of how you got there. It seems strange to be in São Paulo, to be alive, to speak Portuguese. I look behind me and see some hundred-reais bills inside a half-open bag. Lots of hundred-reais bills. I don't know if I'm hallucinating. The lighter belonging to Diego's friend is on top of the bag. It seems natural to burn the money so it can't be used to buy weapons that end up in the hands of twelve-year-old boys. I'm more afraid than ever, but at the same time I have no doubt that it's what I need to do. The Force is with me—if I concentrate I'll manage to blow up the pickup, run away, past the armed boy, somehow overcome the kilometers that separate me from home, jump over the wall, enter my room, and go to sleep.

Mr. Expedito leaves me at the pharmacy and goes back to his corner. The pharmacist examines me and says I need to go to the first aid station. I can't take aspirin or anything because he suspects it's dengue. I would go, get a taxi and go, but what about Miranda?

I take off my jacket, stick it in the pickup's gas tank, soak it with gasoline, and spread it over the bags. I open two more and see they're also full of money, douse them a little more, spread more gasoline around, the smell is making me nauseous, confused. Suddenly it doesn't make sense to burn money—the fire will produce smoke and pollute the air. The world will turn black and it'll be my fault. The armed boy isn't there, I think he went into the warehouse too. I drag a sack to the outside of the gate, which is ajar, and leave it next to a pile of boxes of cardboard and old newspapers for recycling. I take a second bag, and when I'm in the middle of the path the boy yells from the warehouse door, "She's taking the money!" Without thinking, I return to the pickup and flick the lighter near the bags. The explosion throws me backward. Flame licks my shirt and I catch on fire.

I leave the pharmacy not knowing what to do—the three-lane street looks to be kilometers long. It's empty and that's the only reason I'm not run over despite crossing it so slowly. Where is Miranda? If I go to a first aid station they'll put me in a hospital, and I can't let that happen. But where to start? I can barely breathe, I'm exhausted. I collapse onto the bench at the bus stop, in the center of Panamericana Square, and feel like I'm in the middle of a desert, no one will ever find me here, I'm in the heart of a true desert of sand and high winds. I've been alone for years. Miranda has disappeared, slipped through my fingers, and no one will ever find me again, no one will save me. I need to find Miranda. I black out.

The door to the house is open. Aunt Flora isn't anywhere. Mr. Expedito tells me he left her at the pharmacy. The fog in my head has lifted; I see the entire world, the sun is coming up. I find Aunt Flora shivering on the bench at the Panamericana bus stop. That's so sad, so lonely. Without anything, without anybody. My aunt all alone. If only I could walk . . . If only I really had the Force . . .

I wake up two days later. Miranda is at the foot of my bed, reading a newspaper and laughing about an article saying that people at a recycling center found a garbage bag with more than 100,000 reais. No one has been able to explain where the money came from.

Miranda tells me about her adventure.

"And what happened when you were blown backward?"

"When I was falling, Diego left the warehouse and saw me. We looked at each other. He ran toward me to save me, but then he changed his mind and went to the truck to try and get the money out. I pulled off my shirt and used it to put out the fire. A force took care of me. Diego was in the truck bed with a couple of other men, thrashing their hands on the bills to extinguish the fire. I jumped onto him and pushed his head into the fire, I wanted him to suffocate in the money and burn to death. Later he stopped having any importance for me. All I could think about was you by yourself, here at home, and I wanted to return right away. I left while they were still burning their hands."

"You were courageous to do that—is it all true?"

"All true, except the part where I killed Diego. I made that up. I think I made it up."

FLOW

BY Ferréz

Itapecerica da Serra

The Itapecerica da Serra Highway, a long highway that crosses the Capão Redondo and passes through the town of Itapecerica, which has the famous S hill where at rush hour buses are just like trains, stops and waits for a phantom driver to free up traffic—the driver who, through magic, pauses every day at the same hour.

The highway ascends in the direction of Valo Velho, a district piled with houses and people who, coming from all the pretty places, now try at any cost to color their rough walls the same noble green of their home regions, far-off places where cigarettes are a rarity. Bahia, Piauí, Pernambuco, and today cigarettes from Paraguay with strange and generic names, are resting in their pockets.

Only a few shacks finished, dirt streets, the sun begins to set. She dries her tears, she spent hours watching the television news, the death of MC Daleste will provoke much more clamor. Leaving the shack that today is her home, she speaks the words of the assassinated singer, verses that seemed to be written directly for her, as well as for millions of young people in the periphery. "When I started out, I went through a lotta hardship, and there at home it was unreal, it's revoltin', I know, I felt the taste of poison, we never had a bathroom till I was thirteen." Pride keeps her from looking at the neighbors, she doesn't like the rabble, a proud person doesn't comment, doesn't conspire, doesn't boast.

Waiting at the bus stop, she takes the tiny mirror from her purse, retouches her lipstick, a van passes by, a jitney bus, and a driver who whistles; she looks sidelong and reads the bumper sticker: *Preto Ghóez Lives Forever*. She understands it as a homage to someone newly deceased, maybe a van driver, maybe one of those has-been rappers who older guys play in bars.

She loves it when dominoes clack onto the table, the aluminum ones have the best sounds, followed by a shout—"Take that, fool!!!"—so loud that instead of offending, it makes everybody laugh.

Cards are silent, flattering like the poor who love the rich people closest to them, whether because they have a better job or because they once had one.

The unemployed from large firms are more valued than the employed at midsized or small companies, she knows that very well from her mother, always coming home lifeless, her legs swollen.

She feels good among those potbellied men who have done well with their robberies, or, as they put it, their businesses.

Some of them dress well, calling it business casual, sneakers, long-sleeved shirts, the most up-to-date dress pants, a sporty watch that clashes with everything, and gel in their hair, the less fortunate trying to stay closer to the lucky ones.

They all follow the games, nodding as if all four players are going to win.

The plastic chairs, the table with garish beer ads, none of it sounds like the old days, the noise is no longer muted, the dominoes are bone, an uninteresting clap of one dull plastic on another, beer in an aluminum can, what has become of the sweating bottles, the cloth on the shoulder or at the waist of the bartender to wipe away the sweat, to dry what drips from the bottle onto the table, where is the delicacy of serving the beer—no foam, please.

And before, there were the raids, hands against the wall, explain why you have two cell phones, where do you work, nowadays everyone is afraid of hoodies and covered faces, of gunshots and meaningless questions, of rage and massacre.

And all of that reminds her of her father, and embraces, and chocolate she received at the edge of the counter.

On the corner of the avenue, where like a river it feeds lesser streets, just beyond the new Skol Pit Stop—a franchising trend that has caught on in recent months in the outlying hillsides.

"Jão, you come in with sixty thousand, and they do the rest, you just find the place, they set everything up."

"But isn't it just a kiosk?"

"Yeah, like a trailer, there you sell everything of theirs cheap, people come and buy."

"You get 1.8 reais a bottle and there's the fuckin' special beer that goes for nine."

"Like an opium den, except for beer?"

"Right. And totally legal."

"But you can't drink and drive, and Pit Stop can?"

"You can, easy."

Excess of conversation, loud noise, the conversation trying to override the noise, the smell of beer, meat on skewers, barbecue, mayonnaise, urine, counterfeit perfume, hair cream, sweat. Everything merges and everything confuses his thoughts, for an instant he wonders whether he ought to be at home with his children, with his wife and her endless no's, his quiet masturbation in the double bed, without a lot of movement so she won't notice, coming in his hand, cleaning up quietly in the bathroom.

Every day the same, at five in the morning, Odílio wakes up and looks at the clock, always ten minutes before the alarm goes off. (Why do old people wake up so early?)

Half an hour later he leaves for the bar, where he always has a cup of coffee and milk. He sits at the seat on the right and picks up the newspaper to read all about real estate and cars.

In a few minutes he is ready to go into action, walking down the street, looking at the same houses, sparser and sparser, disdaining the buildings and their colorless residents.

In twenty minutes he arrives at the gas station, greets Claudia, his manager, then shakes the hand of all the employees, goes to the cash register, and begins entering the cash and credit cards from the night before.

Dimenó, a nickname dating back to childhood because of his short stature and his easygoing looks, sticks the nozzle of the hose into the tank, wearing his favorite work sneakers, taking extreme care not to get them dirty, he enjoys looking at license plates, coming from a tumultuous life, *la vida loca*, he tells everyone that he was saved by rap, a rhythm of the outlying districts, with poetry, always with a social message, which led him to read revolutionaries like Malcolm X and Nelson Mandela. From his old life, what remains is the habit of memorizing the initials, because he doesn't remember the model or the color of cars where the enemies he has acquired surely are.

CTO. No, not an enemy.

DCD. Might be, something like DC cut me off on the Marginal.

He surveys the faces of everyone in the car, the bearded driver, yes, him. He cut Dimenó off on the Marginal, DCD beyond a doubt.

The guy with the beard pays and leaves, Dimenó stares, the guy doesn't understand but watches through the rearview mirror.

The cell phone rings, Dimenó picks it up, the face that appears causes him to smile shyly, it's her, he prepares his soft voice, not believing that he ever met such a beautiful girl, and she doesn't have any kids even though she's already sixteen.

She manages to get on the bus, the sleepy-eyed fare collector is listening to the boy beside him, fifteen years old at most, short hair, talking.

"The way we roll is by making waves, man, ya feel me? Pow-pow, bikes revvin' like crazy, don't matter if the pigs show up, they give us heat, we give them hell."

She passes through the turnstile, sits beside a lady eating boiled corn on a small plastic plate, the entire bus smells of corn and butter.

Her friend's house is nearby, she pulls the cord, some guy looks at her legs, she pretends not to notice, she gets out and enters through the alleyway, in a few minutes she's in the home of Cleide, her friend and the sister she never had.

Amid talk about creams, cell phones, the best dance, MC Fininho's new album, they plan the day's activities.

The sun disappears with impressive speed, the poorly lit streets take on a somber tone, at night the only ones who go out are those who can or who think they're going to survive, the evening drizzle will soon fall, brightening the pavement and making the city more sinister.

The spot is getting crowded, they arrive in the middle of the flow, Cleide quickly finds her partner, Dimenó is waiting for his girl, they kiss passionately. Cínthia says goodbye to her friend, she's going to circulate.

She passes by several circles of people talking.

"The house is real cool, bro, it's got a pool, bathtub, of course we gonna split the take, right? But it's cool, five grand, divided, it's cool."

"Except it can't be like Cleiton, who rented it and the owner showed up saying he'd just loaned it to that girl."

"But Cleiton proved it, even had a contract, you shoulda seen all the people, the place was packed."

Cínthia walks a bit farther and stops at the corner, her iPhone 5 at her groin, minishorts frayed at the edges, a tiny black top that displays her belly and her piercing.

"It's like that here, lots of rookies, see? After ten at night the Pit closes, then it's the spot and the motels, you just show up and take your pick, it's all ours."

"Favela dance, favela dance, and young guys ready to fuck if they get the chance."

The cars go by, bringing more throbbing to the heavy beat, erotic poses, the cars go by slowly, attentive gazes, every girl or woman is inspected, the observing eyes blazed.

Odílio wears glasses but not when there is a *night*, now it's *vida loca*, a gold bracelet, platinum chain, an open polo shirt to show the chain, a Tag Heuer watch, loudspeakers at full blast.

"You're crazy—hey, boozehound, you can c'mon in, it's all ours."

Odílio has glasses on, a buttoned dress shirt, carries a binder filled with papers, heading to his next meeting, one more gas station will be open, his son calling and wanting to know about swimming classes. No, he can't take the boy today, he had to leave everything ready, inform his wife, *very busy*, he had to pick up his watch at the repair shop, *is the guy gonna replace the mechanism?* These days that's how it is, the watch'll come back with a Chinese mechanism, for God's sake.

Odílio and his chrome wheels.

Odílio and his meeting till later.

Small businessman—no, entrepreneur. Conservative but out of shape, CDs in the car, polo shirt in the trunk, friends his own age. "Shit, you're not dead, you're pushin' fifty, you gotta live life, you could die tomorrow, your wife'll find someone else right away, put your dick to use, Odílio, find yourself some dynamite pussy."

She is in the flow, in the middle of all the others, the face of a victim.

Odílio stops, his lips trembling, but he pulls himself together. "Get in, baby, wanna go for a ride?"

She gets in, smiles timidly, he kisses her on the cheek.

"What's your name?"

"Cínthia."

"Man, you're beautiful."

The car tears away, its chrome wheels, its tires screeching, the people at the Pit Stop shouting, "That one's heading for a cock-lashing."

He is going to a hotel on the avenue, she places her hand on his leg, "Are we going to Cheiro do Campo?" With that sweet face, anything's possible.

"Sure, Cheiro do Campo."

Odílio glances at his cell phone, answers his wife, she doesn't kiss on the lips, they haven't gotten it on for months, she doesn't even touch him with affection, she doesn't give blow jobs, she's always tired, the kids' classes, the house, shopping, her mother who's always sick, old, washing clothes, taking care of the house, the grandchildren's birthdays, the stepdaughter's wedding.

"Look, love, I'm going to the meeting but I'll be home soon." Little hearts in WhatsApp, nowadays hypocrisy via icons, preestablished sentiments. All you gotta do is choose.

Cínthia enters the bedroom. "Wow, there's a tub!"

She quickly gets a Red Bull, he gets a beer, takes off his shirt, she looks at his hairy chest, his white hair, the platinum crucifix shines more than anything, he sits down rather awkwardly, he's panting, long flights of stairs, poor circulation, a precarious life, always grabbing a bite to eat, not much salad, he saw the doctor, he'd have to cut down on meat, greasy food, fried things, not to mention soft drinks.

Cínthia's tiny shorts, Cínthia's legs, she lets down her dark hair onto her bare shoulders, it brushes his chest while she gives him a peck on the cheek.

"You smell good, love. What's your name?"

"Odílio, princess. Is everything gonna happen today?"

She sticks out her lower lip and forcefully grabs him on top of his pants, he puts his hand in his pocket, takes out two blue pills, and swallows them without her seeing.

Cínthia removes her top, her breasts hard, the blue piercing hits his eyes, the fine hairs below her navel.

Odílio gets up, approaches her, kisses her on the lips, vigorously sucks her tongue, she finds it strange, he's thirsty, he grabs, runs his hand over her ass, vigorously, then looks at her face, steps back a little, still with her taste in his mouth, and slaps her.

"What's this?" She's flustered, speaks in a low voice.

"With me that's how it is, you're gonna get hit in the face, you little whore!"

"Not in my face, love. I don't like it."

"You gotta like it? Keep quiet and take off your shorts."
She lowers her head, feels something hot on her breast: spit.
Odílio didn't even pucker up, it seemed more like hawking,
she dries it with her hand, wipes it on her shorts, examines her
hair, takes out her iPhone 5, it isn't the S but the regular one,
touches the screen twice.

Odílio takes off his pants, now in white undershorts, the
platinum crucifix, the girl unbuttoning her shorts, him on his
third beer. There's a knock on the door.

"Who can that be?"

"Who is it?"

The knock grows louder, he opens the door quickly, she
lifts her head and stops unbuttoning her shorts. Two men
come in, black T-shirts, pistols in hand, one bearded, the other
quite young.

Odílio leans against the wall, the men close the door, the
bearded guy takes out a cell phone.

"It might stick. It's the rapist we was lookin' for."

Odílio a rapist? Odílio hadn't taken his son to swim class,
his daughter of sixteen hadn't asked him for a new cell phone,
she hadn't seen her father, all day at a meeting.

Cínthia, motionless, begins to cry softly, covers her breasts
with her slim arms.

"You rapist son of a bitch, you'll get yours in jail, they'll
screw you in the ass every day."

"Rapist how? I was here with her, she—"

"She's a minor, you sick fuck, look at her. Calm down, girl,
what's your name?"

"Jaqueline."

"Cínthia, you said you—"

"Shut up, you old son of a bitch, the girl was raped, just

look, Esteve, get a photo." The younger one takes out his cell phone, snaps a picture, the girl lowers her head.

"For the love of God, I have a family."

"Everybody's got a family, but nobody goes to their home to rape their daughters. They're gonna ram a broom handle up your ass, you hear? They're gonna spread your legs and kick you in the balls till they're bigger than your belly."

Odílio sits on the floor, his head in his hands.

"Toothpaste, they stick a toothpaste tube up your nose, and then punch it and everything goes in, tearing up your guts, I seen it, the stuff busts up everything."

"My God, they're gonna squeeze you, like they say in the joint."

"They rip off your nipples, rip 'em off with improvised tools, awful sight."

Odílio is crying, takes his hand from his face. He speaks in a low voice: "Can't we come to some kind of agreement?"

"Agreement? Just look at the girl there, for Chrissake. All fucked up, what did you do to her?"

"I didn't touch her, I swear it."

"Swear? You screwed her good, you fucked the girl and now it's *you* who's fucked."

The thin one approaches. "If you took her from behind, it's a violent offense against morality, it can put your ass away for five years."

"Please, let's talk, I can get ahold of some money."

The two men look at each other, the younger one goes up to Odílio.

"Look, my partner is old school, the straight-arrow type, but if you can put your hands on a hundred thousand in cash . . ."

"Damn, that's a lot, I can't raise that much, help me, man, for the love of God."

"Help me to help you—look at the girl there, you're going to be fucked."

"I didn't know, I swear."

"Okay, then get on the phone, goddamnit, your situation ain't easy."

Odílio calls, speaks, calls, speaks.

"I can get thirty thousand . . . thirty, thirty."

"I understood, for fuck's sake." The bearded man looks at him from a distance and shakes his head, the younger one turns to Odílio.

"Look, there's the precinct chief in this deal too, each one gets a cut, he's already in on it, understand? We can't settle for less than fifty."

Odílio calls, speaks. He succeeds.

"And where's the money?"

"In Leste, we have to go get it."

"Shit, that's too far."

"But that's the only place I can get it, a friend has already left some of it at my house, we can go there and add it to mine that I was saving."

"I don't know, Esteve, let's handcuff this guy right now." The bearded man turns his back.

"Please, let's go there, get me out of this."

The younger man makes a show of pity: "What about the girl?"

"Fuck, what're we gonna do with the girl?"

Odílio doesn't answer. What to do about the girl?

"Cínthia, I've got a thousand here in my wallet."

"Not Cínthia, Jaqueline. I don't want your shitty money. Can I get out of here, sir?"

The policeman lets her don her top, and she quickly goes into the bathroom to wash her face, uses the towel to wipe the spittle from her chest, straightens her hair, and leaves without looking back.

Odílio arrives home, everyone is awake.

"What happened, father?"

"What was it, man?"

"Nothing. I need money, did Márcio leave it here?"

"Wait, I'll get it."

"And also the money from the safe beside the bed."

"I'll go, but all of it?"

"All of it, woman, go!"

When he goes to deliver it, the bearded man receives a phone call. "What? The chain? Okay, fuck."

"Your chain there, my brother."

"My chain?"

"Yeah, hand it over, or you want us to go in and explain the situation to your wife?"

The men leave, stop at a nearby gas station, exchange their T-shirts for two regular polos.

"Time to become normal civilians."

They go into the store and buy energy drinks and some snacks.

Jaqueline arrives into the flow that Friday, her iPhone 6 at her waist, her new piercing a platinum crucifix.

"What's your name, sweetheart?"

"Cínthia. What's yours, love?

COFFEE STAIN

by Olivia Maia

Sé

Black coffee: pure, strong, thick. She added five spoonfuls of sugar and stirred until it cooled, until the voices around her penetrated her thoughts as if they were part of them, as if they emerged from them. *Anything else, ma'am?*

It was a Thursday and the restaurant was crowded. *What juices do you have?* The coffee was never strong enough, and she didn't even like coffee, much less sweet coffee. A stupid beverage, and the stupid little sweet sitting there beside the cup, almost crumbling in the saucer. *Can you bring me the check, please?* It's the sugar that gave the liquid that sticky consistency. *Is this dish enough for two?*

She raised the spoon with a bit of coffee and spilled it onto the napkin on the table. Then she lifted the paper to see whether the tablecloth also absorbed any of the liquid. *Is this knife enough to kill someone?*

Who was laughing?

She called herself Lina, mainly because no one would call her anything, and she almost always forgot the name when she introduced herself to someone. She was called by a different name each day. *They say it's a butcher knife, for slicing pork, I don't know.* She didn't like *senhorita*, which seemed as if they were saying she was incapable, incomplete, awaiting the man of her princess dreams. Like one waiting for life to begin without ever risking the initial steps. *Would you like cof-*

fee, senhorita? "Lina" was good, it sounded like a fairy name, something taken from a fantasy book. It wasn't the name she had heard during most of her childhood, but then she remembered almost nothing from her childhood, except an immense desire to laugh at the voices of others. *Who carries a butcher knife in their pocket?*

(And leaves walking down the street.)

At times, the voices were amusing. Lina raised the cup to her lips but stopped when she caught the sweet smell of sugar. She let her hand hover in the air for a time, then spilled part of the drink onto the saucer and the crumbly sweet, carefully so as not to splash her clothes, because no one likes clothes stained with sweetened coffee. She rested the cup on the table and tipped the saucer a bit so the liquid could escape and stain the tablecloth again. She ran a fingernail over the tacky stain and discovered nostalgia lost in memory: the touch of the damp cloth, the friction at the tip of her index finger. *It's seven centimeters, isn't it? I think I read that somewhere on the Internet.* How curious: a reduction to the metric. She had never been very good at math. She vaguely remembered the smile of the elementary school teacher—a red mouth, terribly red. *Thank you, come back soon.* You're welcome. Lina, they're calling you outside. That man who just left, gray suit, graying hair, the face of a politician. How can someone wear a mustache in the twenty-first century, for heaven's sake. Must be a congressman. Or did he actually say he was a congressman? Come on, you're not even going to drink the coffee. Leave five reais on the table and get up.

Who leaves the money on top of the table and then leaves in the twenty-first century? What's happened to customs, the best customs? That cinematic attitude of I know how much I have to pay, I don't want to look the waiter in the eye again.

Let's go, Lina.

A breaded cutlet with sautéed potatoes, please.

The five-reais bill and another of two, just to be sure and because it wasn't going to make any difference. That thick wrinkled wad of money that she had in her pocket, without a wallet. She couldn't remember where she had lost her wallet. *It's gotten cold, hasn't it?* But it's August, what else can be expected in August? Somebody had said it was going to rain. The congressman with the mustache went down the narrow street with his hands in his pants pockets, a wide step, a lazy step, in narrow-toed shoes that looked like nineteenth-century transatlantic liners. A huge mistake, a transatlantic crossing the dirty black-and-white bricks and skirting puddles that even without rain emerge from the bowels of the earth. *But it depends on the organ affected, the size of the cut.* Maybe he was a lawyer, because this area is full of lawyers and what a breed, those lawyers. *They're never congressmen.* A cup of coffee after lunch and back to the office to invent more bureaucracy to delay for another month any case already lost from the start. Where did you hear that, Lina? Since when do you know anything about the law?

This place becomes impossible at night.

The gaze of the woman, you know?, everything the cement and the asphalt and the buzz of cars. The monotonous voice that narrates a repetitive routine of signing documents and copying legal papers, changing a few dates, some names. Always the same boring task; for this she had studied six years? The salary at the end of the month and the bills to pay and the house to clean and clothes to wash and

(but had she told all that?)

maybe it would be better to go back to college and *study something less useful like art or literature or oceanography* (leaning against a dirty wall of some gray building after asking, *Got a light?*).

Because at times she got lost. She trod paths that were not hers and followed steps that merged into the patterns on the sidewalk. Her reflection in a puddle of water: *Do you still remember me?* Maybe she was invisible: *I nearly didn't recognize you in the light of day*, he would have said if he had said anything. What Lina saw was the spotted leopard printed on orangish paper and *Please don't bother me, I need to go back to work*. Or she heard someone calling from the other side of the street, there where a group of ladies gathered inspecting children's T-shirts priced at 3.99. Afterward, she was lost: she read the name of the street—surely the name of some baron or priest or politician from many years ago.

Where else had she witnessed that scene, that trickle of dark liquid sliding along the wet ground and disappearing among the black stones to reemerge among the white stones and later the black ones and later . . . Where else? She didn't remember; perhaps it was the thick coffee on the cheap fabric of the tablecloth. The green-and-white checkered tablecloth. The coffee on the edge and the drops on the floor, in the carpet; the red carpet and—

Listen, Lina: someone is calling.

The knife ought to be here somewhere.

A knife like that can even kill a spotted leopard.

Two transatlantic shoes half-covered in a puddle of water: one with the tip upward toward the cloudy sky at the top of the buildings; the second toppled and tragic. The improbable puddle in the irregular paving of the slope. The tie with blue and green stripes, the shirt stained wet and dirty, and that impossible, probably imaginary silence

(or it was the voices that had suddenly quieted)

the certainty that something was missing from the scene
someone.

Why do you get involved in that kind of story, Lina? Better to get out of there, the problem isn't yours and someone
is going to appear, following the stain on the pavement below
that creeps between the square bricks. The doorman at the
neighboring building pausing for five minutes for a smoke or
one of those bored policemen who don't like people using the
narrow street to make their homes out of cardboard boxes. A
pile of cardboard and empty plastic bags like an abandoned
house, and in the silence, the congressman, his eyes and
mouth open, his mustache stiff, his belly swollen

(and red).

And was that sound in the distance a gunshot? The military police had a habit of killing crazies with no questions
asked; she had seen it on the news the previous week. At the
foot of the slope was the valley and a busy avenue. Was it
already getting dark? When did these passageways become so
deserted? To a casual eye, the politician with the mustache
looked like one of those drunks toward the end of the afternoon. *This is the world, do you see?* Lina enjoyed the company of
that woman, though she didn't much like the cigarette smoke.
But the entire city was smoke, all the time: cigarettes, cars,
buses. The constant smell of filthy wet asphalt. The woman was
also the city, the paleness of the city center, the gray of buildings, the weariness of business employees. She said things like
this, important things: *The city kills because it devours choice.*
Lina didn't know what that meant.

The voices didn't always make sense.

She walked up the slope and made her way to the corner,
felt the cool air of open space, the murmur of the street and
the people. The knife wasn't there, it wasn't anywhere. *How*

can a man die of a stabbing if the knife doesn't exist? Because it wasn't the first time; something told her it wasn't the first time. Despite the crowd in the city center, the military police fired without taking names and people found a dark corner a few steps from the subway entrance to die of knife wounds.

Lina didn't know the woman's name. She was a lawyer; she had to be.

Inconsistent punctuality, she always appeared at that spot at five in the afternoon every other day—or sometimes not. *Good thing it's Friday.* At times Lina didn't know if she was really there, her body leaning against the neoclassical construction, one arm folded over the belly, the other elbow floating in the air next to the cigarette smoke. *What a shitty day.* She cradled the cigarette deep between her index and middle fingers, and when she raised it to her lips it was as if she covered it with her entire hand, as if repenting something she had said; as if

(she seemed incapable of repenting anything at all).

A repeated figure: that desire for importance while the city passed by her indifferently. A voice muffled by the street noise and the cigarette smoke mixing with the exhaust of cars, of buses. Lina spotted the law students lined up on the sidewalk with their backpacks and rolling carts loaded with voluminous books. *I haven't studied at all for that exam on tax law.* The woman said she felt sorry for those children with large egos. She spoke of her day in the office, about a missed deadline, about an irate boss and an incompetent intern.

She said:

They killed a lawyer yesterday in the center of the city, near here.

Stabbed to death;

a nonexistent knife.

If only things could exist through force of the word, by simple syntactical placement or;

(of course she wouldn't think this).

Lina wasn't one to worry about linguistic questions, and since the elementary school teacher there was no teacher at all. *My school is the street*, as the voices repeated at times; sometimes the voices were downright ridiculous. The street didn't teach anyone anything; the street was the street, literally or figuratively, a stretch of asphalt or that dirty setting in which people crossed hurriedly to and from work. *A knife that large can't go unnoticed.* She smelled the suffocating smoke from the cigarette and tried to recall the expression in the eyes of the congressman who wasn't a congressman. That's where the answer would be. *Then they say no one saw anything.* She had seen the knife, she was sure of it. *In the middle of the street, two blocks from a police guard post.* The answer was in the memory shattered by the wrong turn that had led her to notice a pair of transatlantic shoes shipwrecked in a puddle of water. *Do you remember everything you saw today?* Lina didn't understand. *Remember the street kid smoking crack and the couple who passed you on the viaduct?* She remembered the thick texture of the coffee on the checkered tablecloth in the restaurant and didn't understand what those people had to do with a dead lawyer.

She wanted to know how much force was needed to make a knife blade penetrate human flesh

and especially wanted to remember

because there was a knife

if the lawyer had been stabbed

but she kept quiet.

No one ever sees anything.

Or they see and forget. They spend the afternoon and night trying to remember; a half-sensation that merges with the coffee stain between the tablecloth and the wooden table. Lina remembered when two military policemen shot a boy who was running away—shot him in the back and he fell as if he'd lost control of his legs. A dive onto the concrete without even time to protect his head with his hands, elbows, shoulders; thrown forward like a cloth doll and someone screamed before a totally wrong silence flooded the block and another dull thunderclap sealed the fate of the youth sprawled on the sidewalk.

Seems like exaggeration, don't you think?

She shifted her gaze from the students on the corner of the law school and stared at the woman and the cigarette and the smoke. She must have made some comment about knives and spotted leopards, must have stuck her hand in her shorts pocket and shown the lawyer the wrinkled fifty-reais note as if to make sure she knew what a leopard was

(because city people only know the animals printed on currency or)

and they give me money when they encounter me during the day.

The lawyer didn't react and Lina no longer knew why she had the figure of the spotted leopard in her hand. She stuck it back in her pocket, tugged her shorts down a bit, her panties up a little; she looked at the mark the elastic made on her waist because of excess flesh or fat or a bit of each or the shorts being too small. The lawyer had on a skirt and jacket, both gray, and rather worn flats. Hair pulled back and an old green handbag; cheap leather coming apart at the seams. *You shouldn't be in the street, girl,* she said. Perhaps it wasn't the first time she ever said it.

Or had it been another person?

Why don't you go study?

Lina didn't understand what to study for and even why people studied; she didn't understand life in an office and grumbling at the end of the workday and having a car and living in an apartment with security cameras. It seemed to her that everything was the same: work, money, office, street, a dark motel. And after all those years of study the woman didn't even have an answer: a congressman, his transatlantic shoes in a puddle, the nonexistent knife.

(The knife should be there somewhere.)

Nor the voices;

memory a silence.

Don't go around asking about a knife; some may find it strange.

But she—the lawyer, her cigarette finished, the butt tossed into the gutter to join other garbage and filth and an empty yogurt container, a remnant of pink mixed with the soot of exhausts—she the lawyer didn't find that strange at all or; she reappeared and stayed even when Lina didn't have a light, she never did.

If anyone gets the idea that you did something;

but was she following him? she only wanted to ask

(do you still remember me?)

because she remembered him, or was almost sure she did, and there were few times she remembered someone

it's not going to help much to say you're innocent because they never believe people like you.

Lina wanted to know what the discomfort she felt was; whether from the absurd accusation or. Do you know to whom you're speaking, Lina? At times she doubted that presence in flesh and blood, were not the clothes and the work handbag such obvious indications of reality: the fabric frayed by time and the dust of the city infiltrating the fibers. The so ordinary

reality: to realize that her shorts really were tight and consti-
tuted so little cover that she felt a bit cold.

But she only wanted to ask
and he was startled because he recognized her or
the fifty-reais note
two ladies choosing children's T-shirts
three ninety-nine.

*Valtinho grows so fast it doesn't pay to buy clothes for the boy;
you have to take advantage of sales.*

Suddenly the lawyer wasn't there either. Lina heard the
sound of hurried footsteps, or perhaps imagined them; she
heard the wheels of a handcart full of books being dragged by
one of the students from the other side of the corner.

First she saw the ID: a piece of paper laminated in plastic
inside a black wallet, with the shield of the civil police em-
bossed on the cover. He opened and closed it a few times,
to be sure she fully understood the purpose of the visit. Or
because the movement made it impossible to read anything
or closely examine the photograph, the name, or any proof of
authority instead of paying attention to the stitching that was
coming undone or the damp stain on the edges. Lina would
have opened the door without saying anything; standing there
like an interrogation, unmoving.

The name coming from his mouth was unknown and she
didn't know how to react. *Lina*, she wanted to say, but—

I just want to talk.

It was also a repeated discourse, although not so much
by the police investigators who appeared at her door with an
old wallet and an incomprehensible ID. Still at the threshold,
he cited names and Lina didn't know what the thread of the
conversation was. *May I come in?*

No answer, just the subtle movement of her head and the door left open; she returned to the interior of the apartment that in reality was a kitchenette the size of a small bedroom. The kitchen itself was a camping stove with two burners that some crazy guy had thrown in the trash and the neighbor woman had connected to the natural gas outlet with an old piece of hose. No refrigerator, she didn't need it. On the counter was a package of coffee, some bananas, and boxes of crackers.

A couple of fruit flies buzzed above a blackened, somewhat overripe banana.

Were they there before?

They said you are usually near there toward the end of the day.

They said.

Near there.

What did the man want? She told him to have a seat, removed a magazine and some wrinkled clothing from the sofa bed to create a bit of room. *Make yourself comfortable*, she must have said. The words didn't come out? He sat to the side with his arms resting on his legs, his hands clasped together in front, his spine quite straight. She expected more from a police investigator entering with official credentials that left no room to say no. That lack of assertiveness was the same as the lawyers; as the female lawyer and her worn handbag. The congressman who didn't even deign to be a congressman, on the dirty ground with his feet in a puddle. These people are all so common, in their cheap suits and untidy colored ties. Shoes that have seen better shines. Reality was always disappointing and Lina didn't even watch soap operas, she didn't watch television, she didn't like how the voices also repeated themselves in the electronic medium and continued echoing throughout the day. But the images of a more attractive life, less worn-out fabric and fewer tomato stains on the shirt collar—those images were everywhere, in magazine ads and the display windows at the shopping center close to her apartment.

That's where you hang out, isn't it?

Wasn't that how it was said? Hang out? What odd turns words take. He repeated a name. Lina didn't know why the man was there. She distracted herself by thinking of knives and spotted leopards—had she been been robbed of a part of her memory that had been replaced by the vague sensation of running a fingernail along tacky fabric stained with sweetened coffee? She said: *I can make some coffee; do you drink coffee?* Was that how it was, Lina? Sometimes the voices remained silent, and Lina forgot what people did to have a conversation.

Listen, there's no need to worry; I'm not here to talk about your work.

But coffee, mister, she was talking about coffee. He would use one of those gestures with his head and hands like someone saying, *Please, relax,* or, *I'll have some coffee, of course, why not.* Him and his jeans that hadn't been washed in a week, beat up and dirty, wrinkled at the knees and beneath the hips. His sneakers were a soiled white, disguised among exaggerated colors that would never go with the long baggy shirt to conceal the gun stuck in the waistband of his pants so obvious from the motion of sitting down and leaning forward with his elbows on his knees.

The flaking enamel of the small stove that had once been white;

perhaps.

Perhaps she should tell him, explain to him: It was a knife like this, understand? More or less this size, with a wooden handle, the kind that lets you see the continuation of the blade all the way, which is an indication of quality, they say.

Because then—isn't that right?—the blade won't come loose from the handle no matter how much force we use when we are cutting an onion, for example. Cutting an onion can be dangerous. The blade was something like a handspan more or less in length—the flash of the metal impresses and memory tends to exaggerate what we remember, especially when it's replaced by a thick coffee stain. It was there, I'm sure of it. The knife, you understand?

(Don't go around asking people about a knife.)

He got up to avoid the open part of the sofa bed and went to the window with his hands behind his back, just like a television detective and completely wrong given his ordinary presence.

(If someone gets the idea you've done something.)

This is the third time it's happened, and if you help us this time.

Fill the pan with water and light the fire with a depleted lighter still good to produce a spark

(*got a light?*);

open the package of coffee and wait.

(*If you help us this time.*)

Because it wasn't the first time and Lina remembered

the knife

someone.

Are you sure, Lina?

(She never had a light.)

But what could she tell the police investigator if reality had the habit of always taking wrong turns; or she would become confused and needed to ask the time or the price of a pair of shoes, just to be sure the world had not suddenly been replaced by another, unknown. From the back she saw that his shirt had two small holes in it, at waist level. Also the stitching was coming undone in one spot, leaving a piece of yellow thread hanging.

Someone is killing under the nose of the police, in the open air.

A boy running away and the police who shot him in the back, in the open air. Pay more attention, Lina. The voices can teach you something, explain how these people work. She still remembered when she was a child and had gone to the zoo with a class from school. She remembered the spotted leopard and the capuchin monkeys, and some birds with long legs and pink feathers that tucked their necks into their bodies, to rest standing on only one foot.

You're always in that area, girl.

And the guide said, *Now we're going to see the area with the elephants.* Wasn't that how it was? The capuchin monkey picked up trash from the ground and jumped back to what looked like a tree house, full of small doors and windows.

Just what was it the spotted leopard did?

Whose idea had it been to put animals on the back of currency? Lina opened the drawer to get a spoon and stopped with her hand hovering over the cutlery

(please don't bother me, I have to get back to work)

and was it a smile or merely an expression of relief at seeing it was no longer necessary to search.

You were there the whole time?

The investigator continued looking out the window, staring at the dirty wall of the neighboring building. In the silverware drawer the spoon she used to measure the coffee was hidden behind a large knife with a wooden handle, just as she remembered it; the blade wasn't shiny

some fifteen centimeters?,

maybe fourteen.

Lina grabbed the spoon and closed the drawer.

How old are you?

How many spoonfuls of powdered coffee? The perfect

consistency was impossible because of the old filter or the cheap brand of coffee, but she didn't give up trying, ever. She noticed the water boiling and the man at the other side of the apartment observing her and waiting for an answer, any answer. *Can I use the bathroom?* Lina pointed to the narrow door near the entrance and he crossed, once again, the space that separated them, to disappear from view with a click of the latch.

She poured water into the filter full of powder and watched as the black liquid flowed through. Black coffee.

Pure

strong

thick.

She served two cups and went to look in the drawer for a small spoon to stir the sugar. She didn't notice the sounds coming from the bathroom, sounds of someone moving cautiously in a restricted space, lifting clothes and displacing objects. She thought about asking if he wanted sugar; she didn't have artificial sweetener—*they say sweeteners cause cancer*. She approached the bathroom with the cup in her hand just as the door opened and the enormous body of the police investigator appeared. An unexpected gesture and a scream when the hot coffee streamed down the checkered shirt

(*son of a bitch!*)

and to Lina it seemed a multitude of arms when she moved the knife rapidly upward and forward, with force and skill. The man's hands on her shoulders her arm her neck in an effort to grab the weapon in his waistband but the door too narrow and the bathroom a cubicle suddenly painted in red; there was barely space to fall to the floor, slide along the wall, and hit his knee on the toilet. It mattered little that he would reach the weapon in the rear of his waist. Lina wielded the knife until it struck a rib, curved, made contact with the rib on the other side. The investigator's right hand found the pistol while his left closed around the handle of the knife over Lina's hand, without the strength to stop her from raising it and attacking his chest again. On the checkered pattern of his shirt the coffee stain merged with the blood, a dark sticky red that was a little like a lost and then rediscovered happiness; it was the fingernail on the tablecloth stained with sugary coffee, knowing that she no longer needed to remember, that the voices asked no questions, and that reality was more than a shirt with holes in it, an old worn handbag, trash and soot in the gutter, the sound of a law student's wheeled valise jolting over the uneven sidewalk in the city center.

ANY SIMILARITY IS NOT PURELY COINCIDENTAL

BY MARCELINO FREIRE

Guaianases

I t was Luciflor who told me this story.

True, very true. And she sets the scene slowly, bleakly, like a silent film that speaks. She tells me that her district was born more black than white. In the fog, in the darkness of low clouds, in the terror of stairways. "And they get darker all the time. Have you seen the Nigerian immigrants? Everybody's choosing to live here nowadays. All of Africa, for heaven's sake!"

There are many stories. One inside the other. When she arrives to do the cleaning, I only find peace when she leaves for the market. When she buys powdered soap, or *guaraná*. She touts fabric softener. "That one smells good, it's new, lavender. You're a writer, aren't you? One of these days write a story about me. Because my life is a novel, you know? This Mexican life of ours."

Tell me, Luciflor, tell me. So a few weeks ago, she gradually related the strange story of her neighbor Guiomar, who was already a grandmother and found herself pregnant. She began trussing her belly so no one would suspect. What would her only son, who lives next door to her, think? *My mother is a whore.* Her little grandson would get a playmate now. "I turn purple just imagining the harassment of the poor woman. I'm a grandmother too. And I think. Without meaning to, she was capable of killing the fetus. Death by asphyxiation. Such suffering!"

Guiomar was only going to show the offspring to everybody when the offspring was born. The strong girdle that she made was clumsy, awkward. It gave her latitude to put on weight. The child's father was a watchman at a train station near Poá. They slept together several times. Right there, in the ice cream stands. They drank cane juice and beer near the church. Guiomar was never one for drinking beer, but she drank. She even began to make things up. "My belly is growing because of drinking." She's a day worker too. She got sick going to work. The Itaquera subway, you know what it's like—a sardine can.

She secretly went to a doctor. To find out if it was a boy or a girl.

"It was that damned Deusdete who set it up. She knew that in Guaianases there's a quarry. From time to time a bomb goes off. And I'm not talking about a gunshot, like I hear when they shoot at the water tank. I pretend not to listen. I know who's bad, who's good, and who's gonna be saved. There's lots of worthwhile people in the neighborhood. It's just that everywhere there's sons of bitches. Right here, my dear, in this rich area, you're surrounded by a bunch of bad guys. Aren't you, Murilo?"

Luciflor pauses. Overcome by emotion, perhaps. And eats stroganoff with rice.

"Someday I want to make a lunch for the two of us. You'll come, won't you? Say you'll come. You'll like the place where I live. My house is your house. I'll take you to a laying-on of hands, in the home of a woman with the power. Many people come, even from other countries, to be cleaned by her. Guiomar only decided to go after the shit hit the fan. The doctor puttered around, here, there. In a makeshift walk-in clinic with room for nobody. And he spoke, without preparing the old woman's heart. *You're expecting twins. Did you hear that? Twins. Not just one child.* Guiomar was hiding in her immense belly two births.

"Know what happened? It was Deusdete who had the crazy idea. Is reality more literature than literature, or not? More real than that stuff you write? I see something worse, something bigger, happen every day. Deusdete told her to keep just one of the babies. She would sell the other. It would help with the cost. It wasn't poor Guiomar's fault. You think it was wrong? Twins would be a real heavy load. Guiomar would have to stop working. And how would she face her older son with a double dose? Or the daughter-in-law who was already giving her a hard time, the envious woman. Her young grandson would get two playmates to fly kites with, or whatever. The future would be hopeless. Her life wouldn't be easy. And there was already a family in São Paulo who wanted to adopt the kid.

"And that's how it was done. On the morning of the birth, when Guiomar woke up, she had only Betinho in her arms. The other baby was already gone to its destiny. The money was enough to buy a crib and diapers. Deusdete is very dangerous. With one hand she helps the desperate woman. With the other she disappears. We don't forget. Guiomar doesn't forget. But what to do? She came home one night holding a package. Her grown son asked what it was. She didn't answer. She fainted at the entrance. She almost lost the baby from the fall. She was bleeding like a stone, broken there at the quarry. They had to call an ambulance. She was in the hospital a long time. Guiomar and the child, hovering between life and death."

Luciflor exaggerates. She holds back the tears. She incorporates long silences, especially in the unfolding of the facts. She tells me that time has passed. Guaianases, of course, has changed greatly.

"When I moved there, there was nothing but my house on top of the hill. And lots of woods around. Today—shops, markets, lottery stores. It doesn't rain like it used to. That chilly mist is a thing of the past. The end.

"The Arena Corinthians is a stone's throw from here. During the World Cup, I even rented a room to a Haitian, who almost ended up wanting to stay but didn't.

"Like I was saying, Guiomar found her other son, the one she didn't raise. You believe me, don't you? These things happen. It was like something out of a soap opera. She went to work in a successful doctor's apartment and the doctor was the picture of Betinho. The same smile, the spitting image. As soon as she saw him she collapsed on the sofa. Her sight darkened, she blacked out. A tragedy. Guiomar went looking for Deusdete. She wanted to know who the damn woman had sold the little boy to. She had to be certain. And she was dumb enough to bring Deusdete with her to work one day. The assassin took a look at everything. At the doctor's possessions. The modern clothes. The car. He gave them both a ride to the subway."

Luciflor suddenly seems afraid of narrating more details, but she continues: "Deusdete confirmed that it really was the boy, shares the name of the adoptive parents, soy planters. People with dough. The doctor lived by himself in the capital. And you know what that animal Deusdete did? She vanished again, with Guiomar's son. She got the idea of kidnapping the young man. Slowly she came up with a crazy plan."

I laughed. It was easy to guess what happened next. And I

commented as much to Luciflor. Many books have dealt with such a switch. Of identity. I'll bet Guiomar's son Betinho was involved in the kidnapping. He went to live in his doctor brother's home. *Didn't you tell me, on another occasion, that Betinho was studying to be a nurse? Something in that area, in a small clinic, I don't know. That's it, isn't it? Did I get it right?*

Guiomar went to work for Betinho, thinking that Betinho, the son she raised, was the other son she didn't raise. As for the doctor, they got rid of him. Deusdete disappeared again, with the body. *Is that it or isn't it, Luciflor? Tell me it's true. You can tell me.*

Was this how the story ended?

Luciflor became frightened at my excess of commonplace theories. Of clichés. She stopped what she was doing. Looked deep into my eyes. And cried like a lost soul. She was like a sick animal. Suddenly collapsed at my feet. Phantasmagorical. I dashed to get her some water with sugar. I was going to call an ambulance. *Don't you want me to call someone? Luciflor, let me open the windows. Turn on the air. Everything's so stuffy, so hot. Forgive me if I ruined it. If I spoiled your narrative. I have a habit of trying to guess the ending. The outcome of a book, a film. Stay calm. Speak to me, please. What happened, then? Speak, woman.*

She stifled her sobbing. The words died away. Then letting everything out in a single breath. Dramatic.

"I was desperate with terror. And with love. We're running a risk, my son."

And the silence between us remained. For a long time. *You're joking, making it up, Luciflor. Why didn't you ever tell me this story?*

ABOUT THE CONTRIBUTORS

MARÇAL AQUINO was born in Amparo, a city in the interior of the state of São Paulo, in 1958. He is a journalist, writer, and scriptwriter for film and television. He has published, among other books, the short story collections *Faroestes* and *Amor e outros objetos pontiagudos*, for which he received the Jabuti Prize, as well as the novels *O invasor*, *Cabeça a prêmio*, and *Eu receberia as piores notícias dos seus lindos lábios*. He has served as scriptwriter for such films as *Os matadores*, *Ação entre amigos*, and *O cheiro do ralo*. His work has been translated and published in Germany, Spain, France, Mexico, Portugal, and Switzerland.

VANESSA BARBARA was born in São Paulo in 1982, in the Mandaqui district. She is a journalist, translator, and writer, as well as an opinion writer for the international edition of the *New York Times*. In 2012, she was included in *Granta*'s *The Best of Young Brazilian Novelists*. In 2015, she won the Prix du Premier Roman Etranger in France for *Noites de alface*, which has been translated into six languages. In 2014, she was awarded the Paraná Literature Prize for her novel *Operação Impensável*. She has also published *O livro amarelo do Terminal* (winner of the Jabuti Prize for Reporting), the novel *O verão do Chibo* (with Emilio Fraia), and a story collection, *O louco de palestra*.

TONY BELLOTTO was born in São Paulo in 1960 and has lived in Rio de Janeiro for over twenty years. Guitarist and songwriter for Titãs (Titans), one of the most important rock bands in Brazilian musical history, he debuted in literature in 1995 with the novel *Bellini e a esfinge*, which was adapted for film and is being translated into English by Akashic Books. Since 1999, he has hosted *Afinando a língua*, a TV program that uses literature and music to discuss the Portuguese language and forms of expression.

FERNANDO BONASSI was born in São Paulo in 1962. He is a screenwriter for film and television, a playwright, director, and author of diverse works that include the novels *Subúrbio* and *Luxúria*, the children's book *Declaração Universal do Mole-que Invocado*, and a collection of short stories, *São Paulo/Brasil*—the last two were finalists for the Jabuti Prize. He is coauthor of films such as *Os matadores*, *Carandiru*—winner of the TAM Brazilian Cinema Prize for best adapted script of 2003—and *Cazuza: O tempo não para*, winner of the TAM Brazilian Cinema Prize in 2004. From 2008 to 2015 he created and developed, in collaboration with the writer Marçal Aquino, three seasons of the crime serial *Força-Tarefa* and the mini-series *O Caçador* and *Supermax*.

BEATRIZ BRACHER was born in São Paulo in 1961, along the banks of the Pinheiros River. She is a novelist, short story author, and scriptwriter. She has published the novels *Azul e dura*, *Não falei*, *Antonio*, and *Anatomia do paraíso*, and the short story collections *Meu amor* and *Garimpo*—all with Editora 34. With Sérgio Bianchi she wrote the script for the film *Os Inquilinos*, and with Karin Aïnouz the script for the film *O abismo prateado*.

MARIA S. CARVALHOSA was born in São Paulo in 2001 and has lived in Rio de Janeiro since she was six months old. She is currently in the ninth year of primary school. "Panamericana," in collaboration with Beatriz Bracher, is her first published work.

ILANA CASOY was born in São Paulo in 1960. She holds a degree in administration from the Getúlio Vargas Foundation, a specialization in criminology from Instituto Brasileiro de Ciências Criminais (IBCCRIM), and was trained in investigation and homicide forensics by US police instructor teams in Orlando, Florida. She acts as a consultant for TV and film series and documentaries. In the last twenty years she has dedicated herself to rigorous research into serial killers, taking part in actual cases with police, forensic experts, the Department of Justice, and defense lawyers. She is the author of *Arquivos Serial Killers—Louco ou cruel?* and *Made in Brazil.*

FERRÉZ has worked as a clerk, general assistant, and archivist. His first book, *Fortaleza da Desilusão*, was published in 1997, and in 2000, with the publication of *Capão Pecado*, he turned to writing full time. He is the author of the novels *Manual prático do ódio, Deus foi almoçar*, and two short story collections: *Ninguém é inocente em São Paulo* and *Cronista de um tempo ruim.* His story "Os inimigos não levam flores" was adapted for TV, and he wrote for the film *Bróders* and for the Fox serials *Cidade dos Homens* and *9MM.* He was also a scriptwriter for the series *171* on the Universal channel. He continues to work as an editorial consultant for *Le Monde Diplomatique Brasil* and has a blog and a YouTube channel dealing with militancy and culture of the periphery.

MARCELINO FREIRE was born in 1967 in Sertânia, Pernambuco, Brazil. He currently resides in São Paulo, having moved from Recife in 1991. He lived for a time in Guaianazes, in São Paulo's East Zone, the setting of his story in this book. He is the author of the short story collections *Angu de sangue* and *Contos negreiros*—for which he won the Jabuti Prize for Best Book of Short Stories in 2006; and the novel *Nossos ossos,* which won the Machado de Assis Prize in 2014. He is the creator of Balada Literária, an event held annually in the São Paulo district of Vila Madalena since 2006.

CLIFFORD E. LANDERS has introduced over two dozen Brazilian authors to English-speaking readers. The more than thirty novels and one hundred–plus short stories he has translated from Portuguese include such acclaimed writers as Rubem Fonseca, Jorge Amado, Nélida Piñon, and Patrícia Melo. He is a recipient of a prose translation grant from the National Endowment for the Arts and the Mario Ferreira Award. He and his wife, Vasda Bonafini Landers, reside in Naples, Florida.

OLIVIA MAIA was first published in 2006 with the novella *Desumano.* She is the author of two self-published books, *Operação P-2* and *Segunda mão*, as well as two books of crime stories. Her most recent novel, *A última expedição*, was sponsored by the Petrobras Cultural Program. In August 2013, she resigned from her job as a teacher and left São Paulo with only a backpack. After two years and two pairs of boots between Patagonia and the Alps, she settled in the interior of Bahia, in the city of Lençóis, where she teaches classes for children, bathes in the river, and writes.

MARCELO RUBENS PAIVA is a writer, scriptwriter, and playwright. He was born in São Paulo in 1959 and studied at the School of Communications and Arts in the University in São Paulo, pursued a master's degree in literary theory at Unicamp, and was a Knight Journalism Fellow at Stanford University. He is the author of the novels *Feliz ano velho* (winner of the Jabuti Prize in 1982), *Blecaute, Ua:bari, Bala na agulha, Não és tu, Brasil, Malu de bicicleta, A segunda vez que te conheci,* and *Ainda estou aqui.* He has been translated into English, Spanish, French, Italian, German, and Czech, and he has written scripts for Rede Globo and the Multishow channel, as well as for films and documentaries. He is currently a columnist for the newspaper *O Estado de São Paulo* and the *Estadão* website.

MARIO PRATA was born in Minas Gerais in 1946, lived in São Paulo for thirty-five years, and currently resides in Florianópolis. He is the author of plays, telenovelas, miniseries, children's books, and scripts for film and television. He has written fifteen books for adults, the most recent of which is *Mario Prata entrevista uns brasileiros.* Since 2005, he has dedicated himself to writing crime fiction and has published three novels: *Purgatório, Sete de paus,* and *Os Viúvos.* His work has been translated into forty-seven languages, three dead tongues, and thirteen dialects. He uses humor in all his work.

JÔ SOARES is a humorist, actor, comedian, director, writer, producer, and plastic artist. He was born in Rio de Janeiro on January 16, 1938. He studied in the United States and Europe from the age of twelve to eighteen. His acting career began with the film *O homem do Sputnik,* directed by Carlos Manga. In 1960, he moved to São Paulo, where he wrote and participated in the *Dick Farley Show.* He is the author, among other titles, of *O xangô de Baker Street,* a novel published in twelve countries; *O homem que matou Getúlio Vargas,* published in seven countries; and *Assassinatos na Academia Brasileira de Letras.* Since 2000, he has hosted the *Programa do Jô,* a variety show featuring interviews, music, and comedy.

DRAUZIO VARELLA was born in São Paulo and received his medical degree in 1967. Since then, he has been intensely engaged in clinical studies in the field of oncology. In 1989, he began providing volunteer medical services in Carandiru, a prison in São Paulo, which he continues to this day at the women's penitentiary in the city. He is the author of *Estação Carandiru* (winner of the Jabuti Prize in 2000), *Nas ruas do Brás* (winner of the Novos Horizontes Prize in 2002), *O médico doente, Carcereiros, Borboletas da alma, Janelas quebradas, Correr,* and others. *Estação Carandiru* has been published in France, Great Britain, Australia, Portugal, and Poland. He has been a columnist for *Folha de São Paulo* and the magazine *Carta Capital* for almost twenty years. In that time he has produced more than thirty series on health for Rede Globo along with various works dealing with medicine on the radio and the Internet.